Soldier Doll

FRAGILE

AFGHANISTAN
5 1 07
افغانستان

U.S. POSTAGE

VIET NAM
★ 13 8 70 ★
DA NANG

CZECHOSLOVAKIA ★
08 2 1944
★

CANADA POST CORPORATION

DEVON
12¹⁵ PM
23 INE
1918
GREAT BRITAIN

BERLIN
20 APR
1939

SOLDIER DOLL

Jennifer Gold

Second Story Press

Library and Archives Canada Cataloguing in Publication

Gold, Jennifer, author
Soldier doll / Jennifer Gold.

Issued in print and electronic formats.
ISBN 978-1-927583-29-6 (pbk.) .— ISBN 978-1-927583-30-2 (epub)

I. Title.

PS8613.O4317S65 2014   jC813'.6   C2014-900014-6

C2014-900015-4

Edited by Kathryn White
Copyedited by Kathryn Cole and Kate Abrams
Designed by Melissa Kaita

Cover photographs © iStockphoto

Printed and bound in Canada

Second Story Press gratefully acknowledges the support of the Ontario Arts Council and the Canada Council for the Arts for our publishing program. We acknowledge the financial support of the Government of Canada through the Canada Book Fund.

ONTARIO ARTS COUNCIL
CONSEIL DES ARTS DE L'ONTARIO
50 YEARS OF ONTARIO GOVERNMENT SUPPORT OF THE ARTS
50 ANS DE SOUTIEN DU GOUVERNEMENT DE L'ONTARIO AUX ARTS

Canada Council   Conseil des Arts
for the Arts   du Canada

MIX
Paper from
responsible sources
FSC® C004071

Published by
SECOND STORY PRESS
20 Maud Street, Suite 401
Toronto, ON M5V 2M5
www.secondstorypress.ca

For my mother

CHAPTER 1

Toronto, Canada
2007

It looks like a doll—at first. It has a doll's baby face, complete with pink cherubic cheeks and rosebud mouth. The carved and painted hair is soft-looking and yellow-blond. A closer look, however, tells a different story. The little figure is dressed in carefully painted army finery and stands stiffly, arms at his sides, feet together.

Elizabeth looks at the doll with interest. It's been years, of course, since she played with dolls—she's fifteen now and much too old for that sort of thing—but there's something unusual about this one, something compelling that makes her want to take a second glance. It looks less like a soldier than a baby in uniform, its delicate little hands a stark contrast to the gray military coat. She leans forward on the table to get a better look, and it wobbles slightly; she nearly loses a flip-flop trying to steady herself. An old man nearby in a gray wool suit—*Isn't he hot?* she wonders, wiping the sweat from her own forehead—gives her a disapproving stare, the kind adults usually dole out with advice on homework or queries about habits related to dental hygiene. Elizabeth waits until he isn't looking, then sticks out her tongue.

She turns back to the little soldier. Its uniform reminds her a bit of what her dad used to wear, in the old pictures. *Maybe he'd like it.* Her father is a pack rat with a weakness for old junk. His "finds," he calls them affectionately. Back in Vancouver, most of these finds have been banished to the garage by her mother, who has a slightly less favorable view of the broken old clocks and model airplanes. Elizabeth pictures the new house and realizes that it doesn't have a garage. She wonders briefly where the collections of old *Time* magazines and foreign Coca-Cola bottles will make their new home and has a feeling she knows. She has a vision of her mother surreptitiously hauling out the little bottles at night, hiding them in garbage bags and leaving them at the side of the road. She feels some sympathy toward her father, then hardens her heart. *It's his fault for moving us across the country*, she tells herself. *What is it he's always saying? Actions have consequences, Elizabeth.*

She checks the tag that's dangling from the doll's foot: two dollars. The price is right, and besides, she's quickly running out of time. Her dad's birthday is tomorrow. Elizabeth opens her purse and rifles through it for change. She knows it's in there somewhere; she remembers tossing in a handful of coins earlier on. *Katie was right*, she thinks, pulling out a sticky, half-eaten lollipop covered in bits of tissue. *I do need a real wallet.*

Katie. Elizabeth feels a wave of homesickness overtake her.

"Can I help you, dear?" An older woman hovers behind her. *The homeowner, presumably.* Elizabeth hastily drops the sucker back into her bag.

"The doll, please." Elizabeth gestures toward it. She fishes for coins again with her other hand.

"Interesting, isn't it?" The woman picks it up. She looks at it fondly. "Found it on the side of the road not far from here. My grandkids used to call it 'the soldier baby.'"

"It's cool," Elizabeth agrees. She pauses. "Would you take a dollar fifty?"

"One seventy-five," the woman counters. Elizabeth grins. *Tough old lady.*

"Deal."

Elizabeth watches as she wraps it up carefully in newspaper, sealing the ends with Scotch Tape.

"There you go."

Elizabeth takes the parcel and thanks her. She tosses it into her bag, relieved. Even if her dad didn't like it, he'd almost certainly pretend to. He was that sort of father. When she was a little girl, he'd always been overgenerous with praise for her works of "art": scribbles of crayon on the backs of napkins, mis-shapen pottery, paintings where the colors had mixed together to form an unattractive shade of brown. He'd kept all of it.

Where is Dad, anyway? Elizabeth surveys the street. People wander about, trying on old jewelry and thumbing through ancient issues of *National Geographic. How could so many people come out in this heat?* She looks over again at the old man in the suit and feels almost faint. In Vancouver, everyone would have been at the waterfront on a day like this.

It was one of those street sales where one family plans carefully for the day, only to find themselves in competition, at the last minute, with all of their neighbors, who—taking advantage of the free advertising—spread out beach towels and crocheted blankets on their lawns and try to cash in on de-cluttering their homes. Elizabeth walks by a pile of paperbacks with missing covers and one of those old bouncy seats for babies. *Is that vomit on it?* She makes a face. *Yuck.*

Although she pretends she's just letting her dad drag her along, that she's humoring him, Elizabeth secretly enjoys these sales. You never know what people might be giving away. Most of it is junk, of course, but every so often, you find something that makes you forget about all the moth-eaten sweaters and the ties with cartoon characters on them. Once she found a yellow leather jacket with a faux-fur collar. The yellow was perfect: the color of fresh butter. She still gets compliments on that one.

"Miss, would you like some lemonade?" A blonde girl with pigtails waves at her. A boy stands next to her. He's a bit older—maybe a year or two—and brandishing a pitcher. *Miss? Ha.* Elizabeth smiles. She watches them wistfully. She'd been too shy to have a lemonade stand as a kid. It was the kind of thing you did with a brother or sister.

"Sure, I'll have some." Elizabeth begins another search for

coins, cursing silently. This time she comes up with a stale, half-eaten peanut butter cookie that she bought at the Vancouver airport. *Gross.* She looks around for a trash can but doesn't see one. Resigned, she tosses the cookie back in her bag.

"That'll be one dollar." The girl sticks out her hand.

"A dollar?" Elizabeth raises her eyebrows. "Isn't that a bit much?"

The girl gives her a hard look. "The heat drives up demand."

"How old are you?" Elizabeth stares at the pigtails.

"Eight." She still has her hand out.

The brother gives Elizabeth an apologetic look. "Our mom's an economist."

"Right." Amused, Elizabeth counts out four quarters. "There you go, I guess."

The lemonade is a bit too sweet, but it's cold. She drinks it quickly; she's thirsty from the heat. She isn't used to this kind of weather and isn't sure she wants to be, either. *What would I be doing in Vancouver right now? What are Katie and Elise doing today? The beach?*

Elizabeth recalls how her dad first broke the news about the move. Anticipating her reaction, he'd brought home Pad Thai for supper, her favorite. For weeks after, she hadn't been able to look at the stuff; even the thought of rice noodles made her ill. The other news—that he was shipping out in August—came later, over dessert. She should have known the Rocky Road ice cream was a kind of culinary bribe. Elizabeth stares down at her flip-flops and feels a fresh wave of resentment. If her dad was going to Afghanistan, why couldn't she and her mom have stayed in Vancouver?

"Liz!"

There he is. Finally. She waves and walks over.

"Find anything good, hon?"

He's clutching a pair of clunky old lamps. Elizabeth looks at them and recoils. *How much did he pay?* She thinks of how her mother will react to the lamps. *Better you than me, Dad,* she says silently.

He's still talking. Loudly. "I saw some necklaces over there that you might like." He gestures a few houses down. "Beaded stuff, you know? That hippie stuff you always—"

"Thanks, Dad." Elizabeth cuts him off quickly, cringing. *Why does he have to talk so loud? And use embarrassing words like* hippie? She looks around to see if anyone heard, then she remembers that she doesn't know anyone here. *The upside to moving across the country,* she thinks wryly. *Yell away, Dad.*

"Did you find anything interesting?" He peers into her bag. Elizabeth pulls away. "Hey!"

"Sorry, sorry. Did you?"

"Maybe." She's terrible at keeping secrets.

"Not sharing?" He looks hurt.

"Maybe it's a secret." She puts a heavy emphasis on the word secret.

"Huh? *Oh.* Okay. I see." He reaches over and tries to ruffle her hair. "Thanks, sweetheart."

Elizabeth ducks, embarrassed. "Dad!"

"Sorry, sorry!"

They walk together. The new house is only a few streets away. *Should I offer to carry one of those lamps?* Elizabeth looks at them again and groans. The air is thick with humidity; it's too hot for any kind of heavy lifting or being helpful so she decides not to. *It'll be worse than this in Afghanistan*, she reasons. He should be prepared.

"Liz—this way."

Startled, Elizabeth turns; she doesn't have a very good sense of direction. At night, she keeps turning the wrong way to the bathroom from her bedroom. Even with no one watching, she feels stupid. Who gets lost in their own house?

"Do you think Mom will like these lamps?"

Elizabeth looks at her father in disbelief. *Is he joking?*

"I'm thinking they'll look good in the living room. What do you think?"

Elizabeth searches for a diplomatic response. "I think you should ask her."

They reach the front door of the new house. Tall and narrow, it is the opposite of their squat little bungalow back in Vancouver. The real estate agent called it a "Victorian"; Elizabeth figures that's some kind of adult double-speak for ancient. The brick is painted a color that isn't white and isn't beige but an in-between shade. Elizabeth's favorite part is the door, which is bright red. She holds it open for her dad, who is still struggling with his cumbersome purchases.

"Phew," he says. "It's hot out there. Humid." He drops the lamps onto the ceramic floor, and the sound reverberates through the hall. "Amanda—you home?"

7

Elizabeth kicks off her sandals and navigates her way through the maze of boxes. She notices one in her own handwriting labeled "underwear." *How did that end up downstairs?* Discreetly, she kicks it to one side.

"Where have you two been?" Her mother sticks her head into the hall from the kitchen. Her hair is in a ponytail, and she looks sweaty despite the blasting air-conditioning. "I've been home for an hour. What happened to unpacking?"

"There was a yard sale." Elizabeth avoids her mother's gaze.

"A yard sale?" Her voice rises. She comes into the foyer, brandishing a box-cutter. She waves it, looking dangerous. "We haven't even unpacked the junk we already have!"

Elizabeth looks at her, wary. She stares out at the hallway full of boxes and feels guilty; she never should have agreed to go.

"This house doesn't even have a garage, John. We discussed this—" Her mother stops talking and gasps. She's spotted the lamps. *Here it comes*, thinks Elizabeth. She takes two steps back and braces herself.

"What. Are. Those? You're not honestly thinking those are coming in the house, are you?"

"What's wrong with them?" Elizabeth's father looks miffed. "They're really nice. I thought they could go in the living room."

"The living room! They're orange-and-green plaid."

"So? They're early twentieth-century Scottish, I think, very interesting—"

"Interesting? I think you mean ugly. I don't care when or

8

where they're from, our living room is painted red, for God's sake—"

Time to make my exit, Elizabeth thinks. "Guys? I'm going to my room to unpack."

They don't even hear her now; they're too busy arguing intensely. Rolling her eyes, Elizabeth grabs the box containing her underwear and retreats upstairs.

"One of my patients recommended this place to me." Elizabeth's mother leans across the table and offers her a container of Shanghai noodles. "He said they do great takeout."

Elizabeth takes the box and unceremoniously dumps some on her plate. She pokes at it with her chopsticks. The noodles seem soggy, and the broccoli is wilted.

"They definitely don't look like Asian Garden's noodles." Elizabeth thinks of the birthday meal they celebrated for her father last year, in Vancouver's Chinatown. This food doesn't look nearly as good. For one thing, it's all gray.

Her dad takes a bite of his General Tao chicken. "This isn't bad." He offers the foil container to Elizabeth, who peers inside and makes a face.

"No, thanks." She reaches for an eggplant dish. "I'm thinking of becoming a vegetarian."

Her father looks up, surprised. "Since when?"

"Since seeing this General Tao."

"Funny." Her mother takes the chicken from her dad, picking and choosing from among the pieces, and adds three to her plate.

"What kind of person would recommend this place?" Elizabeth toys with her eggplant. It's too mushy; the consistency reminds her of white bread soaked in milk. "Does he have a taste bud disease?"

"Yes, actually." Her mother pours herself a glass of wine. "It's an entirely new disease. I discovered it. I'm going to be famous. Also rich. The other dermatologists at the practice are all really jealous."

"Great. Maybe we can pay someone to unpack all these boxes, then." Elizabeth takes a tiny bite of her noodles and makes another face. She puts her chopsticks down.

"We really need to get moving on these boxes." Her mother gives them a hard look. "It's nearly two weeks, and we've made almost no progress. Of course, some people here ran off and went junk shopping when they were supposed to be helping out."

Elizabeth and her dad exchange a guilty glance. Her father clears his throat. "Liz, try the chicken, really. It's not bad at all."

Elizabeth shudders. "No, thanks. It looks like brains."

"Brains!" Now her dad makes a face. "Thanks a lot." He puts down his own chopsticks.

"Brains are a delicacy in France." Her mom spears a piece of chicken and points it at her family.

"I'm really glad I live in Canada, then," Elizabeth says. She pushes away her plate and eyes the bakery box on the counter, its telltale white string coming untied. *It won't be as good as The Sweet Shoppe*, she thinks, wondering where it's from. She pictures her fifteenth birthday cake: pink frosting with yellow flowers. The good kind of frosting, the sort that's almost crispy on the outside.

Her mom notices her staring at the box. "You'll be pleased to hear that the patient in question didn't recommend the cake."

"Finally, some good news. Where'd you get it?"

"Actually, the grocery store. It's chocolate."

"Chocolate's good. Is the icing chocolate or vanilla?"

"Vanilla. Does that matter?"

"Of course it matters. How could it not matter?"

Her father chimes in. "Isn't it my cake? What if I wanted lemon?"

"Dad, please. Lemon cake? What's wrong with you?"

"She has a point, John. Can someone pass the brains?"

"Mom!"

When it's time, her father says they shouldn't bother with candles on the cake. "Too many this year," he jokes. "You'll have to call the fire department."

Elizabeth rolls her eyes again. Her dad has made the same joke every birthday for the past ten years. Possibly longer, she realizes, since her memory only goes back about that long.

"Nonsense," her mom says. She's rummaging through a box labeled "kitchen—miscellaneous."

"Here we go." She sticks a candle into the cake. "Uh-oh. Anyone have a match?" Reflexively, she reaches for the cupboard over the sink, where they kept the matches in Vancouver.

Her father looks stumped. "I think we threw out the match jar while we were packing."

"I might have some," offers Elizabeth.

"You have matches? Why do you have matches?" Her mother turns to give her a penetrating stare.

"Sometimes I play with them. When I'm not smoking." Elizabeth rolls her eyes. "It's for my scented candles. Remember my candles? All, like, twenty-seven of them?"

"Funny. Right. Candles." Her mom gives her another look. "You're a real comedian."

"It's a coping mechanism."

Her dad looks up. "What do you mean, Liz?"

"It means that otherwise I'd focus on having no friends. Also, no life."

"Ah, well in that case, I think you mean a defense mechanism." Her mom licks some icing off her fingers.

"Whatever. What's the difference, anyway?"

"Don't they teach you anything in school?" her mother says.

"Not really. Wait. We did spend a lot of time learning about isotherms."

Her dad shakes his head. "I think you mean isotopes."

"I'm sure it was isotherms."

"No, Liz. Isotopes. You're dad's right. Like in chemistry, when a molecule has two shapes or something."

"Actually, Amanda, I think those are isomers." Her dad looks delighted. It's not often he gets to prove her mother wrong. He drums his fingers happily on the table.

"You're both crazy." Elizabeth pushes her chair back and stands up. "I haven't even taken chemistry. These have something to do with geography. Like in the tundra?"

"What is tundra again?" Her mother frowns.

"Near the Arctic. Like, in between where it's cold and really, really cold." Elizabeth walks toward the door. "I'll go get the matches."

Elizabeth hurries up the stairs. She'd found the matches yesterday, in the underwear box. She hadn't exactly been careful about what went in which box when packing. At the time, it didn't seem like a big deal: So what if she packed her hair products with her textbooks? Now, though, finding her belongings is like an ongoing scavenger hunt, only there are no clues. Worse, her history textbook is completely covered in mousse.

Matches in hand, she returns to the kitchen. "Liz, any idea why this was in a box marked *dishes*?" Her mother holds up a pair of lab goggles. Elizabeth has a vague memory of tossing them in after a particularly difficult ninth grade science lab involving hydrochloric acid. She hopes her mom plans on running the dishes through the dishwasher before serving food on them again.

"Sorry. Why is there a nine on Dad's cake?"

"It was the only candle I could find."

"Wouldn't no candle be better?"

"Don't be ridiculous. This is a birthday cake." Her mother takes a match and lights the nine-shaped candle, which is pink and cracked. The cake is iced white with green trim and blue roses, only the roses have melted slightly in the afternoon heat and now look more like blobs of finger paint.

"Dad?"

"I'm not arguing over this one, sweetie. I have to pick my battles."

"Oh, right. The lamps."

Her dad blows out his candle. Her mother uses a carving knife to slice the cake; she can't find the cake server.

"That looks scary, Mom." Elizabeth nods at the knife, which cuts easily through the layers of cake and icing. "Freakish."

"Just be glad I found it. Otherwise I would have had to use a box-cutter."

"Gross."

Elizabeth takes a large bite. "The icing is too creamy," she says.

"Oh, well, sorry, Your Highness," says her mom. "Should I take your piece, then?"

"Ha. You did name me after the queen, you know. And no, I'll keep it. It's better than starving."

"All right, Princess. Do you have a gift for the King here?"

"Of course." Elizabeth reaches under the table, where she's stowed her purse. She pulls out the little parcel and hands it to her father. "Happy ninth birthday, Dad."

"This is wrapped so nicely, Liz," he says. Thank you."

"It's newspaper, Dad."

"I know, but it's so neat."

Elizabeth rolls her eyes. "Just open it!"

He peels back the tape and carefully unwraps the paper, picking up the wooden soldier inside with both hands.

"Oh, Liz." He turns it over, examining it. His hands are

large, and the little doll looks tiny by comparison. "This is wonderful. Thank you."

Her mom peers over his shoulder, interested. "Strange," she says. "It looks like a baby doll, doesn't it? But it's been painted as a soldier."

Elizabeth nods. "The woman at the yard sale called it a 'soldier baby,'" she says.

Her mother shoots her a grateful look. "Thank you for picking something so small."

"What happened to the lamps, Mom?"

"Boiler room."

"Ah."

Her dad shakes his head. "So unfair. They were such an interesting plaid," he says. He looks down at the doll again. "Thank you, honey. I love it. I'll take it with me to Kabul. A good luck charm."

"I thought the outfit looked a little like what you wore in the old pictures," says Elizabeth shyly. "Before you switched to engineering." Her dad had been a pilot before becoming an aeronautical engineer.

He smiles, remembering. "It does a bit, doesn't it?"

Her mother stares at the doll, frowning. Her father notices and clutches it protectively to his chest. "I'm not getting rid of it. This isn't junk, it's—"

"No, no." Her mom shakes her head. "It just reminds me of something. But I can't remember what, exactly."

"Really? You've seen something like this before?" He looks interested.

"No. Yes. I'm not sure." She shakes her head again. "It feels like it's on the tip of my tongue."

"Maybe there are lots of these," suggests Elizabeth. "Was it a toy or something way back?"

"That's not it," her mom says. She's still frowning.

"I'm sure it will come to you," says her father. He pats her on the arm.

"I feel like I'm losing it."

"Have you put your keys in the dishwasher or anything?"

"Huh?" Her parents both turn to look at Elizabeth.

"It was a joke. Sort of. I saw this thing on TV about Alzheimer's. It showed people in the early stages putting things in the wrong place. The example they gave was keys in the dishwasher."

"I'm forty, not four hundred." Her mom looks offended now. "You know, if I had said something like that to my mother, I would have been slapped."

Her father laughs. "My dad used to threaten to drop me off at the orphanage."

"Are there still orphanages?" asks Elizabeth, curious.

"Not in Canada. Now children have foster parents if there's no one to look after them."

Her mother nods. "Doesn't have quite the same ring to it. If you're so unhappy here, maybe we should take you to live with a foster family!"

"My mom used to wash our mouths out with soap. How about you?"

"Oh, absolutely." Her mother eyes Elizabeth.

"Don't even think about it." Elizabeth stares back defiantly. "Do you want me to go live with a foster family?"

They're laughing now. Elizabeth watches her mother. She closes her eyes when she laughs. She closes them tight and scrunches up her nose and cheeks. It's not exactly flattering, but her good humor is infectious. When her mom laughs, people usually join in.

"Has it come to you?" Her dad turns to her mom. "About the doll?"

"No, not yet," she says. She shakes her head again. "I'll let you know."

"Thanks again, sweetie." He leans over and gives Elizabeth a kiss on the cheek, quickly, so she doesn't have a chance to move away. "I really like it. Very thoughtful."

"You're welcome, Dad."

"My turn." Her mom smiles. "It's outside."

Elizabeth looks at her eagerly. "Is it a new car?"

"Sadly, no. But I think it will make your father very happy. Go look out the window to the backyard."

The new kitchen opens to a large family room with a double set of glass French doors to the back deck. The three go over and stand, staring.

"What are we looking at, Mom?"

"Look at the far left corner." She points.

It's a small shed that looks almost like a little barn. It's painted black and white with a bright red door, just like their new house.

"I had it delivered from Home Depot this morning."

"Oh, Amanda. Thank you." Her father presses his face against the glass to get a better look, and then turns back to his wife. "For my finds?"

"Yes. A junk shed. Since we don't have a garage here."

"Oh, sweetheart." He puts his arm around her.

Elizabeth watches her parents and wonders how old you have to be to get excited over a shed as a birthday present. She hopes it's a long way away.

"You're welcome, Johnny."

Johnny? Ugh. Her parents are entwined now, like a pair of middle schoolers slow dancing in a school gym. They're kissing, too. They always get like this on special occasions. *Gross.* She looks away, embarrassed, then turns back to the kitchen. She sees the half-eaten cake out of the corner of her eye. It hasn't yet been put away.

Couldn't hurt to have another slice, she reasons. Attacking it directly with a fork, she shaves some off one of the edges and takes a large bite. *Maybe the icing isn't so bad after all.* She scoops the remaining flowers off the top.

"Any plans for the weekend?"

Elizabeth looks up from her laptop. *Is he serious?* "I do, actually," she says. Her voice is riddled with sarcasm. "I plan to buy myself a bag of barbecue chips. Then I plan to eat the whole bag."

Her dad sighs. Elizabeth watches him. He's unpacking a box of utensils. He can tell she's upset, but the sarcasm is lost on him; he's too earnest. Looking uncertain, he holds up a potato masher. "Any idea where this goes?"

"That depends." Elizabeth eyes it suspiciously. What is it?"

"It's for mashing potatoes."

"Why do we have that?"

"What do you mean?" Her father looks confused.

"Has anyone here ever mashed potatoes?" Elizabeth goes back to typing. She ducks her head behind her laptop so her dad can't tell she's rolling her eyes.

"Your mother makes mashed potatoes all the time."

"They come from a package, Dad."

"Do they? Really?"

"Yeah."

"They're so good though."

"That's why we don't need a potato masher."

"Right." Her father looks around. "I'll just stick it in this drawer."

Elizabeth sighs, exasperated. She stops typing again. "Throw it out!"

"I think it might have been a wedding present." Her dad looks guiltily at the potato masher.

Elizabeth rolls her eyes again, this time not bothering to duck behind the screen. "You've been married for, like, fifty years. You can throw it out now."

"Seventeen," her father corrects her, looking affronted. "And what if it was from someone important?"

"Like who? The pope?"

"Funny. Like Granny?"

"Who do you think taught Mom about the instant potatoes?"

He puts the masher on the counter. "I'll let your mother deal with it," he says. He sits down at the table next to Elizabeth. "I'm sorry about the weekend question. I guess that was stupid."

"Kind of."

"I forgot."

"Which part? That I don't have any friends here?" Elizabeth's face flushes. Hearing herself say the words out loud makes it more real, and she feels her heart speed up in fear at the truth of the statement. *I have no friends.* She shudders.

"I'm really sorry. It was thoughtless. I'm an idiot."

"Yeah."

He leans over and peers at her computer screen. "That's Facebook?" he asks, curious.

"Dad!" Elizabeth protests. She twists the screen out of his line of vision. "That's private!"

"Sorry, sorry! I'm not trying to spy. I'm just interested."

"It's not so interesting. I'm just talking to Katie."

"How's she doing?"

Elizabeth looks at her father's face. He looks so kind, so sincere. For a moment she says nothing. Then she feels her resolve crumble, and she gestures toward the screen. "Everyone went on a hike yesterday." The unspoken words *without me* hang in the air between them. She avoids her father's stare and looks at a spot on the wall beyond him, where he's just put up a calendar. She closes her eyes; she doesn't want to see that, either. It's already mid-July. *Less than two months to go until school.*

"I'm sorry, hon." He pauses. "Have you thought about trying to meet some people before school starts?"

"I've thought about it."

"And?"

"Dad. You don't just decide to meet people. Think about what you just said."

"I'm zero for two, aren't I?"

"Unfortunately."

"Maybe your mother has some ideas." He sounds half-hearted, as if even he doesn't truly believe what he's saying. Now he avoids her gaze. He stares at a nick in the wood table that wasn't there before the move.

Elizabeth raises her eyebrows. "Sure," she says. "We'll ask her. Put it on the list with the potato masher."

"Zero for three?" he asks.

"Yup."

"I guess suggesting you go to the community center would be like digging my own grave at this point."

"Community center, really? Have we unpacked the shovel?"

Grave. Elizabeth suddenly thinks of Afghanistan and feels a twinge of guilt. *What if something happens to him?* She pushes the feelings aside, buries them. "Sorry, Dad. I just need some alone time right now. Okay?"

"Absolutely." He stands up and pats her awkwardly on the back. "I'll go tackle the basement," he says. He fiddles with his watch for a second, then disappears.

Elizabeth watches him go, before turning back to her

computer. Katie is online, and she wants to know all about the new house.

> how's ur room?

> ok. big. have my own bathroom here.

> lucky!! i have to share with andrew. he's disgusting, there was PUBIC HAIR in the sink. WHAT is he doing in there???

> EW!

> I know. Anyway—talk later? My mom is screaming about something.

> OK. bye. Say hi to Elise and everyone.

Elizabeth stares at the screen. *What would it be like to share a bathroom with a brother?* Brother. The concept is foreign to her. When she was little, she found it harder, being an only child. It was more obvious back then, at friends' houses or at the playground. As she got older, she grew more comfortable with not having brothers or sisters around. Even so, there were moments when she still felt that emptiness, that sense that someone was missing from her life. Worse, her parents never talked about it, and she knew they had wanted more children. When she was little, she'd sometimes catch her parents whispering; she heard words like "miscarriage" and "infertility." She hadn't known what they meant then, but she did now. She would have liked to talk about it, but she worried it would hurt her mother. She didn't want to see her cry. Not about that. Not again.

Elizabeth remembers that day clearly: first grade. How proud she'd felt! Miss James had singled her Popsicle-stick picture frame out for praise, complimenting her choice of color. Light blue—Mom's favorite—she recalls. She'd had to mix the white and blue paints carefully to get the right shade.

Where was her mom, anyway? Only six, Elizabeth had been confused. It wasn't like her mother not to be waiting at the front door when she came home from school, waiting to ask her questions about what she'd learned and whom she'd played with. Bewildered, Elizabeth had walked around the house, then up the stairs, searching. Why was the bedroom door closed? It was always open. She listened. What was that inside? Was she on the phone? Elizabeth listened closer. Was that crying? She took a step back, frightened, then peered into her parents' room.

Her mother sat huddled on the bed, holding an old sleeper of Elizabeth's and crying. The sleeper was pink and faded. Her mother brought it to her face. She gave a stifled sob and closed her eyes.

Elizabeth had stood at the door, clutching her frame. Should she go in? Give her a hug? The frame? She watched her mother for another moment. Then, frame in hand, she turned and walked away. She never told her mother what she'd seen.

Only child. She sometimes hates that term. It makes her feel as if there's something wrong with her, with her family. There aren't labels for other families. No one says to Katie,

"Oh, you're a pair-child." It annoys her. It feels like judgment. Now, though, Elizabeth can't help wondering what it might have been like to have a sibling to share this move with—even if it was a brother like Andrew. Built-in company that wasn't your parents: the idea feels foreign to her.

Elizabeth takes a last look at the new photos on Katie's Facebook page and snaps the laptop shut. *Enough self-torture for one day*. She looks around the kitchen. It's bigger than their old one, and brighter. Everything is white: the cabinets, the counters. The walls. She pictures the old house in Vancouver. Everything had been smaller there, but it hadn't felt cramped. It had been cozy. It felt like home. What's the new family like? She thinks of someone else living in her room and feels strange, as if someone is watching her, a prickly feeling on the back of her neck. This new house isn't bad, but it's not quite home. Not yet, anyway.

Elizabeth's gaze falls upon the little soldier doll, which is perched on the kitchen counter next to an unpacked box labeled "fancy dishes." *That is so Dad*. She rolls her eyes. Her father has an annoying habit of leaving his things in a trail around the house, Hansel and Gretel style. It drives her mother crazy. *It's going to end up with the potato masher*, she thinks. She goes over to pick it up, to move it to safety. It looks back at her, unblinking. "You really are a weird little thing, aren't you?" she muses. She settles it carefully on the fireplace mantle.

CHAPTER 2
Toronto, Canada
2007

"Do you think you'll ever leave the house?" Her mother is unloading the dishwasher. She carefully sets a mug on the counter and looks at Elizabeth, who sticks out her tongue.

"I leave the house all the time."

"Going to the corner store for ice-cream sandwiches doesn't count."

"Why doesn't it count?"

Her mom sighs. "I'm surprised at you, Liz. This is a great neighborhood. Lots of good stuff. Used clothing stores. Stuff you'd like."

Elizabeth looks away. "I've been busy."

"Going on the Facebook isn't *busy*."

Elizabeth cringes. "It's just Facebook. There's no *the*."

"Does it matter?" Her mother throws her hands up in the air. Elizabeth feels a small sense of satisfaction and doesn't answer. *It does matter. You don't know what you're talking about. You don't know everything.*

"Why don't you go for a walk tomorrow instead of sitting at your computer all day?"

"Whatever." Elizabeth scowls. "Fine."

Her mom rolls her eyes. "You know, the whole surly teenager thing doesn't really suit you," she says. Her voice is light. "I know you're trying hard at it, but it might be time to try a different stereotype."

Elizabeth scowls again. She's really angry now. Her fists are clenched and her mouth is twisted up on the left, the way it always gets when she loses her temper. "Stop doing that!"

"What did I do?"

"You know. Making fun of me. It's not fair. I'm allowed to be upset."

"You are. But you need to get outside. You can't sit around moping. It's been weeks."

"I have no one to go out with." *Not here*, she adds silently.

"You used to spend hours walking around the city by yourself in Vancouver! All those used clothing stores—"

That's it. "Vintage!" She's shouting now. Her mother, looking startled, loses her train of thought. Her voice trails off, and there is silence between them.

"It's vintage clothing," says Elizabeth quietly. "Not *used*. You want me to go out?" She stands up. Her eyes are flashing, and her cheeks are hot with anger. "Fine! I'll go!"

"Liz—"

Elizabeth doesn't answer. She slams the front door on her way out.

The night air feels thick and stale with heat. Even the trees look hot, their branches drooping dejectedly in the face of such oppressive temperatures. As she walks, Elizabeth feels increasingly uncomfortable. Her clothes quickly take on an irritating sticky quality, as if they've been washed in corn syrup and only half dried. Little droplets of sweat trickle with an almost predictable rhythm from her forehead down one side of her nose. Elizabeth doesn't wear much makeup, but she's sure the little she did bother to put on that morning is melting off at a rapid pace. *I can almost feel my hair frizzing.* She examines a strand and makes a face. I must look like a witch. Turning a corner, she passes the high school. She notices some girls about her own age camped out under a maple tree; they're laughing about something. Elizabeth hurries past, feeling shy.

Despite the weather, the city is pulsing with life. Restaurants have crammed extra seating onto already tiny patios, leaving diners struggling to use their cutlery without elbowing strangers at the next table. The line at the ice-cream store extends almost around the block. Children with water guns chase each other and are, in turn, chased by their parents. Couples walk close to one another but don't hold hands; it isn't really hand-holding weather. Elizabeth watches a group of girls slightly older than her try to attract the attention of two oblivious boys. They're all dressed alike; all wearing tiny shorts and skimpy tank tops. *How do they tell each other apart?* She stares, wondering if they go to her new high school.

Elizabeth stops to buy herself a Popsicle at the grocery store. Her favorite—cherry. It isn't quite as good as an ice cream, but not having to wait in line for it makes it taste better than it might have on an ordinary night. She passes by two vintage clothing stores right next to each other. They're closed for the evening, but the window displays are enticing. A red crocodile-skin purse with a jeweled clasp catches her eye, as does a lavender wrap dress that she thinks might be designer. One store is advertising a shoe sale. *Mom was right*, she thinks. *It's good to get out*. She feels a pang of guilt but keeps walking.

Elizabeth feels a sudden drop of cool water hit her neck. She looks up at the sky, but it's a clear night. She looks up again and sees the offending agent, an air conditioner. Old and clunky, it's practically groaning with effort to do its job in the stifling heat. A steady stream of water leaks onto the pavement below.

Elizabeth peeks into the store underneath. "Read It Again, Sam" says the sign above the window. Inside, the lights are on, and she can see shelves and tables stacked haphazardly with books. She pushes the door open, and a bell tinkles, announcing her entry.

Elizabeth inhales deeply, smelling that familiar odor of dust, aging paper, and old glue. She loves to read, but it's more than that, really. She loves books. When she loves a story, she wants to own it. Not just to read it again, though of course that's a part of it. There is something about having a copy of a book you love on the shelf, knowing that the book is yours and yours alone. She likes how when she reads a book again, she can sometimes recall where she'd been, or what she'd been doing, the other times she'd read it. A faint stain of dripped tea or the lingering scent of a candle or perfume—each triggers its own memories, its own set of thoughts.

"Hi, can I help you?"

Elizabeth stares at the clerk. He's about her age. Tall, he's wearing faded cutoffs and a green concert T-shirt listing tour dates in 1982 for a band she's never heard of. He has glasses and the kind of hair that sticks up in a bunch of different directions. Elizabeth thinks of her own sweaty, frizzing hair and feels herself go slightly pink.

"Thanks—I'm just looking," she says.

"As long as you're not selling." He looks relieved. "If I have to do any more inventory today, I'm quitting."

"So you buy old books here?"

"Yeah. We buy and sell. Most of our stuff's used. You probably noticed." He gestures around him.

Elizabeth nods and tries to think of something clever to say. *What was that?* She recoils, feeling something brush against her leg. Something furry. "What the—argh!" She gives a small shriek and jumps back.

"Oh no! Sorry!" The clerk rushes out from behind the desk. "That's just Boris," he explains. "Sometimes I let him out of the cage at night, when there aren't a lot of customers."

An enormous black-and-white rabbit lumbers, curious, around Elizabeth's ankles. He's sniffing her chipping purple toe polish suspiciously.

"Are you okay with him doing that? He's a good rabbit, I promise."

"Yeah, of course." Elizabeth grins and reaches down to pet Boris gently between the ears. "I've never heard of a rabbit in a bookstore before. Usually it's a cat." Boris's ears twitch, as if he knows they're talking about him. "He's huge."

The boy nods. "Sam—that's the owner—had a baby, and the kid was allergic to poor Boris. So he brought him here. He's a really good rabbit, very friendly. He is huge though. People are always shocked."

"I think he's eating my flip-flop."

"Oh no! Boris! Cut that out."

"It's okay."

The clerk puts out his hand. "I'm Evan."

"Elizabeth." They shake hands.

"Do you live around here?"

"Yeah. We just moved."

"Really?" Evan looks interested. "From where?"

"Vancouver."

"Oh wow! So you, like, really moved. Not just houses." Evan sounds impressed. "That's really cool."

"It is?"

"Yeah, for sure. Vancouver's awesome. I was there once. Snowboarding. I guess you board, right?"

Elizabeth blushes again. "No."

"No? Why?"

"Bad experience."

"How bad?"

"Bad."

"Bad, like, a full-body cast?"

"Something like that." Elizabeth doesn't elaborate. She certainly isn't going to tell Evan the story of how, at age nine, she'd gone for skiing lessons and her new braces had got stuck on the rope tow. She'd been screaming in fear, and the evil contraption had taken advantage of her open-mouthed expression. The hill had been shut down for over an hour while paramedics had been called in to disentangle Elizabeth's orthodontia from the yellow twine.

"Are you going to Westwood?" Evan is talking again.

Just hearing the name of the high school is enough to set off the butterflies in Elizabeth's stomach. "Yeah," she says. An old poster catches her eye; it's for *Gone with the Wind*. Her mom's favorite. The butterflies morph into a knife-like feeling, which she ignores.

"Me too. I mean, I go there." He leans back on his elbows against the desk. "Do you—oh no!" He swears under his breath as a small pile of books crashes to the floor.

Elizabeth bends down. "Let me help."

"No, no. You don't have to do that." He stoops over and tries to take the books she's collecting.

"Well, I'm not going to just let Boris eat this copy of *The Fountainhead*."

"Boris!"

Elizabeth hands the remaining books to Evan. On the top of the pile is a copy of Margaret Merriweather's *Autumn Evening*. "Oh, I love that one." She takes it back and turns it over in her hands.

"Which one?" Evan peers at the cover. "Oh, yeah," he says. "It's great. Did you do it in ninth grade?"

"Yes! You too?"

"Yeah. Sometimes teachers pick really crappy books for class, but most people like that one." Evan runs his hand through his hair, making it look even messier.

Elizabeth opens the novel and reads the first paragraph.

"Have you read any of her other stuff?" Evan is watching her.

She stops reading, embarrassed. "I thought this was her only novel."

"It is. You don't read poetry?"

"I didn't know she wrote poetry." Elizabeth looks away, pretending to be absorbed by a display of science fiction from the seventies.

"Really?" Evan looks surprised. "You didn't do 'The Soldier Doll' in tenth grade?"

"No. Well, not yet. I'm going into ten. Wait—" Elizabeth looks up at him. "What did you say?"

"Huh? What did I say?" He looks confused. "I'm going into eleven, by the way."

"Sorry." Elizabeth shakes her head. "The poem. Did you say 'The Soldier Doll'?"

"Yeah, why?" Evan is giving her a curious look. He gathers up some books and stacks them in a haphazard pile.

"I've just never heard of it," she says evasively. She puts the Merriweather book down and picks up an old recipe book, studying the cover intently.

Evan doesn't notice. "Apparently it's really famous," he says. He adds another book to the pile, which looks as if it might collapse. "You know, like, with adults. It's about war. We did it at the same time as 'In Flanders Fields.'"

"That's the poem about the poppies?" Finally, something she knows. Relieved, Elizabeth looks up again.

"Yeah."

"What's the poem about—'The Soldier Doll'?" Elizabeth tries to sound casual.

"Actually, it's really interesting." Evan leans against the desk again, this time accidentally knocking over a container of pens. Elizabeth tries not to smile as they roll off the desk and onto the weather-beaten parquet floor. Boris hops over eagerly to sniff them; realizing they are not food, his nose twitches and he turns his back, dejected. Evan scoops up the pens and continues without missing a beat. "It's apparently based on a real doll, but it went missing."

"Missing?" Involuntarily, Elizabeth leans toward him and notices he has a dimple on his left cheek. She feels herself blushing again and averts her eyes back to the sci-fi.

"Yeah," he says. "That's what my teacher said, anyway. Lost in a war or something. People are always looking for it and whatever." He looks pleased to see that Elizabeth is so enthralled. He grins, smug with his knowledge, as he carefully places the pens back in their container.

"A real soldier doll?" Elizabeth feels her heart start to pound. Any louder and it's going to overtake the noise of the air conditioner.

"Yeah. It's the symbolism, right? The idea of innocence in war." Evan brightens. "Let me see if I have a copy of Merriweather's poetry." He goes over to the computer.

Elizabeth watches Evan type something on the keyboard, which is old and clunky. It looks as if it was probably once white but is now worn and yellowed. *You're being silly*, she tells herself. She picks up the copy of *Autumn Evening* again and stares at the cover. *It's just a coincidence.*

"Good news." Evan is talking again. "We have one!"

"I'll take it!" Elizabeth feels a thrill of excitement. Her fingers clutch the copy of *Autumn Evening* tightly; she feels the cover dig into her palm.

"Great. One sec." Evan walks to the back of the store, where the poetry section is apparently located. She watches him climb onto a rickety step stool, cursing under his breath again as it creaks beneath him. He comes back, triumphantly waving a slim hardcover. It's old and battered-looking.

"More good news," he says. "It's only two bucks."

Elizabeth reaches into her bag, and out of the corner of her eye, she sees the lollipop again. She carefully avoids it.

"You know what?" Evan reaches into his pocket and fishes out two dollars. "It's on me."

"No!" Elizabeth blushes again. "I can't. I just met you!"

"You might hate it though, and I made you buy it."

"You're recommending it. You work in a bookstore. That's your job."

"I insist." He drops the money into the cash register. "There. Done. Nothing you can do now."

"Well, thanks. That was really unnecessary." Elizabeth takes the book. Her hand touches his for just a second; it feels cool.

"I hope you like it," he says.

"I'm sure I will." Elizabeth pauses. *Should I leave now? Or say something more?*

"Are you on Facebook?" Evan pulls out his phone. "What's your full name?"

"Elizabeth Bryant." She spells it for him. "Yeah, I'm on Facebook."

"I'll find you. Do you have a cell phone? What's your number?"

Elizabeth pauses. *Damn.* "This is awful, but I don't remember. And I left it at home." She curses silently; a string of expletives runs through her head like subtitles in a foreign film.

"You don't remember? Is that a hint?" Evan raises his eyebrows.

"A hint? At what?" Elizabeth looks at him, bewildered.

"That you'd rather never hear from me again?" Evan winks at her mischievously.

"Huh? Oh! No!" Elizabeth shakes her head furiously. "I'm just bad with numbers, and it's a new one. I feel really stupid."

"Fair explanation." Evan grins. "We'll see if you'll accept my Facebook invitation."

"I will, I swear!"

Evan tucks his phone back in his pocket. "Nice meeting you, Elizabeth."

"You too. And thanks for the book." Their eyes meet.

Elizabeth notices his are an unusual green color, almost like a cat's. Elizabeth smiles at him but turns quickly away. She doesn't want Evan to see her blush again as she leaves the bookstore.

"I'm sorry, Liz."

Her mother is hovering near the door, worried, when she returns. She exhales loudly when she sees Elizabeth, clearly relieved. She's in her pajamas now, pacing the black-and-white tiled hallway between two piles of empty boxes her dad hasn't yet gotten around to flattening.

"It's okay. You were right," Elizabeth says softly, dropping her purse to the ground.

"It's just that—wait. Did you just say I was right?"

"Maybe." Elizabeth walks toward the kitchen. "I'm starving." She opens the pantry. There isn't much, other than a box of cornflakes and a bag of pretzels. She opts for the pretzels, opening the bag with her teeth. She cuts her gums on the hard plastic and winces, running her tongue along the wound.

"Hold on, I want get to get that on tape." Her mom follows her into the kitchen.

"On tape?" Leaning against the kitchen counter, Elizabeth rolls her eyes and bites into a pretzel. "I'm not even sure they *make* tapes anymore."

"They do so." Her mother fills a kettle with water and places it on the stove.

"Don't think so." Elizabeth's voice is muffled by a mouth full of pretzel.

"I have a Dictaphone at work. It uses tapes. So there." Her mother looks triumphant.

"A Dictaphone?" Elizabeth looks bewildered.

"It's like a miniature tape recorder." Her mother takes out two mugs and places tea bags in each: peppermint, Elizabeth's favorite.

"I have no idea what you're talking about. Did you have to order it special, like, from the Smithsonian?"

"Very funny. What was I saying?" The kettle is whistling. Her mom pauses. She turns toward the stove and turns it off as the whistling grows louder and more insistent. Carefully, she pours the steaming water into each mug and hands one to her daughter.

"Thanks." Elizabeth takes the mug and sips her tea. "You were nagging me about something, probably. Pretzel?" She offers her mother the bag.

"No, thanks. Anyway, I'm sorry about earlier." She puts a hand on Liz's shoulder. "I was being unfair. If my parents moved me across the country at fifteen, I'd have probably run away."

"Is that advice?"

"Don't even joke." Her mother puts down her mug and gives her a tentative hug.

"I'm sorry too, Mom." Elizabeth hugs her back tightly. She can feel her clothes clinging to her back like they've been pasted on, still sticky with sweat from her walk.

"So you had a nice walk?" Her mother picks up her mug of tea and inhales the minty aroma before taking a sip.

"Yeah." Elizabeth is about to say more, but decides not to. She takes a sip of her own tea. "It's a nice neighborhood," she says finally.

"I won't say I told you so." Her mom smiles. "Was anything open?"

"Some stuff. I need to go back during the day. Maybe tomorrow."

"That's great," her mother yawns. "I should go to bed. I have a patient coming in before eight." She brings the mug to her lips a final time before setting it in the kitchen sink.

Elizabeth shudders. *Eight.* A full three hours before she plans on even getting out of bed.

"Shut off all the lights before you come up, okay?"

"Sure, Mom. Night." Elizabeth listens as her mother climbs the creaking stairs. Most of the house has been completely renovated by previous owners, but the staircase is part of the original house.

Elizabeth waits until the noise stops. She goes back into the hall and grabs the book from her bag. *The Soldier Doll. So weird*, she thinks. She peels the lollipop off the back cover and marches to the trash, tossing the half-eaten candy in with relish. Leaning against the counter, she reaches for another pretzel and flips the book open to the poem. As she reads, she feels her heart speed up, thumping loudly against her chest.

"Cherubic face and eyes of blue/His boots are shined, his rifle new." She reads it twice before carefully placing the book facedown on the counter to mark her place. She walks over to the fireplace. *Could it be?* she wonders. Evan said people have been searching for it. Elizabeth looks up at the little soldier. He stares back at her from his place on the mantle, serene and full of secrets. Could the little figure really be the soldier doll from the poem? But if it is, how on earth did he make his way to the yard sale? And, more importantly, where could he have been hiding all these years?

CHAPTER 3
Devon, England
1918

"Meg! Megsy! Wait for me!"

Meg paused and looked over her shoulder. Ned had almost slipped running along the grass, still slick with yesterday's rain. "I shouldn't think so!" she shouted. "You have to catch me!" Laughing, she lifted her skirts and continued her dash toward the river, long hair flying loose behind her like a kite's streamers on a windy day, the kind that children flew at summer picnics. The sun was strong and warm though now and then a brisk breeze would rattle the trees, cooling the April air.

Meg saw Ned groan and force himself along, out of breath from running. She sprawled out on the grass, lazily braiding her hair.

"Why so slow, lazy bones?" Meg's green eyes twinkled as

he approached. She kicked off her shoes and wiggled her toes. "My feet are sore from running so much quicker than you." She grinned and looked out at the river. Spring was coming—there were signs of it all around—but the water would still be too cold for swimming or wading until perhaps June.

Ned collapsed next to her. "You really must stop that, Meg." He coughed, his shoulders shaking slightly. "It's harder for me to keep up with you now." He plucked a blade of grass and rubbed it between his fingers.

"Nonsense." Meg looked away. "Don't be silly. You're well now. The doctor said it himself." She found a stone and picked it up. With surprising force, she tossed it toward the river. It skipped once before sinking; they both watched it go down.

Ned coughed again. "I am on the mend, but I'm out of practice. I'm not quite ready yet for running races to the water." He gave her an apologetic look and a hopeful smile. He took the blade of grass and ran it behind her ear, tickling her skin.

Meg brushed his hand away and stared at the ground. Ned had taken ill just past Christmas. She had been permitted to visit and had done so every day, bringing him books, soups, and freshly baked bread. The entire time, Meg had stubbornly refused to acknowledge Ned's pneumonia directly.

"You'll be on your feet again any day now!" she'd exclaimed whenever Ned had gently tried to broach the subject of his illness. But the days had turned into weeks, and the weeks, months. And then finally, a week ago, Dr. Porter had given Ned a clean bill of health. At last.

Ned touched her shoulder. "Megsy, I know you refused to

believe I was really ill." He let his hand rest there for a moment, feeling her hair.

"I did not!" Meg glared at him. "I knew you were, Ned. I came every day, did I not?" *Even when you were too ill to know I was there,* she added silently. She yanked a small daisy from the ground and twisted it in her hands. Angry, she plucked off a petal and tossed the daisy aside.

Ned grinned and shook his head. "There's no arguing with you, is there." It wasn't a question. "I say, Meg. You're the most stubborn creature on earth."

Meg rolled her eyes. "You're always saying that."

"Because it's true! I reckon you get it from your father."

Her mother had taken ill and died when Meg was only seven. Her father, a cabinetmaker, had raised Meg himself. He had never remarried. His reputation for stubbornness in the village was legendary. When his wife had died, he had mulishly refused repeated well-intentioned offers from the village's women to help care for Meg. "I can take care of my child just fine on my own," he'd insisted. He had pointedly ignored parcels of food left on his doorstep, despite the acrid smell of burned meals emanating from his own kitchen as he attempted to assume his wife's former duties. It had paid off, though—with little Meg's help, he'd quickly learned how to cook basic dinners and manage a household.

"I am not stubborn."

"You are! You are even being stubborn about not being stubborn! Confess. You're stubborn as a mule."

"A mule! Now you've offended me, Edwin Roberts." Meg turned away, trying not to laugh.

Ned sighed. "I'll say it again. There's no winning with you. Do you know that you have never once admitted that I've won an argument?" He buried his head in his hands in mock frustration.

"I can't help it if you're never right, Ned. That's something you need to work on yourself. Blaming me is unfair, really," Meg replied cheerfully. She tapped Ned playfully on the shoulder.

Ned raised his palms in defeat. "Fine, then," he said. He was smiling now. "We don't have to talk about it." He coughed and reached over to give her braid a tug.

Meg stole an anxious glance at him. "You are better, Ned, are you not?" She had picked up the daisy again and now twirled it nervously. Meg thought of her mother and tried to remember how her cough had sounded before she'd died.

"I believe so, yes." Ned took a deep breath. "That's why I wanted to talk to you today. Alone." He fidgeted nervously.

What could be wrong with him now? Meg looked at Ned, feeling worried. "Whatever is the matter?" She studied his face. He looked pale. "You are well now, aren't you? You haven't taken ill again?"

"I'm fine." Ned moved closer to her. "But I had my eighteenth birthday last month. And Dr. Porter, he says I'm healthy now." He put his hand on hers tentatively.

"You just said that, Ned." Meg continued to look puzzled.

Suddenly, she understood. Her expression turned to one of comprehension and then of horror.

"No!" She jumped up, accidentally squashing a patch of budding daffodils. "No!" Ned grabbed her arm, but she tore away from him, shaking off his grip. "No!" she wailed a third time. She started to run off but stopped after a few strides, sinking down again onto a rock. "No," she said again. This time her voice was quiet.

"Please, Meg." He looked pained. "I have no choice." His voice was soft now. He crouched down beside her. A tendril of golden hair had come loose from her braid. Gently, Ned tucked it behind her ear. "Every man who can fight must go. You know that, Meg. It's the law."

Meg glared at him. "You cannot go." She was furious. She stamped her foot on the grass, intentionally crushing a small patch of violets. "You were just *ill*! You've not yet fully recovered. You're still coughing!" She stomped on the flowers a second time, taking pleasure in watching them wilt to the ground.

"Megsy." Ned reached over and took her chin. "I have no choice. You know that. And even if I did—how could I not go like all the other men in town? What would people say about me? I would get a white feather. Please. Think about it." His eyes were pleading. The sun, so strong just moments before, now seemed to have disappeared behind the clouds. Without its glow to warm them, Meg suddenly felt cold. Ned coughed into his arm, then reached over again toward her.

Meg pulled away. "Tom Jeffries, Peter Maines, George

Taylor—none of them came back." She stared at the river, refusing to meet his eyes.

"I'll come back. I know I will." Ned reached for her again. "Please, Meg. I don't have a choice. Can I ask you not to make this any more difficult for me than it is already?" A gust of wind shook them. Ned buttoned his coat.

"You can't even keep pace with me," she said through gritted teeth as her eyes filled with tears. "How will you march off to war?" Her voice was bitter now. She wrapped her shawl around her shoulders and pulled it tight.

"I'm not leaving quite yet." Ned met her gaze. "And there's training. I'll be ready by then. Dr. Porter said—"

"That's it!" Meg leaped up again. "We shall speak with Dr. Porter. We'll explain to him that he must tell the officials you are still much too ill to be signing up." Her eyes blazed with inspiration.

"No, Megsy." Ned shook his head. He grasped her hands and held them tightly, pulling her back down next to him. "No. Please, darling. Listen to me. I have to go. I must—"

Meg shook her head, cutting him off. "You shan't. Dr. Porter is a close friend of my father's. We'll explain to him, and he will—"

"No, Meg." Ned's voice was firm now. "Dr. Porter can't do that. He took an oath, as a physician. And even if he would do it—I would not want him to. It's not proper. I must go, and I shall. How would I feel, knowing that I was the only one in the town who did not fight?"

Meg didn't answer. She pictured Tom and George and all the others who had waved good-bye in their uniforms, so eager to go.

"Fine, Ned." Her voice was dull now. "I can see I'm not going to convince you. No matter what I say, you're going to go." She pulled again at her shawl, her shoulders slumping, and shivered.

Ned was taken aback. "Did I just win an argument?" He gave her a teasing smile, but she didn't respond.

"Meg?" He put an arm around her. "I have to go. And as soon as it's all over, I'll come right back." He pulled her closer. For a moment, Meg let herself lean against him. His skin felt cool to the touch.

"Of course." Meg's voice was brusque as she pulled away from him again. "Brrr!" She stood up. "It's getting colder. We should be heading back, really. I must start Father's tea." She gathered her skirts and began walking, her pace hurried. She wrapped her arms around herself for warmth, still trembling.

"Meg—wait!" Close at her heels, Ned grabbed her by the wrist and pulled her back to him. He took her hand and looked into her eyes. "Meg—I love you. You know that, right? I've always loved you. Since we were children." He licked his lips, looking nervous.

Startled, Meg looked up at him. She wasn't sure how to respond. "Oh," she managed, her voice shaking. "Well, I love you too, Ned. You know that." Blinking in surprise, she let go of his hand and stumbled back a few paces. Ned quickly made up the distance between them and grabbed her hand again.

He was sweating despite the cold, and his cheeks were flushed a bright pink.

"Well, then. Not exactly how I rehearsed it, but…" Ned's voice trailed off. He took a deep breath and bent down on one knee. Meg watched, shocked, as he reached into his pocket and pulled out a small wooden box. Her heart was beating so fast, she could barely hear his words as he spoke. He released her hand to open the box and retrieved from inside a small gold ring. Meg breathed in sharply.

"I know it's not much." He looked apologetic, his cheeks almost purple now. "But one day, if the printing business does well—"

"Sh," said Meg. She put a finger to his lips, and then allowed him to slip the ring on her finger. "A perfect fit." She looked up at him, eyes moist. "It's beautiful, Ned." She held her hand up to get a better look at the ring. She stared at it, admiring, turning her hand in different directions, preening slightly. Ned watched her. She remembered he was there and dropped her hand back to her side, her own cheeks reddening.

"I gather that's a yes, then?" Ned coughed. He was smiling now but still looked anxious, fiddling with the box and shuffling his feet. "I asked your father's permission."

"Did you?" Meg laughed. She pictured her father's embarrassed reaction and gruff response. "Poor Father. I imagine he got quite flustered."

"Well, a bit." Ned grinned. His color was returning to normal now. "But he gave it. Didn't seem all that surprised that I was asking. I suppose everyone will have seen this coming."

Meg stared at her new ring again. "Shall we be wed soon, then, Ned? Before you leave?" The sun had come out again. In the sunlight, the gold of the ring glittered brightly. Rainbows scattered in every direction.

"Well…" Ned fidgeted with his hands. "I've been giving this quite a bit of thought. The thing is, I'd prefer to wait until I return. You're so very young, after all. And we can plan a proper wedding that way."

Meg waved her hand dismissively. "I don't need a fancy wedding." She shook her head. "Whatever for? I just want to be wed to you." She laughed lightheartedly. She twirled a lock of hair around her newly adorned ring finger. In the sun, the color was almost a match to the ring.

"No." It was Ned's turn to be stubborn. "I want you to have a nice wedding like all the other girls, with a proper dress. You deserve it. You're the prettiest and smartest of them all."

"Ned," Meg sighed in frustration. She rolled her eyes. "I don't care about a silly wedding and a silly dress. I think we should be wed as soon as possible. Before you leave."

"No, Meg." Ned took her hand in his and stared at the ring. "We'll have a beautiful wedding. Even if you don't want it, *I* want it for you." He looked at her, earnest.

Meg bit her lip. She could see this meant a lot to Ned. She willed herself not to stomp her foot.

"Fine, then, Ned." She laid her head gently on his shoulder. "We'll have your fancy wedding. When you return." The breeze was picking up again, stronger now. Meg gritted her teeth, determined, and closed her eyes as the breeze became a wind, whipping against her face with increasing ferocity.

"So, did he do it, then?" Jim Merriweather gave his daughter an appraising look and put his hammer down as she entered the small cottage. He was building a kitchen pantry for the Thomas family next door. He picked up a rag and wiped the sweat from his forehead. His large size and wild hair gave him a rather intimidating appearance, but his eyes were kind and his soul gentle.

"That's romantic, Father." Meg's voice was dry as she hung up her shawl. "What if he hadn't? You'd have ruined the surprise."

"Bah," Mr. Merriweather picked up the hammer again. "He couldn't have kept it a secret. Boy was never much good at hiding things. Feelings written all over his face."

"Well, the answer is yes." Meg grinned. She held out her hand to show off her new ring. "He did ask, and I accepted."

Mr. Merriweather nodded his approval. "He's a good chap." He hammered a nail into the door of the pantry. "You'll be happy with him. Promised me he'd take good care of you."

"He's going off to war, you know." Meg tried to sound casual, but her father looked up. He was a perceptive man and caught the change in her tone immediately.

"He's a strong boy," said her father, his tone brusque. "Doctor says he's in good shape now. He'll do fine. Everyone is saying the war will be over soon. He'll be back in no time at all. You'll see." His voice was strong and reassuring, but he didn't look at her. He busied himself with the hammer in his hands, as if inspecting it for some sudden and previously overlooked defect.

"Tom and George didn't come back." Meg sat down across from her father in the little chair he'd made especially for her so she could watch him work. It was a touch small for her now, but it was still her favorite place to sit. She folded her hands in her lap and stared down at them, and crossed and uncrossed her feet.

"Now, Margaret." Her father's tone was sharp. "Is that any way to talk? To think, even? You must be strong for Ned." With a loud bang, he hammered another nail into the cabinet.

"I know, Father." Meg looked abashed. "But I can't help worrying. He's been so ill. And then I think of all the boys who haven't come back..." Her voice trailed off.

Mr. Merriweather sighed. "It is a terrible war," he acknowledged. "There's never been one quite like this before."

"He doesn't want to be wed right away," said Meg. "He wants to wait until he returns. He wants a proper wedding. And he says I'm too young."

"That seems sensible. And he's right. You are very young. Little more than a child." Her father put the hammer down and stared across the room, his eyes softening. "Your mother and I, we had a beautiful wedding."

"Oh?" Meg looked at her father in surprise. He rarely spoke of whimsical things like weddings. She waited, hoping he'd say more.

"Oh, yes." Her father had a faraway look in his eyes. "We

didn't have much money, of course. But it was June, and the flowers, they were lovely. Your mother, she must have spent days gathering them. And her dress. Such a pretty white dress. Made it herself, she did. She was a fine seamstress, Bess was. She would have made you a beautiful dress." He looked down at his daughter, his eyes sad now.

"I know, Father." Meg smiled and gently placed a hand on his arm. She sighed inwardly, resigning herself to wait for a fancy wedding. There seemed to be no escaping it. "I'm certainly not a good seamstress, though. I'll have to enlist some help."

"No," admitted her father. "But you have other gifts. Like the writing." His face shone with pride. "Imagine, a daughter of mine who can write like a scholar."

"I'm working on some new poetry, actually." Meg stood up. "I'm going to do some mending, and then I'll get the tea started," she said. "And afterward, I'll read you some of my new poems."

"That sounds lovely." Mr. Merriweather went back to his workbench, and Meg made her way to little the room at the back that was hers. The cottage she shared with her father was small—only four rooms—but it was more than enough space. Made of stone, it had been built over three hundred years earlier. It still had a thatched roof. Some of their neighbors had replaced these roofs in recent years, trading them for modern shingling, but Jim Merriweather wasn't one to fix something that wasn't broken. "It keeps out the rain, and that's good enough for me," he'd say, and Meg tended to agree.

A wicker basket of clothing requiring her attention sat on a corner of the writing desk her father had fashioned just for her. Meg picked up the basket and, in doing so, knocked over the small wooden figure that had been hiding behind it.

Meg crouched to the floor to retrieve the little doll. It had a cherubic face, like a baby's. Her father had made it for her years ago, when her mother died. As a child, the doll she'd named Will had served as a special friend and confidant. Though she didn't play with dolls now, she still frequently spoke to the small figure. She knew it was silly, but her feelings toward her childhood friend were still very tender.

"I'm to be wed, Will," Meg told the doll as it stared back at her blankly. "Imagine that."

"It's to Ned, of course," she went on. "And you don't have to worry. He already knows all about you, so he won't mind if you come and live with us."

With a smile, she laid the doll gently back down on her desk and picked up her writing journal and a pen. There was mending to do, but there were poems to write as well.

"I can't believe it's May already," said Meg, half to herself. Ned was leaving on the fifteenth. When he had received the official letter, the one Meg had so dreaded, May had seemed far away still. Now she felt they were running out of time.

"Don't you fret, dear." Mrs. Tanner, the local seamstress, stuck a pin in the yard of silk she was wrapping around Meg's waist. Meg felt a prick at her hip and winced. "I heard from my cousin in London that the war isn't going to last much longer.

Now, let us try to make you a beautiful dress, shall we?"

Nights were the most difficult. Alone in the dark, Meg's thoughts would turn to Ned and to the stories about the war that she'd read in the papers her father sometimes brought home. Unable to sleep, she would toss and turn with no one to keep her company save the little wooden doll. As she'd done as a small child, Meg would clutch Will to her chest when she felt fearful or couldn't sleep.

The day before Ned was set to leave, Meg asked him to join her on one of their walks to the river. Hand in hand, they strolled in silence. The daffodils were in full bloom now, and they covered the fields so completely with yellow that it was almost as if someone had buttered the landscape.

"Ned," she said, "Have you ever heard of handfasting?"

He laughed. "Like the Scots?"

"Yes, darling. Traditionally, they would hold hands and promise marriage for a year and a day. A trial, of sorts."

"What are you suggesting?"

Meg took a deep breath. "Hold my hands and tell me you're my husband."

"Come now, Meg. We've been through this. We'll have our wedding when I return."

"It's only temporary. Until you get back." Meg's eyes were pleading.

Ned smiled. "This will make you happy? Settle your fears a bit?"

"Yes, Ned. Please?" Meg's voice shook slightly. She moved closer to him.

"Fine, then. What do I do?" Ned was grinning, like it was a game. Meg took a deep breath. "Hold my hands," she said quietly.

Meg grasped his hands and held them firmly. They felt hot. "I will take you to be my husband," she said.

Ned repeated the vow and gave Meg a questioning look. "Is that all?"

"Well traditionally, I think we would exchange rings. You've already given me one. I don't have a ring for you, but..." Meg's voice trailed off. She turned to him and unwrapped the small bundle she had hidden in the apron of her skirt. "I want you to take this with you to the front."

Surprised, Ned looked down to see Meg's little wooden doll. Only now, it had been painted. Meg had carefully decorated the tiny figure in a soldier's uniform: khaki trousers and tunic with tiny buttons. There were even painted breast pockets, shoulder straps, and rifle patches.

"I painted it." Meg's voice was shy now. "I thought it could be a friend for you. When you feel lonely or afraid. It's always been a friend for me." She offered it to him.

Moved, Ned took the wooden doll, staring at its shiny painted boots. "I can't possibly take this, Meg. Your father made it for you." He tried to give it back to her.

"Ned, you must." She pushed the doll back into his hands. "It will comfort me to think Will is with you. And when you look at him, you'll think of me."

"Well," said Ned. He sounded doubtful. "If you really want me to take it, I will. I daresay it will be nice to have some company on the battlefield." He smiled. "I promise to keep him safe, Meg." He took the keepsake and tucked it into the breast pocket of his coat. Ned tapped the pocket and pulled her close.

Meg pulled him to the grass. "There is one other part to the handfasting," she said. She was blushing now, and her heart was beating fast.

"What's that, love?"

"You have to make me your wife, Ned."

It was Ned's turn to blush. "Here? Now?"

"Now."

He took her in his arms.

Ned wrote regularly. This both relieved Meg and put her ill at ease. The euphoria she first felt at seeing his handwriting on an envelope quickly deteriorated into a ceaseless worry as the letters came, first detailing his experiences at the training camp and then describing the trenches in Flanders. Nonetheless, Meg treasured these letters. She slept with them under her pillow while at the same time chastising herself for having turned into a hopeless romantic, the kind of silly girl she would have once mocked. When she looked in the mirror now, clad in her almost-finished wedding dress, a stranger stared back at her. Each day when it was time for the post to arrive, she lurked at the front stoop, pacing nervously. When the postman arrived, she would look up hopefully, searching his face. A grin and a nod meant good news: a new letter! A rueful shake of the head meant another day of waiting and hoping. His latest letter had both comforted and unsettled her.

Dearest Meg,

How are you, love? I do hope you're taking care and keeping dry, as I hear England is nearly as wet as Flanders this spring. I must say, it is quite cold here, and I have never seen rain such as this before. It rains almost constantly. The fields, as a result, are a sea of mud. The mud is almost as dangerous as the Krauts. There is mud everywhere, and I will confess I long for a hot bath and a clean bed!

We are preparing for another battle at a town called Ypres. It is not much different than Vimy Ridge, as far as I can tell. All these small Flemish towns look alike to me, though I suppose one could say the same thing of our little English towns. Trenches are being dug, and the men are getting ready to fight once more— though I must confess, I cling to the rumors that hint that the war will be over any time now.

I do miss Harry Stevens dearly. You remember Harry, whom I mentioned in my early letters? Harry caught pneumonia shortly after the fight at Vimy Ridge. It isn't natural to spend the night in the rain and mud in the trenches. It is hard on the body and on the lungs, I reckon. I am lucky that so far my cough has not worsened. The army doctor says my lungs are functioning well and that I am healthy as an ox. Poor Harry. He had a sweetheart waiting for him at home, too. I do think of her, then think of you, and us, and feel overwhelmed with sadness. What will become of her, his

Violet? I wish I could write to her and tell her of his bravery, but I do not even know her surname.

Never fear, Meg darling, as I still have your little soldier doll. It is a great comfort to me as a token of you as well as a companion during the long, cold nights. I keep it in my breast pocket at all times. The other lads think the doll is lucky and regularly rub it or pat it on the head prior to going down to the trenches. I thought you might find that amusing!

Please take good care of yourself. You are in my thoughts at all times, and not a moment goes by when I do not see your smiling face in my mind's eye.

All my love,
Ned

Meg read the letter over and over. She had replied, of course, right away. Meg wrote even more frequently than Ned did. She hoped that her letters would boost his morale in the endless rain and mud.

Dear Ned, she wrote most recently, *Thank you for your last letter from Ypres. As always, it was wonderful to hear from you. The conditions you describe sound intolerable. It has perhaps been slightly more rainy than usual here, but not to the extent that you are describing. I worry to think of you sleeping in a rain- and mud-filled trench, though I am relieved to hear that you are doing well and that your cough has improved.*

I am so sorry to hear about poor Harry. I will add his Violet to my prayers.

Things here are as they ever were, dear one—pleasantly boring. The most exciting thing that happened since your departure occurred last week. Leaving church on Sunday, Mrs. Tremont stood up, and her skirts and slip were tucked into her stockings! People tried not to laugh but they couldn't help it. Mrs. Allen kept trying to signal to Mrs. T. what the problem was, but she simply was not catching on, and finally, Mrs. A. reached over and yanked them out herself! Poor Mrs. T. was mortified, and of course everyone is still talking about it.

I miss you constantly. I am so pleased that the doll is a comfort to you as it was to me after my mother died. I think of the two of you often, and the fact that you are together gives me much happiness.

I love you, Ned. Keep safe.

Yours,
Meg

The weeks passed. Day after day, the postman would look down regretfully, shaking his head. Soon, he began averting his eyes, as if he couldn't bear the disappointment he saw in hers. Meg grew increasingly worried and despondent.

"He's busy, Meg." Her father dismissed her fretting. "He's at war. Not much time to write when you're busy fighting the enemy. And besides—it's likely that the post is moving much slower than usual, given the war."

58

Meg felt skeptical, but said nothing. The day before, she had realized that she hadn't had her courses since Ned left. She didn't have a mother, but she was privy to the whisperings of the seamstress and the women at church. One month might not mean anything, but three left little room for doubt. Her clothes still fit, but she was sure that was only because her appetite had diminished when Ned left. She touched her stomach. What would her father say? She crossed her arms over her waist protectively: she could endure the shame. Ned had suffered worse.

Ned. Her heart picked up immediately as her body and mind entered into a familiar dialogue. Something must have happened. Ned would never *not* write her for such an extended period of time, no matter how hectic things became. She remembered that when the news had come about Tom, Mrs. Jeffries said she'd already known. That she'd been washing the floors and suddenly the lye smelled differently and there wasn't enough air to breathe, and she'd known her son was gone. Meg pictured Ned's face, the way his gray eyes changed colors depending on his mood or the weather. *Would I feel differently if something happened?* she wondered. She put her hands on her stomach again and closed her eyes, trying to see if she felt anything. She wanted to think she would feel it if he had died or was hurt or ill.

It was a Tuesday when she got the news. She knew it was a Tuesday because on Tuesdays she did the laundry, and she was hanging the clothes to dry when Mr. Roberts—Ned's father—appeared. His face was ashen. Her own father was close at his heels, eyes downcast. Meg felt the ground sway as she dropped a clothespin.

"Meg—" Mr. Roberts took off his hat and twisted it in his hands. She couldn't bring herself to look at him; with his kind gray eyes and wavy brown hair, Ned looked so like him. "Meg, please sit down. I'm afraid I—" his voice broke. He took out a handkerchief and dabbed at his forehead, distressed.

"Meg." Her father came forward and took her firmly by the arm. He sat her down on a nearby wooden bench, taking her face in his hands. "My poor child." He shook his head. He looked away as the tears came, running silently down his face.

"No." Meg's voice was quiet. "No!" She looked, pleading, at Ned's father. "Please, Mr. Roberts." Her hands shook as she brought them together in her lap. "Please tell me that you're not here to tell me…that. He is well? Perhaps just a bit ill again, or injured?" Her eyes searched his face, frantic for some sign of hope.

"I'm sorry, my girl." He took a deep breath and regained some of his composure. "I am truly sorry. But our Ned, he's gone." He patted her self-consciously on the forearm.

"Gone?"

"It was a hero's death." Mr. Robert's voice was feeble. "He died rescuing another boy who'd been shot…" His voice trailed off.

"Thank you for telling me." Meg stood up quickly, avoiding eye contact. "My condolences to you and Mrs. Roberts." She needed to get away, to be alone with her pain. She felt selfish, but she didn't want to comfort Henry Roberts, to sacrifice her own tears on the altar of his loss. She didn't want to compare and wonder whose loss was greater. She turned hurriedly, tripping over the laundry pile. Reflexively, her hands flew to her stomach, and her eyes met Ned's father's as he looked sharply at her abdomen. His eyes widened.

"Meg, wait." She could hear him beckoning her to come back, but feigned deafness. Instead, she ran. Her father shouted something, but she ignored him, too, and ran faster. The kitchen smelled of baking bread when she reached it, and it sickened her. It smelled sweeter than usual, almost like overripe fruit on the verge of decay. It penetrated her senses, and she retched. She wondered how long he had been gone, without her knowing. Was it days or weeks? A month? She retched again, stumbling to her bedroom.

She wasn't sure how much time had passed when her father knocked on the door. "Meg?" He opened the door a crack. "I fetched you some tea." He offered the steaming cup to his daughter, who stared at him blankly. "Tea." he repeated. He looked awkward.

Meg blinked and nodded absently at him. "Thank you." She took the cup and held it with both hands, but did not take a sip. She caught the familiar scent of fresh bread and felt again as if she might be sick.

"I am truly sorry." He sat down at her desk chair. "Ned was a wonderful boy. I often thought of him as a son." His voice choked slightly.

She said nothing, continuing to stare down at her teacup.

Mr. Merriweather reached behind him and pulled out a small box. "The Robertses, they felt you should have these," he said, offering her the box. Meg set the teacup gently on the floor by the bed and took the box from her father. Was this all that was left of him? She opened it.

"His effects," said her father. Inside were his watch, his cap, and a small parcel of her letters, tied neatly with a piece of old cloth. There was also a medal he had been awarded for his bravery, presented to his parents upon his death. Meg turned it over in her hands, disbelieving that this was all that was left of his life.

"Mr. and Mrs. Roberts should have these, really." Meg took out his cap and stared at it.

"No, they felt these things belong to you," said her father. "Henry, he was quite firm about it."

Meg looked again at the objects in the box. Where was the little soldier doll? She shook the contents and checked again. It wasn't there. She wondered what had happened to it.

"Thank you, Father." Meg folded her hands. "I must thank the Roberts's," she said. Then, thinking of facing Ned's mother, her chest tightened.

Her father looked awkward again. "Meg," he said. His face was red.

"Yes?"

"Is there—is there anything you wish to tell me?"

Meg put her hands on her stomach again. "I think you know," she said in a dull voice.

"Oh, Meg."

"We were handfast." Her voice caught. "I'm sorry, Father. The shame—"

"Never mind that." He put a firm hand on her shoulder. "You just take care of yourself now."

"I'll have to tell Mr. and Mrs. Roberts." Meg's eyes were closed, and she was bent forward slightly, breathing heavily as if she was having trouble getting enough air. Her voice betrayed a mixture of fear and grief.

"They'll be pleased, I think. It's not the same as it was. Not with the war."

"I hope so." It was hot in the cottage, but she was shivering. She wrapped her arms tightly around her midsection and tried to take a deep breath.

Her father stood. "I'll leave you now. I'm sure you want time to grieve alone." He made for the door, but before opening it, he turned back to his daughter. "The pain...it does subside eventually. Somewhat." His eyes clouded over.

Meg nodded, but didn't speak, watching as her father quietly closed the door.

Meg looked down at Ned's watch and cap. A tidal wave of grief swept over her, her breath catching as if she'd been knocked to the ground by it. She swam for air.

Her stomach heaved again. Meg grabbed a bowl from the desk and retched. Settling back down, she felt something else: something familiar and unwelcome. The cramps seized her unexpectedly. Meg gasped, and her arms flew protectively across her stomach. The feeling passed, and Meg exhaled, relieved. Tenderly, she stroked her abdomen. "Be well, little one," she whispered softly.

Then it happened again.

The cramping was worse this time. Meg paced the small room until it passed, then collapsed at her desk. When she stood up, she noticed the blood. Just a little—she pretended not to see it, at first. Another wave of cramping overtook her, then more blood. An odd feeling, hot and damp between her legs. She let out a loud moan, hugging her legs together, as if willing the blood to stop.

"No. No, please," she whispered. "Please, not this. Not now."

She sank to the floor, dizzy. She watched the blood as it seeped slowly through her skirts, a red tide of despair.

"I won't even have my son now." The words were a whisper. She thought of her initial worry over the shame of the pregnancy and felt as if she might suffocate, overwhelmed with bitterness and grief. She gasped again. "So much blood spilled," she whispered. "Ned's, mine, the child's. Our child." She pictured Ned, dead in the trenches, and then a baby with Ned's gray eyes, still and silent. "Never even had the chance to wake and see the world. Never felt the sun, never felt love." Meg talked to herself quietly, her shoulders bent as if in prayer. Still, her eyes were dry as she stared down at her ruined skirts. She thought of the dreams she'd had for herself and Ned and the baby, silly childish fantasies that would remain that way forever, now.

When the tears finally came, Meg began to write.

Little soldier, just a boy
Wide-eyed wooden children's toy.
Innocent of ruin and war
Lost and gone, forevermore...

CHAPTER 4

Toronto, Canada
2007

"I thought so—I knew it, actually," says her mother as she reaches for the pizza box.

Elizabeth watches her mother take another slice, her silver bracelet clinking against the watch her dad had bought her for her last birthday. She looks smug, the way someone does when they know something you don't, and they decide that rather than tell you what it is, they'd prefer to draw it out a bit, torture you. Her mother makes a habit of acting superior. Elizabeth wonders if she takes the same tactic with her patients: "You know, Mrs. Smith, you really should have listened to me about the foot cream, because now you—pause, smug look—have a fatal toenail fungus! I'm so sorry." Elizabeth stares at the mix of sauce and grease forming a mustache on her mother's upper lip as she bites into her slice.

"I told you I thought the soldier doll might be important." Her mom spins the box toward her. "More pizza?"

Elizabeth peers into the cardboard box. The grease has soaked through the bottom, leaving a fine slick of oil on the kitchen table. She looks away. "No, thanks."

She's tired of take-out food, of cardboard boxes and foil-lined containers. Admitting this surprises her; she is sure that if two weeks ago someone had offered her the opportunity to eat fast food for an indefinite period, she'd have agreed readily to a happy future of pre-made sandwiches and stapled paper bags. But now, she's sick of prepared food. More than that, it's starting to disgust her. Right now, the stringy pizza cheese is about as appealing to her as a plateful of squirming eels.

"You did not." Her father looks up in protest. He wipes his face with a paper napkin that says Subway, a souvenir from a previous meal. "All *you* said was that the doll reminded you of something, but you couldn't remember what."

"I didn't. I said I thought the doll was important. Liz?"

"I'm on Dad's side here, Mom." Elizabeth raises her eyebrows at her mother, irked. She picks off a mushroom from her pizza and examines it suspiciously.

"Why are you picking off the mushrooms?"

"They look funny."

"How can mushrooms look funny?"

"They just do. Look at this one." Elizabeth holds it between her thumb and forefinger, delicately, as if handling a ticking explosive. "It's all slimy."

"Is that why you're handling it like it's radioactive?"

"Maybe that's what's wrong with it." Elizabeth stabs it with a fork. "What was that place, where they had the nuclear meltdown?"

"Three Mile Island?" Her father looks up.

"No, the other one. The Russian one."

"Oh, Chernobyl." Amanda frowns at her daughter. "It was a huge tragedy."

"I know. Do they export mushrooms?"

"Not funny. Do I need to tell you about the harmful effects of radiation on the body? About the children who got sick? About the—"

Elizabeth yawns. "Spare me the self-righteous indignation," she says. Her tone is cutting. "You want to talk about harming children? Let's talk about eating fast food every day for two weeks! Haven't you heard about the childhood obesity epidemic? Take a hard look at that grease wheel, doctor," she says, pointing at the pizza box.

Her mom deflates, guilty now; her shoulders slump slightly and her cheeks flush pink. Elizabeth knows her mother's weakness and how to exploit it—how she worries that she's a bad mom. She's overheard the conversations with her dad, grandma, and Aunt Elinor: the ruminations over her excessive work hours, the dearth of home-cooked meals, and the prevalence of dust bunnies around the house. Elizabeth feels a cruel sense of satisfaction as she watches her mother droop, like a flower at dusk. She gets the same feeling when she feigns exaggerated disappointment when her mother accidentally breaks the yolks of over-easy eggs.

Her mother is talking and gesturing, waving her hands as she does when she's nervous or guilty. "I know. It's terrible. It's just been impossible, getting everything unpacked and the new job and getting to the supermarket…"

"I'll cook tomorrow," her father suggests, rescuing her. "Something on the barbecue. Chicken?"

"With vegetables?" Elizabeth looks hopeful.

"Good Lord, Amanda, she's asking for vegetables." Her dad fans himself, as if he might faint with shock.

"That's how long it's been since I've had a well-balanced meal," says Elizabeth flatly. "I'm afraid I'm going to die. Or get fat."

"Stop it; you're making your mother feel bad. It's only been a little over a week." Her dad gives her a reproving glance.

"I'm actually craving carrots. What does that say about your parenting?"

"Carrots?" Her mother laughs. "Can I get that on tape?"

"Here we go again with the tape." Elizabeth snorts. "How's your gramophone?"

"It's a Dictaphone, smarty-pants. And I should start bringing it to dinner." Her mother takes a large bite of pizza.

"Excellent idea," her dad pipes up. "Then we could prove you never said anything about the soldier doll."

Elizabeth pushes her plate away. The cheese on the pizza is cool now, congealed. It has turned hard and sticks stubbornly to parts of the plate. "What do you guys think about it? The doll, I mean. It's weird isn't it, that—"

The lights flicker, and a crash of thunder shakes the kitchen. The oppressive heat has finally given way to a violent thunderstorm, with rain whipping angrily on the doors and windows with a loud splattering sound, falling almost sideways, as if the house is under attack by an army brandishing water guns and garden hoses. Outside somewhere, wind chimes hit one another with force, sounding more like cymbals. Her mother shifts slightly in her seat.

"You okay, Mom? You don't have to be afraid of the thunder. Remember? It's just angels bowling." Storms had frightened Elizabeth when she was small. They still did sometimes, if they were at night; the darkness unnerves her. She can still recall being woken by storms as a little girl and the terror she'd felt from the noise and the dark; the internal debate over whether to take the risk and make a run for her parents' room and the warmth and comfort of their more generous bed, or whether it might be safer to lie very still in her own bed, lest something—she was never sure what, exactly—catch her in transit. Her mother had always let her into their bed, had always sleepily pulled back the duvet and helped her crawl up. Remembering, Elizabeth feels a twinge of guilt for baiting her mother. Their eyes meet, and Elizabeth looks away first.

"Did I use that one? I'm surprised you even noticed thunder as a kid, what with your father's snoring shaking the entire house every night." A smile creeps across her mother's face, and Elizabeth feels relieved.

Her father pouts. "I have an adenoid problem. And a deviated septum."

"Ew, Dad! Don't use words like that." Elizabeth looks away, embarrassed.

"What did I say?"

"Septum." Elizabeth reddens.

Her mother gives her an odd look. "The septum is the cartilage dividing your nose."

"Is it?" Elizabeth looks abashed. "Never mind, then."

Elizabeth hastily steers the conversation back to the soldier doll. "Anyway, as I was saying—it's strange, isn't it? About the doll? Apparently the soldier doll from the poem has been missing for, like, a hundred years or something."

Elizabeth had felt triumphant informing her parents about the poem. She likes the feeling of knowing something special they don't know, of having news. It was like bringing home a good report card or gossip, only even more interesting. She also mentioned Boris the enormous rabbit and the bookshop, though she left out Evan.

"I wonder if there's a way to know for sure?" Her mother looks thoughtful. She's drumming her fingers on the kitchen table. "Carbon dating or something like that."

"Carbon dating?" Elizabeth looks puzzled. "What's that?"

Her dad pipes up. "It's a way of figuring out how old something is. It uses radioactive carbon isotopes." He looks proud to know such detailed scientific information.

"Can we do it at home?" Elizabeth leans forward eagerly.

Her father laughs. "Afraid not. I might know someone who could help you, though." He reaches for his mobile phone and pauses, setting it flat on the table, tapping on it slowly with his index fingers like a novice typist. Elizabeth smirks; she'd long ago given up suggesting he use his thumbs to text like any normal person. "Here it is. Madeleine McLeod."

"That sounds familiar." Her mother furrows her eyebrows.

"I met her at that conference in Seattle. Do you remember the one?"

"The time when you forgot to turn the stove off and left for the airport?" Her mother's eyebrows are raised, and she sounds like she's trying to suppress a laugh.

"No. That was San Diego. Will you ever stop bringing that up?" Her father casts his eyes to the ceiling and folds his arms across his chest, embarrassed.

"Probably not." Her mom grins at him.

"Right." He rolls his eyes at her. "Seattle was that conference I went to on artifacts and antiques."

"The junk conference!" Her mother brightens. She reaches for a pizza crust and nibbles on it, looking thoughtful. "I remember now. Why do I know that name, though?"

"I contacted her once. About that butter dish." Her father looks embarrassed again.

"Ah. The butter dish incident!" Her mother puts her pizza crust down. Her eyes meet her daughter's again, and they both grin. Elizabeth coughs into her sleeve; it's now her turn to make the effort not to laugh.

When she was in seventh grade, her dad had developed an obsession with the *Titanic*. It had been triggered by an episode of *Antiques on the Road* featuring a woman who'd found a menu from the legendary ship. She'd unearthed it from under a pile of junk at a local garage sale. As the audience oohed and aahed, John sat on the edge of his recliner, entranced by the spectacle of this woman's success—in contrast to his own regular disappointment—in hunting down valuable antiques. After that, her father had become convinced that there were *Titanic* memorabilia lurking in every flea market and yard sale on the West Coast.

"It was a huge ship," he reasoned. "I should be able to find something."

"John, it sank. As in, underwater." Her mother would look at him, amused, and shake her head. "You're being irrational."

But her dad refused to give up. "You're just being negative," he would say stubbornly. And one day, he'd presented them with a silver-edged butter dish with the signature red-and-gold White Star Line logo on it. White Star Line was the company that had owned the famous ship. "There!" he'd gloated, placing the dish gently on the kitchen table as they crowded around. "Have a look at that!" Now, he blushes at the memory. "How was I supposed to know it was a fake?"

"John, you bought it on eBay from an anonymous seller. It didn't even look real."

"It did so."

"The logo washed away in the sink, hon. With water."

"All right, maybe. She was really nice about it though. Dr. McLeod, I mean. When I took it her to be authenticated."

"What does she do, Dad?" Elizabeth is finished her pizza. She is lining up her mushrooms in a neat little row, dragging them around her plate with her fork.

"She's an archeologist and historian. Twentieth century." He reaches for the last slice of the pie and picks at the cheese. It strips off easily now, in a single sheet. He folds it into his mouth and discards the now-naked crust back into the empty box.

"So, you think she would know about the doll?" Elizabeth says.

"Possibly. It couldn't hurt to ask, anyway. Should I send her an e-mail?"

"Sure, Dad." Elizabeth thinks of Evan. He hasn't been in touch with her yet on Facebook, but she hasn't checked in— she glances at the clock—two hours. She would check again soon. "Thanks."

The lights flicker again and then go out. The screen of her father's phone projects a beam of light onto the ceiling from the center of the table, as if they are gathered around a virtual bonfire. Elizabeth waits for the lights to come back on. Nothing. "Now what?" She thinks of Facebook and Evan and sighs, annoyed at the fickleness of electricity.

"Is that ice cream you bought still in the freezer?" asks her mother.

"Yeah," Elizabeth replies. She'd bought some earlier in the week. "Well, some of it. Why?"

"Well, we wouldn't want it to melt, would we?" Her mom is grinning pointedly.

"Your mother's right, Liz." Her dad rubs his hands together in anticipation. "We don't like to waste food in this family."

Elizabeth stands up. "Where did we put the bowls again?"

"Just grab three spoons, honey." Her dad waves his hand dismissively.

"Seriously?" Elizabeth gapes at her father. He is not the spoon-in-the-ice-cream-tub kind of person.

"Why not?"

Elizabeth opens the freezer and finds a half-eaten container of pralines and cream in the relative blackness of the kitchen. She finds some spoons in a pile of unpacked silverware on the counter.

Elizabeth slides the spoons across the table and peels back the lid, intentionally swiping the underside with her fingers and licking them. "Me first," she says, picking up her spoon and digging in.

"It's room 223." Her father holds the stairwell door open for Elizabeth. "I think this is the second floor."

Elizabeth looks around. She had expected the university building to be old and grand, with stone walls and archways and overgrown ivy. Turrets, possibly. But this building looks more like the hospital where she'd had her tonsils out back in the third grade. The walls are painted a sickly olive. The floors are linoleum, the kind that never looks entirely clean. It's hard to tell what color they might have been originally. Overhead, fluorescent lights hum.

"This way."

Elizabeth follows her father through a narrow corridor. Reflexively, she feels inside her bag again. Still there. She rests her hand lightly on the bundled package within.

"She was in New York, at a conference." Her dad is explaining why it took nearly two weeks to get in touch with Madeleine McLeod. "She's pretty well-known, I think, in her field. Here we are—223." He knocks, and they wait.

Dr. McLeod opens the door. She is a tall woman, one of the tallest people Elizabeth has ever met. Her hair is short, a fiery auburn color, and she wears it tucked haphazardly behind her ears. Unusually dressed, she is wearing a long, green lace skirt paired with a men's gray suit jacket. On her feet are tan construction boots; hanging from her ears are what look like bright blue parrot feathers. Elizabeth likes her immediately.

"John." Her voice is warm. She ushers them into her office. "Good to see you. So you're living in Toronto now, I guess. Settling in okay?"

"Getting there," he says. He smiles and shakes her hand in greeting. "I'm doing some contract work with the air force, Trenton base."

"Isn't that quite far?" Dr. McLeod frowns. "It's about two hours away, no?"

"It is," he agrees. "But Amanda got a great job at one of the hospitals here, so we decided on Toronto."

"Long commute," she observes.

"I'm shipping out in October," he explains. "To Afghanistan. They need engineers over there."

"Afghanistan!" Dr. McLeod looks surprised. Her father quickly looks over at Elizabeth, who stares back at him, impassive.

"How long will you be out there?"

"A year. But I get a couple weeks' leave at Christmas and then again next summer." He looks around. "Great space you have here."

The office is large but has a cozy feel. Elizabeth looks at the faded rug, patterned with small blue-and-white squares. An odd assortment of pictures crowds the walls. It feels more like their old living room back in Vancouver than a workplace. The walls are a soft yellow, and an impressive collection of books rests in oak bookcases that decorate the perimeter. Tucked away at the back is a comfortable-looking pair of worn blue armchairs with a paisley pattern; in the center is a round wooden table with mismatched chairs. The desk is in a corner, pushed to one side, covered in books and papers. Elizabeth wonders, briefly, how it doesn't collapse beneath the weight of so many books. She stares at the room, impressed that an adult has succeeded in making such a spectacular mess.

"It does the job." Dr. McLeod smiles, her parrot earrings swinging. "You must be Elizabeth. Having a good summer vacation?"

"Not bad, thanks." Elizabeth suddenly feels shy and small. She fingers the long rope of faux pink pearls she rescued from a box her mother had marked for donation before the move. "I like your earrings."

"Thanks!"

Dr. McLeod claps her hands together. "So!" she says. She motions them over to the meeting table, urging them to sit. Like the desk, it's a disaster. Elizabeth stares at the clutter of scientific journals, folders, and different-colored pens. Dr.

McLeod apologizes and clears some space so they can all see each other. "What brings you both here? A big find, I hope." She grins, dropping a stack of magazines to the floor. They all turn and watch as the stack topples.

"Well," says Elizabeth's dad. He looks over at her. "It's actually Elizabeth's find, really. She was the one who spotted it. At a yard sale," he adds.

Elizabeth blushes. She reaches into her bag and brings out the soft pink bundle. Carefully, she unwraps the blanket and lays the doll on the table. She looks up at Dr. McLeod. "It's a soldier doll," she says.

"A soldier doll," repeats Dr. McLeod. Her eyebrows narrow and she frowns, looking puzzled. Then, her eyes widen as her confusion transforms, becomes comprehension. "Not *the* soldier doll? From the Margaret Merriweather poem?" She gives them a sharp glance and leans in to get a closer look at the little figure.

"Actually," says Elizabeth's father, "that's what we'd like to find out."

Elizabeth and her dad both gaze at her, looking hopeful.

"Well," she says. She shakes her head. She picks up the doll and stares at it. "Well," she repeats.

Dr. McLeod studies the doll. Elizabeth watches as she turns it over and over in her hands, taking note of its features. She does this for some time. After a while, she looks up at them and gingerly places it back on the table.

"Okay," she says. She trades the doll for a purple pen, clicking it on and off repeatedly. "I need to run some tests. And do some research. But I can tell you that this doll appears to have been made some time very early in the twentieth century." She reaches for a notepad and jots something down.

"So it could be the soldier doll? The real one?" Elizabeth leans toward her eagerly.

"It could be. But it's too early to say for sure." Dr. McLeod makes detailed notes on the doll now. She turns the figure to the left, then the right. She scribbles again in her notebook.

"It's not another *Titanic* dish, though." Elizabeth looks over at her dad, who is looking at the professor with some concern.

"What? Oh! That." Dr. McLeod laughs. "That was funny, wasn't it? Well, it's too early to say. This could very well be the real thing. I need to run more tests, though." She turns the doll back over, gives it a penetrating stare.

"There's something, though, something odd—" She frowns, thinking. Her voice trails off. She gets up and goes over to one of the bookcases and pulls an older-looking volume from the shelf. Reading, she frowns again.

"Uh-oh. Bad news?" Elizabeth's voice is light, but she's concerned.

"Not bad, necessarily. Just strange." Dr. McLeod points at the book. "The uniform. It's the wrong color for a British soldier. Merriweather was English, and she wrote the poem some time during World War I. The doll should be wearing a British uniform." She turns the textbook out so they can see the illustration she's referring to. The soldiers in the photograph are wearing thick woolen tunics dyed khaki.

They all look over at the doll; it stares back at them blankly.

"It actually looks more like the German uniform from the First World War." Dr. McLeod opens the book to another page, showing them the gray-clad soldiers. Elizabeth peers at the photograph, realizing the professor is right.

"What does that mean?" Elizabeth asks curiously.

"It means we need to do more investigating. I need to run some tests. Send it to the lab." She picks up the doll and touches its coat. "Odd," she says again.

Elizabeth thinks of her dad in their old family pictures, waving at the camera in full military regalia. Of course different countries would have different uniforms. She'd never given it much thought before, but it makes sense, like in sports: you need know who's on your team. She thinks of Afghanistan and of camouflage and rifles and the desert, wondering if her father's uniform will protect him. From dust. From the sun. From bullets and shrapnel. Her stomach tightens.

Dr. McLeod stands again. "Come back in a week. I'll send it off to the lab. I should have some results for you by next Thursday." She leads them to the door. "And don't worry. We'll take good care of the little guy."

She shakes hands with both Elizabeth and her father. "The soldier doll! Imagine." Dr. McLeod has a faraway look on her face now, as if she has traveled into the silent figure's past and somehow found herself stuck there. "It's too bad he can't talk," she says, half to herself. "He must have so many stories to tell. I wonder where he's been."

CHAPTER 5
Berlin, Germany
1939

"Papa?" Hanna Roth peered around the storeroom door of her father's Auguststrasse antique shop. "What's this?" Carefully, she presented her father with the small wooden doll she'd found wrapped in an old blanket and tucked in a dark corner of the back cupboard. Now that she was forbidden from attending school, she often helped her father out with tasks around the shop. Cleaning the back cupboard was a job she'd taken on without being asked—her father was an excellent businessman, but a hopeless housekeeper.

Franz Roth blinked twice as he looked up from his book-keeping to stare at the wooden figure before him. It had been years since he'd seen or even thought of the little thing, or the strange circumstances under which he had acquired it. He took off his glasses and placed them on his desk to take a better look.

"Ah," he said. He took the figurine from his daughter and sat back in his chair.

"It's strange, is it not, Papa?" Hanna peered over his shoulder. "I've never seen such a toy."

"No." Franz nodded. His voice sounded far away. "It is very unusual, indeed." He set the doll down on his desk and stared at it hard, remembering. He was silent for a few moments.

"Papa?" said Hanna, questioning. "Is everything all right?"

"Of course, *Liebchen*." Franz straightened. "I was just thinking about the doll. About how I came to have it."

Hanna's curiosity was piqued. "Is it not just an ordinary toy, then?" She searched her father's expression. "There is something special about it?"

"You could say that, yes." Franz put his glasses back on and sat back in his chair once again. "Sit down, Hanna. I will tell you the story of the little soldier doll."

It was at Ypres. "What kind of name is Ypres?" he remembers joking with his friend Max. "Never trust a town that starts with a *Y*." He and Max had found this enormously funny at the time. He had met Max Reinholz his first day of training, when they were both seventeen, and despite their very different backgrounds—Max was the son of a prominent Christian lawyer; he, the son of a Jewish shopkeeper—they had quickly become inseparable. "There go the Troublesome Twins," people would joke when they went by. "Troublesome" they earned because they were always engaged in some sort of prank. If a soldier came back to his camp to find his undergarments waving bravely from a pole, he could be sure the Troublesome Twins were behind it. Their commanding officer threatened them daily with everything from disgraceful discharge to a public whipping, but in reality he enjoyed their hijinks as a welcome distraction from the monotony of trench warfare and the hours spent in cold rain in muddy little holes, picking at lice and bargaining with God not to be annihilated by the latest round of shelling.

It wasn't raining when he found the doll. He remembers because it was one of the only moments of reprieve from rain in his entire two years of service. It never seemed to stop pouring in those cursed fields, the endless pounding of icy water that permeated even the warmest of undershirts and the toughest of boots. It was also nighttime, he recalls, rendering the memories somewhat fuzzy—full of shadows and shrouded in darkness. He and Max were huddled deep in their waterlogged trench looking at a picture of Max's girlfriend, Leni, waiting for an opportunity to enter, undetected, into no-man's-land: that desolate area in between German and British lines that contained the ruined bodies of friends. It was their job to bring these comrades—and any of their severed arms and legs, or worse—back to the camp so they could be dignified with a proper burial. Also identified, if possible, so their mothers could be informed of their deaths in the form letters lauding their sons' bravery and sacrifices to the Fatherland.

"She's *schön*, eh, Franz?" Max asked for the hundredth time, whispering and waving the photograph of Leni.

Franz grinned. He finished his cigarette, dropping the singed remains into a puddle at his feet. It disappeared quickly in the murky water. Franz felt the wetness against his feet and shivered as it seeped through invisible, tiny cracks in his boots and then again through the woolen socks his mother sent regularly from Berlin. He peered out. It looked clear, for once.

"Let's go," he said quietly to Max. "We'll move out on my count."

"I'm not finished my cigarette," Max grumbled, dropping it into the pool at his feet. He took a last look at Leni before stuffing the photograph back into his pocket. "The things I do for you."

"For me? This is for the Fatherland, *Herr* Reinholz. If it were up to me, we'd be on leave at a warm inn somewhere with a bottle of wine."

"Or beer. And hot food. Sausages, maybe."

"And a soft bed."

The two men crouched low as they moved, clutching their rifles close to their chests. They moved as quickly as they could, but it was difficult; the mud was thick and viscous as blackstrap molasses, trapping their feet with suctioning noises that reminded Franz of breathing through a gas mask. His thoughts strayed to the mustard gas and the screams of the men who had been exposed to it. A memory of an English boy screeching and tearing at his eyes came to him, and he pushed it away, walking faster, lulling his mind into submission by staring at the unchanging terrain at his feet.

Suddenly, there was an explosion, and the ground beneath

them shook. Startled, Franz dropped his rifle, swearing loudly. "*Scheisse!*"

"What the devil?" shouted Max over the noise. "The major said there wasn't going to be any fighting until dawn, that *Dummkopf.*"

"I think someone set off a mine," said Franz, shaken. "Our British counterparts, I suppose." There was always a chance of encountering enemy soldiers on a similar mission at night. He cursed their bad luck. Frantically, he searched the mud for his rifle. In the distance, now, was the distinct sound of gunfire.

"My rifle." Franz's voice was desperate. "Max, do you see it?"

"Oh God." Max looked at his friend in horror, realizing he had no weapon. "Where did you drop it?"

Franz gestured helplessly at the expanse of mud and stagnant water. "Somewhere here," he said.

Max poked furiously at the mud with his own gun, kicking at puddles with his feet. "I think I see it," he said suddenly, as he bent down to retrieve the lost weapon, tearing at the mud with his hands.

Franz turned to his friend in relief. "Thank God, I—"

His voice died as he caught sight of a British soldier with a rifle pointed in the general direction of Max's back. The *Englischer* was still a ways off, but close enough to kill if he wanted to, and Franz didn't doubt his motive.

"No!" he cried, lunging on top of Max. With force, he pulled Max into a tiny shell hole at their feet, just in time. Max was safe, but the bullet had pierced Franz's right shoulder, the pain hitting him like an explosion. He felt a roaring in his ears as he rolled over, retching.

Max stared at him. "You saved my life," he said. He was shaking as he watched Franz's blood mingle with the Flemish mud across his coat. "You saved my life," he repeated. He sounded stunned.

Franz groaned in pain. "I shouldn't have," he said, trying to grin in spite of himself. "Look where it got me! I'll never play the violin again."

Max snorted; Franz was tone deaf. "Tell you what, *mein freund*," he said, bending over Franz to examine the gaping wound. "When we get home, I will personally pay for some violin lessons." He tore a strip off his uniform and tied it tightly around Franz's upper arm. Franz gave a small howl of pain as Max pulled the makeshift bandage even tighter.

"You won't have to waste your money," gasped Franz. He looked at the bandage, which was covered in a mix of soil and blood. He felt faint. "I'm going to die."

"I won't let you." Max gave him a hard look. "Anyway, what are you complaining about? It's not like you were shot in the heart. You're acting like a girl, Franz."

Suddenly, Max shushed Franz. "I hear an *Englischer*," he hissed. Cautiously, he lifted his head out of their hiding place, only to come face-to-face with a mud-encrusted pair of enemy boots.

"You're still alive." The boy, younger even than himself by the telltale hairless chin, stared at him blankly. Franz looked up at him from the shell hole.

"You don't say, old boy." Max's voice was sarcastic. He had been to the best schools and spoke English well. "Bad shot. Give my best to the king."

Flushed, the boy reached again for his rifle, but Max beat him to it. "This is for Franz," he said. He shot him once, quickly. The bullet grazed the soldier's knee. With a cry of pain, the British soldier collapsed to the ground, his body skidding a bit in the mud.

"Max, don't." Franz winced as the boy writhed on his back in the muck like a farm animal, like a pig. He thought of his younger brother, David, who had started his service a month ago—he was a boy, barely out of short pants. "He's about twelve years old. Look at his uniform: it's hanging off of him. They couldn't even find one small enough."

"He tried to kill you!"

"Just take him prisoner. Please."

Max shrugged. Hoisting himself out of the hole, he reached over and grabbed the soldier by the jacket collar and hauled him toward the tiny trench. The soldier flailed wildly, shrieking with pain. It was raining again now. It had started abruptly, the way it always did, and was coming down in sheets. Water and mud splashed in every direction as the boy kicked his legs.

"Charles?" a new voice, distressed, came from behind a barbed-wire fence. Another *Englischer*. Franz craned his neck to try to see what was going on above. "Charles? Where are you?"

"Ned!" The boy waved, frantic, from the ground. "Ned, save me! I've been shot! They're trying to kill me, Ned!"

Franz watched, wincing as he tried to shift his arm to a more comfortable position, and Max threw up his hands and looked at the sky that was still vomiting water.

"*Gott in Himmel*, would you listen to this *Dummkopf?*" Max muttered. He turned his back on the boy to check on Franz's shoulder. He tightened the bandage.

Franz was about to reply when he caught sight of the other *Englischer*, the one called Ned, swiftly making his way over to where Charles was lying on the ground. Ned fumbled for some bandaging cloth in his left breast pocket as Max shifted quickly and pointed his rifle at the second soldier.

"It's not too bad." Ned's voice was soothing, reminding Franz of Max's own tenderness moments before. "You're going to be fine." He didn't notice Max as he wrapped the bandage haphazardly around Charles's knee and then straightened. "I'm going to fetch some help," Ned promised him. "You rest here for a moment—" As he turned to go, Ned noticed Max's rifle pointed directly at his heart.

"Hello, *Englischer*," Max drawled, his voice cold. "I gather you're the senior one here. The one who ordered the attack on my friend."

"What?" Ned looked around, confused. "Attack?"

Max pointed his gun at Ned's heart. "Any final words?"

"Please." Ned put out his hand toward Max, who pulled away. "Please, we were just collecting the bodies, we heard the explosion, we thought…" his voice trailed off.

Franz felt a stab of pity for him as he turned away. This second soldier was no boy, and Franz knew that trying to convince Max to be merciful a second time would be a waste of breath. Besides, it was getting more and more difficult to speak as the moments passed.

As Franz closed his eyes, he heard a howl of protest and the sound of gunfire, followed by a stream of curse words from Max. Curiosity overtook him, and Franz opened his eyes, recoiling at the chaotic scene before him. The boy, Charles, was dead now; where his abdomen had once been was now a gaping hole. Franz gagged as he watched the last of the boy's innards unravel to the ground like a dropped spool of thread. Beside him, the other soldier, the one called Ned, lay prostrate in the mud, his head in a puddle, his helmet half off. Sharp, crackling noises could be heard as his chest moved slowly up and down, each rise a momentous effort. Franz knew from experience that when a man's breathing sounded like rocks being scraped against one another, his time was nearly at an end.

"*Mein Gott*, Max, what happened?"

Max blinked, startled. His hand that held the rifle trembled. He brought it back to his side. "The boy." He nodded at Charles, wincing as he caught sight of his distended viscera. "He tried to rally and shoot me, but shot his friend instead. I had to kill him, he had his rifle aimed at me."

Franz nodded, but didn't say anything. It was quiet for a moment, and he realized the rain had stopped.

"The other one is going to die too," he said softly. "Listen." The crunching breathing noises had grown worse; Franz was reminded of his mother grinding pepper with the little mortar and pestle Papa had bought her.

"Shall I shoot him?" Max's face was grim.

"It would be humane," Franz said. His voice was weaker now; his own injury was taking its toll.

He watched Max lean over Ned's body with his rifle. "I'm sorry, *Englischer*," he whispered.

Ned blinked and gasped. His lungs heaved as he tried to speak. "Not…not your fault." His lips were blue now. "The war."

"Yes," echoed Max. "The war."

"Please." Ned's voice was barely audible. "Do it now."

Franz watched as Max fired a single shot at Ned. The crackling ceased, and the two men were silent for a moment.

"*Auf Wiedersehen, Englischer*," said Max softly. He bent forward to close Ned's eyes then began tugging at his coat, as if looking for something.

"What are you doing, Max?" Franz frowned as Max bent over the body.

"Looking for cigarettes."

Max rummaged under the soldier's jacket, searching. He thrust his hand into the breast pocket and frowned. "What is this?" He pulled out a small object and examined it. It was a little wooden figure—a doll. A doll dressed as a soldier. "Odd," mused Max, turning it over in his hands.

"What is it?" Franz tried to get a closer look.

"Some kind of doll. You take it," said Max. He pressed the toy into his friend's hands. "Maybe you can sell it in your father's shop."

"Thanks," said Franz. He looked at it again. So strange—a baby doll, in a British soldier's uniform.

Max suddenly seemed to remember his friend's injuries. "We need to get you to a medic." He looked around. "I don't want to leave you here. Can you hold on to me if I hoist you out?" He offered Franz his arm.

Franz grunted. "I think so," he said. "It's a small wound, really."

With Max's help, he tucked the soldier doll into his pocket, and the two escaped into the night.

After the armistice, when they were finally allowed to come home, Franz did indeed bring the doll back to his father's shop. The painted uniform was peeling; the rain and muck from the trenches had been hard on the little doll. Franz carefully restored the uniform with his own paints—but he modeled it after his own German uniform.

For some time, he displayed the little soldier on his desk, after he took over the shop following his father's passing. But when the Nazis began their rise to power, he grew tired of its eyes on him. It reminded him of the war, and his service and medal in the war meant nothing to the new regime. According to Hitler, he was not even a German at all, but a Jew: a second-class citizen, or worse. First the doll went into a drawer, out of sight. But when he stumbled on it one day while looking for some old accounts, he inflated with rage. Earlier that day, he had been spit on by a boy, an ordinary boy, no older than eight or ten. Shock and fear had mingled with humiliation and wounded pride as he stood very still, listening to the boy's anti-Semitic insults, torn between an overwhelming urge to commit an act of violence and the simpler desire to cry. Looking at the doll that afternoon, he toyed briefly with the idea of selling it in the shop, but remembered the last moments of the English soldier and found he could not. Bitter and determined, he wrapped it in an old blanket and put it where he would never have to see it again.

"And so, Hanna," said Franz, settling back once again in his chair, "that is the story of the little soldier doll."

Hanna, who had been listening with rapt attention, gazed at the toy. She picked it up and examined it. "I wonder why the soldier was carrying a doll."

"Most likely it was a token from a girlfriend or wife." Her father's voice was knowing. "I carried a silly embroidered scarf from your mother the entire time I was in Flanders. It had roses on it, for goodness sake. Roses! Pink ones. But we were courting then—I cherished it." He grinned at the memory. "Max gave me a terrible time about it."

"What happened to Max?" asked Hanna, curious. Her father's story surprised her, as she had not heard him mention Max before. "Why have I never met him?"

"Oh, but you have, *Liebchen*—only you were just born at the time." Franz smiled. "He came to see you when you were born. He lives in Frankfurt now, a prominent lawyer there, as I understand it. We used to correspond frequently. But since the Nazis…" her father's voice trailed off.

"Is he a Nazi, then?" Hanna's expression turned cold.

"No, no. But I stopped corresponding with him; I didn't want him to have to be associated with a Jew and risk his career, his connections. He kept writing, but when I didn't respond, the letters eventually stopped coming." Franz looked wistful and sad.

Hanna shook her head at her father. "He was your friend." She looked reproachful. "I don't agree with you, Papa."

"I know you don't." He shrugged his shoulders, looking rueful. "But you're young still. Only sixteen. Wait until you've been around as long as I have. You'll see how the world works."

Hanna protested, but he shushed her with his hand. "Hanna, I must get back to my accounts now," he said firmly. "You can have the doll if you'd like—it's yours. Go upstairs to your mother. I'm sure she is expecting your help with supper."

Hanna sighed. She scooped up the soldier doll with care, the way she did the other antiques in the shop, and clattered up the steps to the apartment she shared with her parents. She gave her father a final, disapproving look before disappearing through the door.

Franz Roth shook his head. To be young again like Hanna, and to approach life with such passion! He rubbed his temples as he looked down at the books in front of him. He finally had the money to get what he needed: three tickets on a ship bound for Palestine. He intended to get his family out as soon as possible. Now all he needed was the proper papers. How odd that Hanna had brought the doll to him now, today of all days. He picked up his pen and toyed with it. Should he ask Max, after all these years? It would put them both in possible jeopardy should the correspondence be intercepted. He groaned. The internal wrestling over whether or not to write had been going on for days. Franz had tossed and turned for three nights over the matter. On the third night his wife, Sarah, had angrily banished him to the living-room settee. "I cannot listen to this another minute, Franz!" she had admonished. "You must do it. Think of your daughter."

He thought of Hanna. His wife was right, of course. He dipped his pen in the inkwell and began to write to his old friend.

It was dusk when they first heard the shattering of broken glass.

"What was that?" Franz Roth started at the sound and put down his novel. Sarah paused too, looking up from her needlepoint, concerned. "Go check outside, Franz—make sure no one is hurt."

There was another sound of glass being broken, followed by shouting. This time, the sound was closer. Franz and Sarah exchanged fearful glances, and Franz stood abruptly.

Hanna rushed in the room, eyes wide and frightened. "Mama, they're smashing the windows!" She gestured wildly. "They've gone mad!"

"What windows? What do you mean?" Her father looked at her in alarm and rushed toward the kitchen where the view of the street was clearest. Below, an angry mob advanced down the Auguststrasse, deliberately smashing storefronts. Blinking in disbelief, Franz watched, open mouthed, as two young men smashed the Goldstein's bakery window just two doors down. Good-looking young men in quality clothing with neat haircuts. They didn't look like thugs. Franz looked closer at the mob. The people didn't look remarkable in any way—they looked like ordinary citizens. Mostly men, but a number of women too.

"Death to Jews!" Someone shouted. Everyone cheered.

"What is it, Franz? What's going on?" Sarah rose from the table and glanced at her husband fearfully. Instinctively, she moved to stand in front of Hanna. "What's all that racket?"

Franz looked grim. "People gone mad," he whispered dully. He paused for a moment, thinking. Then, decisively, he turned to his wife and daughter. "Go." His voice was urgent now. "Turn off all the lights, and wait in the sewing room. It looks like a closet; no one would think to check there if they came up. Close the door, and stay there until this passes."

They stared at him dumbly. "You think they're coming up? Here?" Sarah's voice cracked with fear. Hanna stared at her father as if he, too, had lost his mind.

"Now!" He was practically shouting. "Now!" Obediently, the two grasped hands and made their way to the little room at the back.

Taking a deep breath, Franz went back to the window. The Goldstein's sixteen-year-old son, Joseph, had come down from his apartment over the store to take stock of the damage to the bakery. Bewildered, Joseph had thrown an overcoat on top of what appeared to be a pair of green striped pajamas. The mob turned on him with a fury.

"Dirty Jew," a younger man shouted at Joseph, eyes blazing. "Get out of our country!" The mob cheered again. Someone heaved a large rock at the broken bakery window, triggering a second round of shattering glass. He saw a woman toward the back of the crowd hold up a young child—about two or three, by the look of him—who was clapping his hands in delight at his mother's coaxing. Joseph felt his stomach heave with nausea and turned away.

"No!" he heard someone scream. He turned quickly back to the window, where Anna Goldstein was shrieking in fear as the mob pushed and swore at her son. But nobody acknowledged her as the mob whisked Joseph Goldstein away. His mother's screams grew louder and more desperate. Franz shuddered. What would they do to Joseph? He was only a year older than Hanna, and he was no match for the mob. A small boy, he had neither the brains nor the brawn to outwit or defeat his pursuers. He had to go down there, to intervene. David, Joseph's father, was bedridden; he'd had an apoplexy in July and hadn't recovered. There wasn't anyone else to help. Franz's heart filled with fear, but how could he not help the boy? What else would a decent person do? He imagined if it were Hanna, and he were in David's place, and he quickly made up his mind.

Franz grabbed his coat from the front closet and pulled his cap on tight over his ears. He put his hand on the doorknob and paused. Turning, he rushed back to the sewing room where he'd ordered Sarah and Hanna to hide, and he flung the door open. Inside, his wife and daughter huddled together in the corner. They looked up at him, frightened. "I'm going down there to help Joe Goldstein." He tried to sound calm. "If I don't come back, find Max Reinholz. I've written him about you both."

Hanna jumped, startled. "Joe Goldstein?" Her high-pitched voice trembled. "What do you mean? Have they hurt him?" She hugged her arms across her chest. "Not Joe." She started to cry. Her mother gave her a knowing glance and put her arms around her.

"It will be all right, *Mammale*," she said soothingly. "Joe will be fine. I know it. Your father will go down and make sure of it." She gave Franz a troubled look.

Hanna took a deep breath. She started, as if she'd just remembered something. "Papa." She reached into her skirt pocket. "Take this. It might protect you." She pressed the little wooden soldier doll into his hands. "It was lucky for you before."

Franz kissed both his women on the head, pocketing the doll. He left the room without turning back.

Down on the street, the mob continued its path of destruction. The noise of shattering windowpanes competed with the sound of broken glass crunching under the feet of the angry crowd, a symphony of devastation. Recalling his army training, Franz kept his head down and moved quickly amid the rabble. What had happened to Goldstein?

Suddenly, he heard a terrible sound, like an animal being slaughtered. *What was that?* Franz looked around frantically, eyes searching. Then he saw. Joseph Goldstein was crouched on the ground, shrieking in pain and terror as a gang of teenagers took turns kicking him, their boots covered in pieces of broken glass and blood.

Franz took a deep breath and went over. "Enough!" he

commanded bravely. His voice shook. "Leave him. He's half your size. What has he done to you?"

One of the young men, a short, red-haired boy of about fourteen, snarled at him. "What's it to you, Jew?" he sneered. "You're next." His mouth twisted with hatred.

With Joseph momentarily forgotten, the miniature mob moved to circle Franz. The red-haired boy grabbed a splintering plank of wood and hit Franz square in the face. The wood clattered to the ground, and Franz, tasting blood, noticed that this makeshift weapon had only hours before graced the storefront of Katz's butcher shop as a sign. It was barely recognizable now: the *K* and the *A* were both missing.

Reeling, Franz grabbed the plank and raised it, threatening the boys. He took Joseph by the arm and tugged him away. Was it safe to go back yet? He wasn't sure where to go. He paused.

"Not so fast, Jews." The voice came from behind. Its tone was one of both amusement and cruelty, and it commanded authority. "No one is running anywhere."

Franz and Joseph turned around slowly. A police officer stared back at them. His face was flushed with excitement; he had definitely been partaking in the bacchanal of destruction and was not there to help.

The officer looked at the boys. "Run off now, *Jungen*," he said. "I'll take over from here." The boys scattered. The red-haired one gave Franz and Joseph a final menacing glance before turning to follow his friends.

"Now, Jews," drawled the officer. He clapped his gloved

hands together. "What shall we do with you?" Joseph and Franz exchanged a quick, worried glance. They no longer harbored even the smallest hope that the officer had intervened to help them.

"Ah, I see you're frightened!" He snorted with laughter. "What is it with you Jews?" He winked at them. "Surely you have money to pay me off. You Jews are rich. You eat well and prosper while good hardworking Germans starve." His eyes were as cold as the Rhine on an icy January morning.

Franz's heart sank. Neither he nor Joseph was wealthy. The wealthy Jews—the financiers, the physicians—had all left Germany months ago for places like London or New York. If the officer was expecting a bribe, there was almost certainly no way he or Joseph could afford to pay it. He glanced sidelong at Joseph, whose face revealed terror. There was a gash above his right eye, and his nose trickled a steady stream of blood.

"No bribe, then?" the bemused tone persisted. "You disappoint me, Jews. I wanted an opportunity to spit on your money. I wouldn't touch money belonging to a Jew." He puffed out his chest. "I am an honest man."

Franz and Joseph waited expectantly. The officer grabbed Franz by the collar. "Nothing to say for yourself?"

Franz cleared his throat. "I, too, am an honest man," he replied with forced calm. He was trembling. "I am a poor shopkeeper. And a veteran of the Great War. I won a medal for bravery fighting for this country." Pushing his fear aside, he lifted his chin with pride.

The officer made a noise and spat on Franz's shoes. Franz

stood very still as the officer spat again, this time in his face. He felt the saliva slide slowly down his left ear and bit back tears of humiliation, of rage.

"You've done nothing for this country except pollute it." The officer's face twisted with hatred as he stared at Franz with unfocused eyes. Abruptly, he grabbed the men by their arms. "You're arrested," he said. "Follow me."

"Arrested?" Joseph spoke up now. "For what?"

The officer snorted again. "Haven't you heard? We've permission now to round up and arrest any Jews we find."

Franz made a small noise. His insides burned with outrage. What was happening to this country? His heart filled with sorrow as he recalled the Berlin of his boyhood. And then he thought, *Please, God, let Max come through with those tickets.* He pictured Hanna's face, her shining, honey-colored hair, and closed his eyes briefly.

"Mr. Roth?" Joseph looked tired. Huddled in the corner of a small holding cell at the police station, he gave a shuddering cough into his arm. The cell, designed to hold perhaps two people, was crammed full with at least twenty men. Most of them were quite similar to Franz and Joseph: middle-aged Jewish shopkeepers and their sons.

"What is it, Joe? Are you not well?" Franz peered at the boy. He was an only child, and his mother would be frantic by now.

"I don't know." Joseph coughed again. "I need to get out of here. It's been over twenty-four hours, I think. Why are they holding us?" His eyes betrayed his exhaustion. "Do you think my parents are safe? And Hanna?" A shadow crossed his face.

"I don't know, Joe." Franz looked unhappy. "I don't know any more than you do."

The boy sighed. He was quiet for a moment. He turned away from Franz and appeared deep in thought. Then he spoke up. His face was flushed. "Mr. Roth?"

"Yes, Joe?" Franz looked at him curiously. The boy seemed nervous.

"I—I need to talk to you about something. It's not about this. It's not really great timing, but I think maybe no time would be a good time, really, so I think I should just go ahead and ask, because maybe I won't have the courage to do it later, and also I'm—"

"Joe." Franz cut him off. "What is it?"

"Hanna." Joseph blurted out her name. He blushed again. "I—we—I love her."

Franz stared at him. He said nothing. Joseph turned an even deeper shade of red, yet continued.

"I've loved her for years." He was getting more confident. "She loves me, too. She told me. We—we want to get married. Not yet; first I need to finish school, but—"

Franz continued to stare at him. This boy, this simpleton, marry his Hanna? Hanna, the smartest girl in her class? Hanna, with her beautiful eyes and hair, marry this *Schlemiel*? He closed his eyes and took a deep breath; the cell seemed even smaller now, as if the walls were closing in on him.

"I promise I will treat her well. I promise I…" Joseph trailed off as he stared at Franz, his eyes anxious.

"Joe. It is...not the time." Franz massaged his temples, his head spinning. "I can't think of such matters right now."

"Of course, Mr. Roth. Sorry, sir." Joseph was stammering now, his entire face flaming scarlet. "But maybe you'll think about it?"

"Maybe." Franz exhaled. He thought of Hanna's concern for Joseph and felt a twinge of guilt. He imagined her reproving eyes and avoided looking into Joseph's. He stared instead at a spider in a corner of the ceiling, oblivious to the men below as it carefully spun its web.

"We can talk about it later, when we get out," Joseph babbled. "When do you think we'll be let out?"

A young man from the other side of the cell—the last to have been tossed in late that night—spoke up now, quietly. "I heard they're deporting people. Sending them to camps." He looked grim.

"Camps?" Franz sat up straighter now and grabbed his elbow. "What kind of camps? Where did you hear this?"

The man shrugged, pulling away. "I overheard a couple of the police talking when I was brought in."

The cell exploded with violent noise as the men digested this new development. "Let us out!" someone yelled. "We haven't done anything!" Others joined in, as men pounded on the bars.

A guard came in, his teeth bared and his face flushed in anger. "Silence!" he yelled, smashing a rifle against the bars. "Shut up! All of you!"

"How long are you going to keep us here?" shouted one

man. "You have no right!" The others chimed in. "Let us out!" they cried. "Let us out—out!"

"Shut up!" Through the bars, the guard grabbed one of the men by the ear and pointed his gun. "Another word and I will shoot this fellow."

The men quickly quieted down as the guard let the man go, pushing him forcefully. He tapped his rifle against the bars and glared at the men inside. "So you want out?" His voice was calmly mocking. "Good news. You'll all be getting out."

There was a buzz as the men sighed with relief and cheered quietly. Joe relaxed visibly. "Thank God." Franz hugged himself, feeling somewhat reassured.

"Oh." The guard spoke up again. He was grinning now. "Did you think we were going to send you home? Bad news, *Juden*. You're all to be deported to prison camps."

The men cried in protest and banged the bars again as the guard reached into his pocket to retrieve a key. "We weren't going to do it until morning, but if you're so eager to go, we can load you into the trucks right now. A lovely way to spend the night!" He chuckled to himself again as he jerked his thumb to the right. "You are all to walk single file through that door. And if anyone tries anything, he will be shot immediately."

The shouts of revolt intensified. The guard cocked his rifle at the ceiling and fired a single shot. There was instant silence. "Have I made my point?" he shouted. "Silence!"

The men filed silently from the room and were led outside where they would be packed into trucks. Joseph stayed close to Franz at first. The older man could sense his fear, and Franz patted his arm in what he hoped was a reassuring manner. His hand at Joseph's shoulder, he caught a flash of gold out of the corner of his left eye. *My wedding band*, he thought suddenly. He twisted it off. When it was his turn, he leaned in toward the guard—a different one now—and pressed the ring into his hand.

"Please, officer." His voice was quiet. "Let the boy go." He gestured toward Joseph, now several men behind him in the line and out of hearing range.

The guard looked down at his palm and pushed the ring back at Franz. "Keep it," he said quietly, looking away.

"Please, officer. He's just a boy."

"I can't."

Franz's eyes met the guard's briefly, and Franz was surprised to see what looked like pity.

"Please, sir. Please." Franz sank to his knees. "Let the boy go."

"Get up, man." The guard, cheeks flushed, turned away, as if embarrassed at the spectacle of Franz's begging. "I can't help you."

"You could. You could let him go when no one is looking."

"I can't! Do you know what they'd do to me?" The guard cringed.

"Please. You're a good man, I can tell. Try." Franz grasped at the officer's sleeve in desperation.

Their fearful eyes met again. Franz reached out his hand and again offered him the ring. "Take it. You could melt it down. A nice trinket for your wife, your girlfriend."

"It's your wedding ring." The man recoiled. "It's yours."

"You'll try, then? The boy?"

The guard looked around him, furtively, to see if anyone was listening. "I'll do what I can," he snapped. He was sweating now. A bead of perspiration trickled down the side of his face slowly, like a tear.

"You." The guard motioned at Joseph. "Step over here. You need to be inspected." He motioned to the left. "And you," he said, turning to Franz. "You go there." He pointed to the right with his gun, where a truck was waiting.

Joseph's eyes widened. "Oh, no." His tone was pleading. "Officer, please. Let us go in the same truck. Please, officer, we—"

"Joe." Franz cut him off. "Do as the man says."

"Mr. Roth? Please, I—"

"Now!"

Joseph hurried over to where the guard was pointing and waited, cowering. He stared fearfully at the guard's gun.

The guard took his rifle and tapped it against Franz's back. "Move it, old man," he said loudly. "Into the truck." Franz gave him gave a grateful glance, and the soldier gave an imperceptible nod as he turned toward Joseph. Shaking with the euphoria of conquered fear and relief, Franz climbed into the truck.

The hours passed slowly. Like the cells, it was crowded in the truck. The men, desperate and humiliated, were forced to relieve themselves without the benefit of facilities, and it began to stink. The initial camaraderie quickly faded in the cramped and squalid conditions: the men bickered and not infrequently came to blows. Franz, grateful for a space in the corner, huddled in his coat, watching his breath dissolve in little puffs of smoke. Remembering the soldier doll, he retrieved it from his pocket and gave it a hard look. *Turns out you are not so lucky after all.* He stared into its eyes. *Good thing I didn't leave you with Hanna.* He touched the uniform he had so lovingly repainted and thought of his service to Germany in the War. His medal for bravery. What had it all been for?

Bitter, he continued to stare at the little doll dressed like a German soldier. He thought again of Hanna and Sarah. When would he see them again? Would Joseph find them? He shivered. It was so cold. He squeezed at the doll's neck, as if trying to strangle it. He imagined it suffocating or snapping in two and felt a perverse flash of pleasure. Another man's cough brought him back to reality, and he stared at his hands, revolted at wanting to destroy a plaything, like an angry child. Ashamed of himself, he stuffed the doll back in his pocket and closed his eyes. He heard the engine roar to life, and the truck lurched along the desolate road.

CHAPTER 6

Toronto, Canada
2007

Elizabeth clutches a banker's box of books to her chest, making an effort not to trip as she navigates her way along the busy sidewalk. *Maybe this wasn't such a good idea*, she thinks. *Maybe he doesn't even have a shift today, or maybe there's a reason he hasn't been in touch on Facebook.* It's too late now, though; she can't exactly leave the box of books on the side of the road. There are people milling about. Someone will see and stop her, and how would she explain abandoning a box of books? A woman pushing a sleeping baby in an oversized stroller rolls over her green-sandaled foot. Elizabeth winces; its wheels are like tires. It's a bit like being hit by a car, she imagines, if she knew what being hit by a car felt like, which, thankfully, she doesn't.

"Sorry, sorry," the woman apologizes. The baby wakes up at the sound of his mother's voice and wails loudly.

"It's okay," replies Elizabeth, hurrying past. As she walks, she can see from underneath the vast expanse of the banker's box that the turquoise polish on three of her left toenails is now cracked. She makes a face, recalling how carefully she'd painted them the night before.

The bell tinkles as Elizabeth backs into the bookshop door, still carefully balancing the box. Safely inside, she drops it to the floor. Her arms ache and there are red marks near the elbows. The humidity has broken, but it's still hot out. She is sweating, and her face, especially, feels damp. With one swift movement, she wipes her forehead and smooths her hair.

"You!" Evan comes over. He's wearing one of those T-shirts that has a fake "Hello, My Name Is" sticker on it, with "Satan" written in the blank.

"Hi, Satan." Elizabeth kicks the box in the direction of the desk. "I've got some books for you."

"You must really hate me." Evan looks at the box despondently. "Do you know how long it's going to take me to go through all that?"

"It's not as bad as it looks. A lot of them are the same sort of thing: medical thrillers. My mom loves them."

"Are you sure she doesn't want to keep them, then?"

"Pretty sure—she said you could have them for free, as long as you take them away."

"Actually, that does make it easier. Sam's system of working out how much to pay for each book is as complicated as an algebra textbook."

"I take it you don't like algebra," Elizabeth says, wiping a hand over her face. She notices her makeup is melting off and cringes.

"How did you guess?" Evan picks up the box and heaves it onto the desk. Boris, who is nibbling on some lettuce near the cash register, jumps, startled.

Elizabeth reaches over and pats him affectionately on the head. "Hi, Boris." His ears twitch.

"So." Evan turns to her. "Do you know how many Elizabeth Bryants there are?"

"Huh?"

"On Facebook. Elizabeth Bryants. There are, like, a hundred. I tried to find one with a picture of you but didn't see anything. Have you blocked your page?"

"No." Elizabeth looks surprised. "I do have a picture."

"Are you sure?"

"Yeah. Oh, wait a second." Elizabeth feels her face go red. "It's, ah, not exactly a picture of me."

"What's it a picture of, then?"

She feels hot with embarrassment. "A turtle."

"A turtle? Why?"

"It's a special turtle. It has wheels instead of front claws."

"Seriously?" Evan looks at her with raised eyebrows.

"It had to have its front claws amputated, so they replaced them with wheels. I thought it was cool." Elizabeth has a fleeting thought of making a run for the door, but decides that would be even more humiliating at this point.

"I don't remember seeing it," Evan says with a frown.

"Then again, I was looking for a picture of a girl with long blonde hair."

"Blonde? It's brown." Feeling better, Elizabeth hides a smile.

"It's sort of, like, in between. Like maple syrup." Their eyes meet. Evan is blushing now. He looks away, and it's quiet for a moment.

Evan clears his throat. "Did you like the Margaret Merriweather poetry?"

"Actually, it's kind of a long story." Elizabeth leans on the desk and picks up a pen. She twirls it between two fingers.

"A long story? Does that mean no?" Evan looks disappointed.

"No. I mean, no, it doesn't. It's complicated. Do you have a minute?" Elizabeth puts down the pen and takes a deep breath.

"Sure." Evan gestures. The store is empty. "We aren't exactly busy here today."

"Okay." Elizabeth leans against the desk again, making herself more comfortable. "So, you know the soldier doll?"

"Yeah."

"I think I might have found it!" Elizabeth feels herself blush again as she makes her announcement. She doesn't look directly at Evan; her eyes fix on a bookcase behind him labeled *Fantasy and Science Fiction*.

Evan is quiet again for a minute. "Um, *I* found it for you. In the poetry section. Remember?" He looks at Elizabeth, his eyes question marks.

"No, not the poem." Elizabeth shakes her head. Nervous, she makes a cradling motion with her arms. "The doll. You know—the one you said was missing?"

Evan stares at her and takes a small step back. Elizabeth watches his feet. He's wearing navy runners, but the laces have been removed.

"Wow, okay. So, since reading the poem, you managed to go out and track down the soldier doll? Busy couple of weeks for you, Elizabeth." Evan raises his eyebrows. She can tell he doesn't believe her. Probably he's wondering if maybe she's not all there, a little crazy. She doesn't blame him.

"Call me Liz." She brushes a stray hair out of her eyes. "And I'm not crazy." He averts his gaze and hefts Boris up, creating a furry, white barrier between them. "I found the doll *before* you told me about the poem. I just didn't want to say anything until I knew more. I found it at a garage sale." She goes on to tell him the whole story, ending with Dr. McLeod's verdict and the tests she said she'd run on the little wooden figure.

"I can't believe this." Evan gently places Boris on the ground. He hops away happily, sniffing at a stack of yet-to-be-shelved romance novels. "It's too weird. You come in here, we talk about Margaret Merriweather, and you have the soldier doll sitting in, like, your kitchen that whole time?" His eyes are wide, and he's gesturing more than usual with his hands. His voice betrays a mix of surprise and hurt.

"Well, it was only five days. I haven't had it that long," Elizabeth says apologetically. She plays with a strand of hair, nervously weaving it around her fingers.

"Whatever." Evan waves his hand dismissively. "You really didn't know about it when you bought it? You'd never heard of the poem?" He still looks skeptical.

"Nope. If you hadn't mentioned it that day, I'd probably never have known." Elizabeth's tone is firm and honest. She moves closer to Evan and smiles. "I owe you one."

Evan smiles back. "I'll say!" His voice his teasing now. "You can give me my half of the million dollars when you sell it."

"Funny." Elizabeth starts to roll her eyes, then pauses. "You think it's worth a million dollars?"

"I don't know. It'll be worth a lot though." Evan shakes his head. "What are you going to do with it? Sell it at one of those auction houses or something? It's too valuable for eBay or whatever."

"I don't know." Surprised, Elizabeth realizes she hasn't thought that far ahead. "I guess I was waiting to see if it's real."

"You should have a plan, though. It's, like, a historical artifact."

"I guess." Elizabeth looks outside. The rain has started again. It's not raining hard, but the droplets are fat, and they hit the glass storefront like little water balloons. Elizabeth is reminded of Vancouver and feels wistful. She stares at the window, momentarily quiet.

"Is Margaret Merriweather still alive?" Evan asks suddenly, eyes bright.

"Huh?" Elizabeth is stirred from her reverie. She stares blankly for a moment, then recovers and does some quick math in her head. "I doubt it," she says finally. She'd have to be at least a hundred."

"But it's possible," says Evan thoughtfully. He leans his weight against one of the wobblier looking bookcases, jumping back when the books start to sway precariously.

"I guess. Do you have Internet access on that thing?" She nods at the computer on the desk. It's clunky and archaic-looking, with one of those giant, boxy monitors that look like the old TVs.

"Good thinking!" Evan brightens and sits down at the desk. "Wikipedia will know."

Evan pulls up the online encyclopedia and types in the author's name. Elizabeth comes around behind him so she can get a look at the screen. Even Boris seems interested. He is shuffling around their feet, nibbling at the strap of one of Elizabeth's sandals. "Cut that out, Boris," she says. "Those are vintage espadrilles." She scoops up the rabbit and settles him back on the desk. He rediscovers the forgotten lettuce leaf and busies himself, content.

"She's still alive!"

Elizabeth stares at the screen in disbelief, but Evan is right: Margaret Merriweather is still alive and living in London.

Evan whistles. "Still alive but ancient. Wow!"

"Yeah." Elizabeth is looking at the photograph of the author. It's black-and-white. Her hair is similar to Elizabeth's own. Unconsciously, Elizabeth reaches up and touches her hair. She wraps a thick lock around her left hand and lets it unravel. It still holds the curl a bit when she lets go.

"You should get in contact with her." Evan is excited now. He paces the length of the desk. "She would know whether it's the real doll or not!"

"That's true." Elizabeth nods. "It's also hers. I think we'd have to give it back."

Evan feigns disappointment. "What about the million dollars?"

Elizabeth grins. "Maybe she'll give us a reward!"

"Yeah, right. I once returned a guy's laptop. It was a really good one, and he gave me a dollar." He scowls at the memory.

"That was generous." Elizabeth laughs and hoists herself up onto the desk so that she's facing Evan. Her legs dangle off the edge and she swings them back and forth.

"Ha. So are you going to get in touch with her, then?" Evan is curious. He clicks on something. "There's her publisher; she doesn't have her personal address online, obviously."

"Right," says Elizabeth, grinning. "She needs her privacy from all those wild and crazy *Autumn Evening* fans."

"Actually, more like crazy soldier doll hunters. Of which you are now one." He taps her leg playfully.

"True." Elizabeth smiles again and runs a hand through her hair.

Evan is tapping away at the keyboard. "Can I send you the link?"

"Sure, that would be great." She gives him her e-mail address and watches the back of his head as he types. His hair is still sticking up in a variety of directions. She suppresses an urge to reach over and pat it down.

"I need to get back," she says, noting the time on the computer.

"I'll send you a message tonight. I'll look for a bionic turtle."

Elizabeth blushes. "I need to change it."

"Don't, it's weird." He pauses. "In a good way." He pauses again. "I like it."

"You don't have to be nice."

"I'm not. I like turtles. Maybe I'll get one for the store. A pet for Boris. Boris, do you want a turtle, my little hare?" Evan chuckles at his own joke.

Boris eyes him suspiciously, then goes back to the lettuce, turning his considerable backside toward Evan.

"Right. Maybe not." He grins again. "I'll talk to you later. You know, there are some parties and stuff going on. Like, with kids from school. You should come. I could introduce you to people."

"Thanks! That's really nice of you." Elizabeth is at the door now. The rain has stopped, but the humidity has returned. When she opens the door, a wall of steam envelops her.

"Bye, Evan."

"Later, Turtle Girl."

Outside, Elizabeth loses her footing on the wet pavement and slips slightly. She catches herself, but the polish on her right toes is now totally scraped away, too. She barely notices. She plays with a strand of her hair again and wonders with what picture of herself she should replace the turtle.

CHAPTER 7
Terezín, Czechoslovakia
1944

Eva awoke with a start. It took her a moment to puzzle out what was wrong. Then she realized what it was: she was freezing. Shivering, she struggled to wrap the thin gray cotton blanket around her more tightly. It was cold for June. She wondered what it must have been like here in the winter and shuddered, feeling thankful that her family at least had the good fortune to have been deported here in the spring.

It was still dark, but a very thin stream of light came in through a little hole in the roof. *It must be almost dawn*, she thought to herself, though it was difficult to tell. There were no windows in the barracks, and the walls were made of a thick concrete that was always cold to the touch. The floors were concrete too. Eva thought of how they felt beneath her bare feet and winced. She sat up carefully in her bed. When she'd first arrived, she'd often hit her head on the bunk above her by sitting up too quickly, but she was more cautious now. The beds were small, cramped, and stacked, and the mattresses were very thin, but Eva didn't complain. She'd heard there were barracks where people shared mattresses on the floor, piled on top of one another like cats in a barn. She thought again of the cold cement and shivered.

Eva looked around her; everyone else was still asleep. She wondered if they had nightmares too. At bedtime, you could usually hear someone crying into a pillow. As a rule, Eva tried not to cry. She had been luckier than most; she still had her parents. She wished she could stay with them, sleep in the same place, but that wasn't permitted here at Terezín. Even her mother and father had to live apart in separate men's and women's barracks. Eva waited all day for evening, when she was allowed to see them briefly. Closing her eyes, Eva pictured her mother as she had looked before, in their Prague apartment, on the settee in their parlor, mending Papa's shirts or knitting Eva a new sweater. Her mother's hair had been long and dark and curly then. And unlike the other mothers, she'd often worn it loose about her shoulders. If she concentrated hard, Eva could even smell her: a faint scent of lavender and clean laundry. Eva suddenly felt tears pricking at the corners of her eyes. *Don't cry.* She hugged herself tightly around the knees. *You have to be brave.*

Eva looked around furtively. No one else was awake. Carefully, she reached into a hidden skirt pocket and retrieved a little wooden figure. "The soldier doll," she had called it when first presented with the toy. It was a great comfort to her during moments like these, when she remembered her life before. Eva had since named the little fellow Piotr, after her best friend at school. Piotr had continued to come and visit her, even after the Nazis said she couldn't go to classes anymore. "You're so lucky, Eva!" he would exclaim. "No math work. No long list of dates to memorize." He didn't look directly at her when he said these things; he'd play with his cap or fidget with his pocketknife. Eva had missed school terribly, but never complained to Piotr; she didn't want him to stop coming by.

Piotr didn't care that she was Jewish; and his parents didn't agree with the Nazis and talked often of escaping to Russia. Piotr wanted to be a Russian soldier. She wondered if the war would go on long enough for him to be able to enlist, and then she felt depressed.

The doll was a curious thing: it had a face like a baby's, but it was painted to look like a soldier. Eva held it tightly to her chest. She knew that at twelve she was almost too old for dolls, but Piotr was all she had. Stroking his head, she thought of the day she had been given the doll; it was during her first week at Terezín, and she had been lost and scared. She'd wandered accidentally from the children's barracks and found herself on the main road, alone. She was huddled near a broken lamppost when an old, disheveled-looking man with worn-out shoes and missing teeth had approached her.

"Hanna, my daughter!" He spoke in German. "I thought

I would never see you again!" He grasped her shoulders and drew her to him.

Eva stiffened, but didn't pull away. He wasn't scary, somehow, and his eyes were sad.

"No, no, sir." She replied carefully, in her best German. "I am sorry, but I am Eva, not Hanna." Her tone was gentle, polite.

Startled, the man pulled back and studied her, his hand still on her arm. "Of course you are not Hanna," he said after a moment. "My Hanna would be almost twenty-one now! A young woman. Not a little girl." His shoulders sagged as he released her, and his eyes glanced at the ground, downcast.

Eva's chest puffed out, her pride wounded. "I am not a little girl," she had replied, indignant. "I am twelve!"

"Oh, twelve!" The man looked at her gravely, eyes twinkling. "Well that's different, *Fräulein*. I didn't realize. You are a young lady now." He laughed, and when he did so, Eva realized he was much younger than she had first thought. *What happened to him, to make him look so old and broken?* Eva wondered. *And who is Hanna?*

As if reading her mind, he smiled at her again. "Miss Eva, you look very much like my own dear Hanna." He extended his hand. "My name is Franz."

Pleased at the grown-up gesture, Eva grasped his hand and shook it firmly. "A pleasure to meet you, Franz."

"And you, Eva!" He studied her. "You're new here, I gather?"

Eva's eyebrows shot up in surprise. "Yes, we just arrived. From Prague. But how did you know?"

Franz coughed. His whole body shook with the effort, and Eva pulled back slightly, afraid. "Because you are not starving, my dear. Because you are not yet coughing."

"We did not have much to eat in Prague, either." It was true. It felt like years since her belly had been full.

"Of course you didn't, child. These are terrible times." He reached into his pocket and retrieved a stale bread crust. "Take this." He pressed it into her hand.

"Oh no, Franz. I couldn't take your ration." She tried to give it back to him, but he refused.

"I am an old man," he said. "You take the bread. I would hope someone would do the same for Hanna."

Eva thanked him and ate it ravenously. She knew she should have pocketed it for later, but it was hard, being so hungry all the time. She looked up at Franz, ashamed, but he was nodding approvingly. "Good girl," he said, patting her head. "You need your strength."

Eva looked at him. "Your daughter…Hanna…" Her voice was tentative. "What happened to her?"

Franz sighed. His face sagged again. "I don't know." He put his face in his hands. He was quiet for a moment. "Not everyone is lucky enough to end up at Terezín." He sounded bitter.

"Lucky?" Eva looked around. *How could anyone feel lucky to be here?*

"Yes, lucky, Eva," said Franz. He gave her a twisted

smile. "This is the luxury camp, don't you know? I was a war hero. I won a medal of bravery in the Great War, fighting for Germany. They had to find a place for me and others like me; they couldn't just deport us. So the war heroes, the artists, the musicians—we were sent here." He started coughing again. "You think this is bad, Eva? There are worse camps."

At the time, Eva had been sure he was exaggerating. *Worse than Terezín?* When they arrived she had heard her mother describe the place as hell. She'd never heard her mother curse before. Of course, she knew better now. She had heard rumors. There were places worse than Terezín—much more hellish.

"Eva." Franz's face softened. "I want you to have something."

Crouching down, he lifted his pant leg to reveal a small pocket. He reached in and carefully pulled out a little wooden object.

"What's that?" Eva was curious. She hadn't seen a toy in so long.

"It's a little soldier doll." He sounded wistful. "Maybe I'll tell you the whole story another time. But my Hanna, she insisted I take it that night. To protect me." He paused, remembering. "When I was arrested, I thought it might be bad luck after all, but here I am, still alive." His voice was now full of grief, his eyes downcast. "I wish I'd known it was lucky. I would have insisted she keep it." He reached out to hand Eva the doll. "Now, my dear, I'm giving it to you. May it protect you as it has protected me."

Eva took the doll from Franz and gazed at it tenderly.

She touched its pink cheek and looked up at the strange man. "Thank you." She said, grateful. "Thank you, Franz." For the first time in days, Eva felt something close to happiness. She had brought several treasured possessions with her to Terezín, but the guards had confiscated all of them. Having something of her own made her feel hopeful again.

"Please keep it safe," Franz said in a soft tone. He touched her cheek gently and smiled.

"Of course." Eva patted the doll's head and tucked it into her inside skirt pocket. "I'll take very good care of him."

Franz reached out and touched Eva's cheek. "You should be heading back to the children's house now, Eva," he said. Seeing her lost expression, he smiled gently and pointed her in the right direction.

"Will I see you again soon?" Eva paused to turn back and look at Franz, but he had already gone. She hadn't seen him again, not since that first week. If she hadn't had the doll, she might have thought she'd dreamed him up in a fit of loneliness and hunger.

Now, Eva held the doll close to her and crooned to it, the way her mother used to do for her when she was afraid. "Don't be frightened, little Piotr," she whispered. "Papa says the war is going to end soon, that the Americans are coming, and the Russians too, and they will save us." Eva hoped this was true, but she knew from the maps at school that America was very far away. How would the Americans find her here?

"Who are you talking to, Eva?" Ilona, who slept on the upper bunk, peered down at Eva curiously. Ilona had very pretty gold, curly hair that bounced when she walked. It now tumbled in the air between the two beds as Ilona looked at Eva upside-down.

"Just to myself." Hastily, Eva shoved the doll back into her pocket. "I had a nightmare."

"Oh." Ilona was sympathetic. She swung down from her bed and hopped into Eva's like the monkeys Eva used to watch at the Prague Zoo. "Don't fret, Eva," she said, hugging her around the middle. "It was just a dream." She sprang back up. "Did you hear about the Red Cross? They're coming here, to visit. My cousin Felix said so, and he's older; he's with the men." She paused to take a breath. Ilona liked to talk and tended to do so at a rapid pace. "They're cleaning up Terezín for the visit. Everything is going to be nice, and we're going to get clothes and food and books…" Her excited voice trailed off.

"The Red Cross? Really?" Eva was surprised. "I haven't heard anything about it from Mama or Papa."

Ilona nodded enthusiastically, her curls bobbing up and down. "It's still a secret," she said, lowering her voice. "Felix is going to be on the beautification committee, so he knows things others don't yet. He's going to be planting grass and trees. Can you imagine?" She motioned around her. "It's going to be green here!"

Eva nodded at Ilona and tried to look excited, but didn't say anything. She was skeptical; it sounded to her like what Papa called "propaganda." When the Nazis first came to Prague, they had been shown a film in school about the Nazi government in Germany. In the film, they were portrayed as

123

saviors and heroes who had brought food, clothing, and prosperity to their country. When Eva had mentioned the film to her parents, her father had disgustedly dismissed it as "Nazi propaganda." He explained to her that the Nazis wanted to win the hearts and minds of the Czech people, and so they presented them with a false, embellished version of what life was like with the Nazis in charge. "They only show the good things, what suits them," Papa had said. "They don't show you the Jews and the Gypsies being tortured and rounded up in the streets like cattle."

Eva had understood immediately what he meant. Now, she listened to Ilona's well-intentioned prattle with a mindful ear. Dressing up the ghetto for the Red Cross would almost certainly qualify as propaganda. She wondered, skeptically, if Ilona's information was even true. It seemed odd, far-fetched, that the Nazis would let anyone in, let alone the Red Cross, and that the camp would be cleaned up. Certainly nothing she'd seen here since her arrival suggested it was true. Just yesterday, she'd watched a pair of guards kick an old, sick man in the street. Over and over again they had kicked him, for no reason at all. When they'd finally stopped kicking, the man had been still, blood trickling from his left ear. Eva had been too afraid to go over and see if he was alive. Like everyone else present, she had turned away, afraid of provoking the guards into choosing their next victim. Later, Eva had heard someone say he was a Rabbi, and she felt ill.

But Ilona looked happy and hopeful, and so Eva said nothing. She wished she were more like Ilona. "That's wonderful news," she said instead, with forced sincerity. She hugged her friend and hoped she was right.

To Eva's surprise, Ilona proved to be correct. By the end of that week, everyone was talking about the upcoming Red Cross visit. Committees of all kinds were created. The goal, people said, was to transform the filthy concentration camp into a quaint-looking town in record time. Even the children were put to work. Eva and Ilona were to perform in the children's opera *Brundibár* with the famous Jewish composer Hans Krása. Eva thought it was a good play. It was about a sister and brother whose mother needs milk to recover from illness. To raise money to buy her the milk, they decide to sing in the market, but the organ grinder, Brundibár, keeps chasing them away. However, with the help of a sparrow, cat, and dog, as well as the children of the town, they succeed in chasing away the evil organ grinder and are able to sing in the town square.

Ilona had been cast in a play before, at the orphanage in Prague with her brother, Emil. Ilona and Emil had been separated from their parents early on in the war, a fate Eva and her parents had managed to avoid. Eva knew her family was lucky, and she was grateful. "Prominents," people called them. Prominent Jews, the kind Franz had mentioned that day on the road. *Professors, artists. People like Hans Krása and Papa*, thought Eva. *Papa was famous. His medical textbook has been translated into German, French, and English.* Eva recalled how, after the occupation, he would leave early in the mornings so that the other men in their building, who were mostly Jewish and no longer allowed to work, wouldn't see him off to his job. "So they don't feel shame," Papa would say. Remembering this, Eva didn't often mention Mama and Papa in front of Ilona, as her friend hadn't seen her own parents in years.

Of course, that didn't stop Ilona from speaking about them constantly. "When the war is over," she told Eva, sounding confident, "I'm going to find my parents, and then we're going to move to America! Emil and Felix, too. I have an aunt there, and cousins. They live in a place called Chicago." She pronounced it very carefully: Shee-ca-go. "They say it's wonderful there. Everyone is allowed to go to school and have a job. And they have a pet cat. My parents might even be there already."

At the mention of the cat, Eva felt wistful. She had had a pet cat, Acedia, whom she missed very much. As an only child, Eva had sometimes felt lonely. Her pet had been good company. When they were forced to leave Prague, Eva had given Acedia to loyal Piotr, who promised to take good care of her while they were gone. "You'll be back soon," he'd said. "I know it. And Acedia will be right here waiting for you."

Eva wondered if Acedia remembered her and felt a pang of sadness. Then she felt ashamed. *Ilona has no idea where her parents are. You have no right to cry over your cat*, she reprimanded herself.

Ilona's chatter had earned them many disapproving looks during *Brundibár* rehearsals. Both girls were in the chorus.

Although Eva was perfectly happy just to be a part of the show, Ilona felt she deserved a better part: she wanted to play the cat.

"I would have been a better choice than that *pitomec* Ella." It was a Monday, and hot. Waiting for Mr. Krása, the children fanned themselves as they got into their places. "My hair is much nicer." Ilona scowled and pointedly tossed her blonde curls.

"Ilona, sh!" Eva looked around, scandalized. "People can hear you!"

"I don't care." Ilona sniffed. "This is ridiculous."

One of the older children in the chorus turned to glare at them. "The two of you are always talking. You need to be quiet." He sounded angry. "Don't you understand? The Red Cross is coming in a week. We need to perform well." There were murmurs of agreement.

"Why?"

The voice came from the back. Heads swerved to see who was talking. It was another boy. He was tall, with a shock of tousled black hair. His eyes were almost as dark, his complexion was sallow, and his expression surly. He leaned against the wall, arms crossed. Eva tried to remember his name.

"What do you mean?" The first boy looked at him, uncertain.

"And why do we have to do well?" asked Eva. *Adam. His name is Adam.*

Someone else spoke up. "So that they'll help us!" It was Ella, the girl playing the cat. "So that they'll help us leave here. Help us find our parents and go home." Others nodded.

Adam gave an empty laugh. "You think that giving a good performance will get us out of here? Are you serious?" He motioned around him. "Look at what's going on here. They're making this place nice. And we all know it's hell." His expression was fierce. "You do understand, don't you? They're making it nice here so that the Red Cross will leave them alone, and they'll leave, and we'll never get *any* help. We're never getting out of here. You can bathe a corpse, but even after scrubbing it, perfuming it, it's still a corpse."

Everyone was quiet. Eva thought about corpses and shuddered, trying to block out the unpleasant imagery Adam's words had evoked. It was true that Terezín had dramatically improved over the last several weeks. There was grass and flowers. And food in the shops! Just yesterday, an empty café had been scrubbed clean, then stocked full of mouth-watering confections to look like a candy store. Brightly colored macarons, chocolate bonbons, pastel gumdrops—everywhere you looked, mountains of sweets. In the center of the display was the most beautifully crafted gingerbread castle Eva had ever seen. It even had a little prince and princess on the top, their carefully iced crowns dotted with red and yellow jewels fashioned from cubes of chiseled sugar. Surrounding the castle were little animals, trees, and cottages made entirely of marzipan: perfect miniature replicas of rabbits, dogs, cats, and evergreen trees. Flowers. Eva had stood and stared at the window for a long time. There had been candy stores in Prague, but nothing like this; the castle was like something out of a fairy tale.

"Like the candy shop," murmured Eva to herself. She remembered how she had felt when Ilona first told her that the Red Cross was coming. *Propaganda.* She felt her stomach sink. *Adam is right.*

Adam had heard her and snapped his fingers. "Exactly! Like the candy shop." He looked at the others. "Haven't you seen it? Do you really think we'll be allowed to eat that beautiful candy?" He snorted. "The guards will eat it all once the visitors are gone. And they'll probably do it in front us, laughing."

Just then, Mr. Krása entered. The room was silent. They were all thinking about what Adam had said. Mr. Krása looked at them with surprise, because usually he had to shout to get them to quiet down.

"Can this be my cast?" he said, eyes twinkling. "Surely not. My singers are much louder than this!"

His smile faded as he noticed the somber faces of the children around him. He looked at them, concerned. "What is the matter, boys and girls?"

A girl called Rosa, who always wore her bright red hair in two thick braids, one on either side of her head, raised her hand.

"Yes, Rosa?" They all waited.

"Mr. Krása, some people are saying it doesn't matter how well we do when the Red Cross is here." She was tearful. "They think that it's all for show, and we won't get any food, and the candy is not for us, and if you bathe a dead person he's still dead." She said it all in a single breath, choking back sobs.

Mr. Krása looked sad. "Listen, my children." As usual, his voice was kind. He took off his cap and looked out at them. "I cannot promise you that the visit of the Red Cross will bring us the help we've all been hoping for. Nor can I tell you whether you will eat any of the food that has been magically appearing in shops—"

"See? I told you." Adam cut him off. He took off his own cap and threw it on the floor.

"But," Mr. Krása continued, ignoring Adam. "But, what I was going to say is, it doesn't matter." His voice was firm.

"It doesn't matter?" Adam interrupted him again. "It doesn't matter if we eat or starve, live or die?" Others echoed him, murmuring to each other in disbelief.

"That's not what I was going to say, Adam." Mr. Krása admonished him gently. "What I meant to say was that we do our best because if we don't—if we put in a poor effort—then the Nazis have already won the war." He paused for effect and took a deep breath. "It means we've given up our belief in ourselves. We have to be like the brother and sister in our opera: we have to sing in the market square, despite the evil Brundibár."

Hans Krása's voice warbled with emotion. "You've worked hard," he went on. "Now, the Nazis say that we are inferior. A subhuman race." He looked at them, eyes blazing. "Well, I say that's a load of *pitomost*. We are going to go out there and perform brilliantly, because we can. We are going to show the Red Cross, the Germans, and everyone else what great performers we are."

Someone started clapping. Soon, the whole room was

alive with thunderous applause. Only Adam failed to join in, his hands firmly at his sides. His eyes flashed with contempt.

"Now, children, if you please." Mr. Krása clapped his hands. "Let's take it from Act Two."

The lists went up that afternoon.

Eva emerged from rehearsal to discover throngs of people moving frantically about, trying to get a glimpse of papers posted on the walls of the buildings. There were wails and sobs as people got close enough to read them. One young woman clutched at her hair and screamed as she sank to the freshly planted grass in horror. A very small boy hovered anxiously about her, grasping her skirt.

Deportations. It had been a month or so since the last round, and Eva had felt relatively safe. "There won't be any before the Red Cross visit," people had been saying. "There won't be any more lists until after they've gone." *They were wrong,* she thought. A wave of despair washed over her and left her as cold as if she'd bathed in ice.

Mama and Papa. She scanned the crowds, frantic, searching for their familiar faces. *What if they're on that list?* Frightened, she began to push her way into the mob, elbowing others in an effort to get closer. Lunging forward, she tripped and tumbled facedown into the dust. It was some moments before she realized, shocked, that she was being stepped on. *I'm going to be trampled to death.* Her mind went numb. She gave a small cry of desperation. "Help," she croaked, but no sound came out. Her mouth was full of dirt, and someone was standing on her hair. She gave another muffled cry and twisted her body in an effort to get back up. She was trapped. She winced as someone else stepped on her left hand.

"Eva, dear, you must get up." A familiar voice, urgent, speaking German. She looked up. "Franz!" His name came out as a strangled cry. Swiftly, he bent down and picked her up, whisking her to a more secluded spot. She coughed and spat out dirt as Franz set her down on the grass. He patted her gently on the back.

"Oh, Franz." She was tearful. "It was terrible. I wanted to check the lists, and I got pushed, and I fell, and…" her voice trailed off. "I never even got to see them!"

"You don't have to worry, *Liebchen*." His voice was dry. "The children were mostly spared, this time. Particularly the ones in the performance. I believe you are in the play?"

Eva was startled. "Me? Oh! I was thinking of my parents."

It was Franz's turn to look surprised. "Your parents?" he said. "They're still here, then? You're still all together?"

Eva nodded. "We were lucky." She was quiet for a moment. She plucked a blade of grass and twirled it between her thumb and forefinger. "Papa was a famous professor at the university. He taught medicine."

"Ah," said Franz. "One of the Prominents. I'm afraid it doesn't mean anything anymore." His face twisted. "Well, at least not for me."

"Oh no, Franz!" Eva's face crumpled with realization. "You're not on the list?"

"I am." He said it without emotion. "But don't cry for

me, Eva. I gave up a long time ago; I am an old man now. But you, you're young. You fight as hard as you can to get out of here." He lowered his voice. "They say the war is going to be over soon. The Americans are coming, and the Russians. It's only a matter of time."

"So it's true, then?" Eva spoke in hushed tones. "I never know whether to believe it or not. America is so far away, Franz. How will they ever find us here?"

Franz turned away. *Was he crying now?*

"They will find you, Eva," he said finally. He turned back to look at her. "I know it. But you have to be strong. You have to make sure you are found." He motioned toward her skirt pocket. "Do you still have the soldier doll I gave you?"

"Yes, Franz." Eva nodded. "I've named him Piotr."

"A good name." Franz stood up. "I should go," he said. "I haven't much time now. But keep the doll safe, and he will keep you safe."

"Are you—are you sure you wouldn't like him back?" Eva's voice was small, and she tried not to look sad. She was, of course, reluctant to part with Piotr, but did not want to seem rude.

"Of course not, *Liebchen*." Franz shook his head. "He's yours."

"Thank you, Franz," she said. A tear rolled down her cheek. "I will pray for you. And for Hanna."

Eva gave Franz a final wave as he walked away. She knew she would never see him again. She stood back up, brushing dust and pine needles off her worn skirt. Catching sight of the mob as she turned, she felt a renewed sense of fear. *Mama and Papa!* Her heart pounded. *What if they're on the list?* She took a deep breath. She'd have to fight her way back through the crowd. She clenched her fists in determination.

"Eva?" A voice, the most wonderful voice in the world! Eva whirled around. "Mama." With a small cry, she stumbled forward into her mother's open arms. She inhaled deeply. Her mother's scent, although faint, was still there. She buried her head in her mother's shoulder. Her father was there, too, and he put his arms around them both.

"Eva." Her mother's voice broke as she stood back to look at her daughter. "You're growing into a beautiful young woman." Her father nodded his head, beaming with pride. "You've been so brave," he said. His voice quavered slightly. He ruffled her hair.

Eva felt the bottom of her stomach fall out. "You're on the list, aren't you." It was more of a statement than a question. Her voice was dull, flat. She looked up at them, expectant.

They exchanged a glance. Her father sighed. "We are, *Miláček.*" His voice was quiet. "We're being deported tomorrow. People are saying they want to empty Terezín for the Red Cross visit. So that it won't seem so overcrowded."

Eva stared at him blankly. She felt her mother's arms encircle her. "I want to go with you." Eva was crying now. "Can't I come? They want fewer people here. I'll go too."

"No!" Her mother's voice was high-pitched. Her parents exchanged another glance, this one filled with horror. Her father, too, was shaking his head vigorously. "Eva." His tone was sharp now. He took her by the shoulders and gave her a small shake. "There are worse places than Terezín. Much worse—you know that. The Americans are coming. You just have to be strong until they get here." He sounded just like Franz.

Eva wrestled free of his grip. "I am tired of hearing about the stupid Americans!" She stamped her foot on the freshly planted grass. "I have no one else! Even Ilona has her brother and her cousin! I have no one!"

Eva burst into tears. Her mother did, too. Her father's face went white and his eyes clouded over. He bit his lower lip and put his head in his hands.

"Eva," he said again, straightening. "*Miláček*, where we're going—they say no one comes back. Do you understand me?" Eva hiccupped: she understood and cried harder.

"What will I do by myself?" Her voice shook. "I can't do it, Mama." She fell into her mother's arms again.

"Eva." Her mother's voice was soft and firm. "You are so brave. Your father and I believe in you. When the war is over, you must get yourself to America. I have a cousin there, in New York. Can you remember that?" Eva nodded, sniffling. Her mother went on, making Eva repeat the name several times, until she was satisfied Eva had committed it to memory.

"You will be safe." She touched Eva's face. "I know it. You will be safe." She pulled her daughter in close and they stood that way for a long time.

It was Ilona who found her, wandering aimlessly. "Eva," she said. "Where have you been? I've been looking for you everywhere."

Eva looked at her, her face empty: a void of expression. "My parents," she managed. "They are...on the list." She couldn't bear to say deported; it felt too final.

Ilona's face softened, and she put an arm around Eva. "I know," she said. "I know how bad it feels. But the war is going to be over soon, and you'll all find each other, and—"

Eva cut her off and pulled away. "Do you honestly believe that, Ilona? Are you an idiot?" She was shouting now. "We're never going to see our parents again, either of us. Haven't you heard the rumors? They say that—"

This time, it was Ilona who cut Eva off. She grabbed her arm.

"I am *not* an idiot, Eva." Her blue eyes were hard, their usual cheeriness gone. Her cheeks flushed, and her mouth twisted in anger. "I know all the rumors. I've heard about the camps, just like you. And you're right, I will probably never see my parents again." She took a deep breath. "I know you think I'm silly. But I try to stay positive because that's the attitude you have to have if you're going to survive." She drew her shoulders back. "That's what my Papa told me when I saw him last. And I'm going to survive, Eva." Ilona sounded fierce now. "I'm going to get out of this disgusting place, and I'm going to get to America, and I'm going to be a nurse and get married and have four children!" She glared at Eva, as if daring her friend to challenge her. Then Ilona started to cry, her strength dissolving. "I'm on the list, Eva." She gave a single, shaking sob.

Ilona—on the list? Eva felt dizzy. The ground swayed beneath her feet. "Ilona," she managed. "Ilona." Her cheeks felt hot with shame. She felt the tears coming again, warm and salty. Not Ilona, surely. Not beautiful Ilona, with her curly, golden hair and her porcelain skin.

Ilona straightened. "Don't cry for me, Eva." She had stopped crying and sounded calm. "I'm going to survive. I know it."

"I'm so sorry. For what I said. I'm so sorry." Eva cried harder.

Ilona reached for Eva's hand and squeezed it. "You don't have to apologize," she said. She gave her friend a little smile. "Promise me you'll try to get some candy. The princess, Eva. Try for the princess. For me."

Eva watched her parents leave the next day. The guards were everywhere, yelling and grabbing people by their shirt collars, hauling them forcibly into cattle cars as people cried and clutched at loved ones. They begged not to be sent. Eva watched as one guard, laughing, tore a sobbing toddler from her parents' arms and tossed her carelessly into a car like a sack of flour. Eva gagged and turned to her parents, filled not only with grief now, but bitterness and bile. She noticed that her mother's hair, once a rich chestnut that tumbled down her back, was now steel gray and cropped short. Her father, the famous professor, stooped instead of standing tall, and most of his hair was now completely gone. Both were pain-fully thin. Eva hugged them tightly, trying to hold on to them in her mind: not only the look of them, but the softness of her mother's hands, the stubble on her father's cheek when she kissed him. Eva stayed, frozen in one spot, until the last car of the train was no longer visible. She clutched the soldier doll, safe in her pocket, for support, tracing her nails along its outline, scraping against its paint.

When the train was finally and truly gone, she slowly turned away, whispering the Jewish prayer for safe travel, the *Tefilat Ha'derech*: "*Yehi ratson mil'fanecha, Adonai eloheinu veilohei avotei-nu. Shetolicheinu l'shalom.*" "*May it be Your will, Eternal One, our God and the God of our ancestors, that You lead us toward peace, emplace our footsteps toward peace.*"

Eva walked away from the station. As she got closer to the barracks, she remembered Ilona wouldn't be there and found she couldn't go on, not just yet. She sat down on a large rock and touched her own plain brown hair, straight and dirty and unremarkable. Why Ilona, with her beautiful golden curls, and not her? It didn't seem fair.

Eva had said her final good-bye to Ilona that morning. Resolute and stoic, Ilona had walked away with Emil and Alex, telling Eva she'd see her in America. She hadn't cried again. With Eva's help, she had pinned back her beautiful hair. "I don't want them to cut it," Ilona had confessed the night before. "I heard they make the girls cut their hair. Maybe if it's pinned, they won't notice it."

The hours passed, and Eva remained seated, still, on her

rock. It was Adam who found her, staring into the distance at nothing.

"Eva?" His voice was uncertain.

She looked up briefly. "Adam."

"You should come to rehearsal."

Eva gave a short laugh. "What for? You were right, you know. It's all nonsense. *Pitomost.*"

"I wasn't. I was wrong." He kicked a rock as he spoke; they both watched as it rolled away in the dust.

"You weren't. They took Ilona, you know."

"I know." He sat down next to her. "My sister, too. She's only five."

Eva felt her eyes fill with tears. *Five years old.* "I'm sorry, Adam."

"Me too." He was hunched forward, his head in his hands. Eva watched as he clutched at his hair: he winced as the wiry black strands came loose. He examined them before tossing them into the wind.

They sat quietly for a moment.

"Krása, he was right, though." Adam spoke up again. He let go of his hair and folded and unfolded his hands in his lap. "I see that now."

"How? They took your sister." Eva's voice was hard.

"Exactly. I'm all that's left of our family." Adam sounded tired, but his voice rang with a quiet resolve. He sat up straighter. "Who will tell Miriam's story? Or my parents', or Ilona's?"

"What does that have to do with anything?" Eva sounded

bitter. She turned away from Adam and stared at a newly planted fir tree. She felt a fresh wave of resentment at its bright green needles.

"It has to do with hope, I think. If we sing, we have hope, still. And if we have hope, we might survive." He put out his hand. "Come with me now."

Eva went to rehearsal. And when the Red Cross came, she sang. She sang as she had never sung before, for her parents, for Adam's sister, for Ilona. She sang in a voice that was loud and clear and true. And she waited, and she hoped. But the Red Cross came and then went. The grass died, and the chocolates disappeared, and the prince and princess crumbled to dust. And the lists went up again.

CHAPTER 8

Toronto, Canada
2007

"Come in, guys." Dr. McLeod is waiting for them when they arrive. They're a few minutes late; finding parking proved to be a challenge today. Usually easy-going and even-tempered, her father becomes Mr. Hyde when driving or parking the car. As she hid in her seat while he swore and railed against other drivers, Elizabeth resolved to make a case for public transportation in the future.

Elizabeth studies Dr. McLeod. She seems cheerful enough—she's smiling, anyway.

Elizabeth and her father exchange a glance. *A good sign?* Elizabeth wonders. Dr. McLeod waves them in, directing them to the table. "I was just on the phone with a colleague overseas," she says. She's wearing a long denim tunic with purple embroidery today and a pair of orange ballet flats. "About your find, actually." She sits down and motions for them to do the same. As she settles into her chair, Elizabeth notes that the pile of journals that toppled over like dominoes last week is still in a heap on the floor. There are also several textbooks strewn around under the table. She tries not to hit any with her chair as she pulls it in closer to Dr. McLeod's desk.

"So." Dr. McLeod looks at them. She crosses and uncrosses her fingers, then crosses them again. She grins mischievously. "How's everyone doing?"

Elizabeth and John look at each other again.

"Okay, thanks," says Elizabeth cautiously. At the same time, John blurts out, "Is it the real thing?"

"Dad!" says Elizabeth, scandalized.

Dr. McLeod laughs. She winks at Elizabeth. "Is he always like this?"

"Worse, usually." Elizabeth rolls her eyes and gives her dad a playful punch on the arm.

"I'm sorry." John looks abashed. He pauses. "But—is it?"

Dr. McLeod smiles. She reaches for a red folder and shuffles some papers. "I can't say for certain, of course. No one can, except perhaps Merriweather, if she's still alive. But in my professional opinion—I would say there is a strong possibility. Probability, even."

John exhales. "Is that as close to 'yes' as we're going to get?" he asks.

Dr. McLeod nods. "I can't say for certain, right? But put it this way: that's as good an answer as you could have hoped for."

John looks triumphant. He reaches over and squeezes Elizabeth's hand. "Quite a birthday present, huh, Liz? Who knew?"

Elizabeth grins. She can't wait to tell Evan. She'd let him know the night before on Facebook that they were coming to see Dr. McLeod today. He'd told her to text him right away when she found out. "Boris and I need to know immediately," he'd messaged back, and she'd laughed.

Dr. McLeod reaches for a pair of purple glasses and opens the folder. "The lab results all match up," she says. "I'll spare you the boring details, but in terms of the wood and stuff, it's all what you would expect for a wooden toy from the southwestern part of England. And it's definitely early twentieth century."

John bangs the table in excitement. "I knew it. I knew it was real! I had a feeling."

Elizabeth pats her father on the arm and exchanges an amused glance with Dr. McLeod. Neither of them mentions the *Titanic* incident or the number of times John's "had a feeling" about something from a garage sale.

"Just a second there, John," says Dr. McLeod kindly. She pushes her glasses back up on her nose; they have slid halfway down it from laughing. "I do think there is a good chance it might be. But there are a few oddities I wish I could explain. They don't threaten the authenticity, really; I just wish I understood what they meant."

"Such as?" John sits up a little straighter. "The uniform color thing you mentioned last time?"

"Exactly," says Dr. McLeod. She's shuffling through some papers now, looking for something. "Another thing that came up was that the boots appear to have been repainted more recently—maybe fifty years ago." She picks up the doll and holds it out so they can see. "I did an analysis, and from what we can tell, that paint was made from organic materials. One of the compounds identified is native to Asia."

They all stare at the boots. "What does that mean?" asks Elizabeth tentatively.

Dr. McLeod looks at her. "It means that our little soldier doll somehow made its way from England, to Germany, to somewhere in Asia, and then—at some point—to Canada." She sits back and lets the others absorb this information.

"Asia!" says Elizabeth, floored. She pauses. "Couldn't it just be that the paint was manufactured there?"

"Good question," says Dr. McLeod approvingly. "But I don't think so. From what we can tell, it's not a commercially prepared paint. It's made from plant materials. In Asia, that kind of paint is usually used for traditional silk screening art."

Elizabeth has no idea what that is, but makes a mental note to Google it later and nods, avoiding eye contact in case someone should ask her thoughts on silk screening. She notices a firefighter calendar hanging on the wall, one of those ones where the firemen aren't wearing any shirts. She fights a sudden urge to laugh.

"I wonder how it got here." Elizabeth's dad is thinking aloud, talking to himself. He reaches for a paper clip and taps it against the table absently.

"Me too," says Dr. McLeod. "Unfortunately, science can only take us so far. I have been thinking, though. If you publicize the find, people may come forward. People who were in possession of the doll." Curious, she looks at them. "What is your plan? Can I ask?"

Elizabeth and her father exchange a glance. A plan is not something they've discussed.

Elizabeth clears her throat. "I kind of want to give it back to her. To Margaret Merriweather. It's hers; she lost it."

Her dad looks surprised. "I didn't know that was your plan," he says.

Elizabeth shrugs. "It doesn't feel right to sell it or whatever," she says. "Not since she's still alive, you know?"

"Is she alive, then?" asks Dr. McLeod. She looks amazed. "I just assumed she had passed. She must be ancient."

"She is," says Elizabeth.

"Well, the women of that generation were a hardy lot," says Dr. McLeod.

Her father gives her another look of surprise. "I didn't realize you'd looked into this, Liz."

"Yeah." She reddens. "Is that okay? I know it was your birthday present, Dad. I'll find you something else. Maybe a nice butter dish?" she smiles slyly.

"Funny." He grins. "It's very admirable of you, Liz."

She shrugs again, embarrassed. "I'm going to e-mail her publisher."

Her father picks up the soldier doll. He gives it a piercing stare, as if willing it to share its secrets.

Dr. McLeod nods at them as she takes off her purple glasses and swaps them for a green pair stuck underneath a sheaf of file folders. "It's been through at least two European wars and then to Asia," she says. "How the heck did it get here? That's what I'd most like to know."

CHAPTER 9
Da Nang, Vietnam
1970

"Here you go, Boots." Mike Stepanek tossed the last cardboard box to the man on his left and sat down next to him, wedging his own box open with his penknife.

"Damn it!" Boots peered inside his C-Ration can and gagged exaggeratedly, turning toward Mike. "Ham and lima beans again! Third day in a row. God hates me, College." He spat at the ground, accidentally hitting one of his oversized boots. The others watched as the saliva trickled down its side, disappearing in the bottomless mud beneath his enormous feet.

"You knew that already, Boots," piped up Red. He stuck a fork in his own can of spaghetti. "Otherwise He wouldn't have sent you here. He would have given you a rich daddy or the brains to go to college." He stole a glance at Mike and blushed, his skin blending with his ginger hair. "Sorry, College."

"No problem," said Mike automatically. He was used to it. The other guys in the platoon couldn't understand why he hadn't applied for a deferral. To be fair, his college friends back in Boston never got it either.

"It's not a fair war, Stepanek." That had been Scott's refrain. He must have repeated it a thousand times, like a responsive reading in church that goes on and on. No matter what Mike said, Scott had only that one answer. "Two weeks ago you're protesting front and center. Now you're going off to war? For what? It's just not *fair,* man."

Karen, too, had begged him not to go when his number came up. "There are options," she'd pleaded. "You could go to Canada. You're being foolish, Mike."

Karen. Mike closed his eyes and tried to picture her, but after months in the jungle her face was fading, somehow, as if he were looking at it through the shallow water that pooled in the rice paddies. Her hair, he could remember that. Long and dark and shiny, the color of coffee when you've added just a bit of cream. It always smelled good: clean and fresh, like Johnson's baby shampoo. Subconsciously, he reached for his own hair. Like the rest of him, it was filthy, caked with a permanent layer of either mud or dust, depending on the season. The filth had been difficult to get used to. When he'd first arrived in the bush, he'd been overwhelmed by the smell, both of the latrines and his comrades.

Now, however, the smell barely registered. A sort of mish-mash of feces and unwashed bodies and cigarette smoke was now nothing more than the olfactory equivalent of white noise. No one noticed it, and thus it went unmentioned.

Six months since he'd landed in Da Nang, Vietnam. Not that long, really, but somehow, like Karen's face, life before was becoming more and more difficult to remember. "The World" the troops called it, referring to the States and home. Mike had found that strange when he'd arrived. Wasn't 'Nam part of the world? But after a trek or two into the jungle, he'd understood. The territory was so strange, so foreign to kids from New York or Kentucky or California that it might as well have been an entirely separate planet: the elephant grass that grew taller than a man and was twice as hard to knock down; the tree canopies that grew so dense that day felt like night and night like death; the heat that felt as if you were being roasted on a stick like a marshmallow at a campfire. You couldn't understand 'Nam until you'd lived it, not if you were a regular kid from Boston or Philly or wherever. And yet somehow, he'd done well here. He often said that he'd been made squad leader only because he'd been lucky enough not to get himself killed in his first five months of service, but he knew that wasn't entirely true. The men looked up to him, trusted him. They listened to what he had to say.

"You're leadership material, Stepanek." Lieutenant Baker was constantly after him to go to officer's school. "You'd do well at Quantico," he'd said again a night or two ago, referring to the officer training school back in Virginia. He'd taken a long drag on his cigarette and offered it to Mike. "You've got the brains, and you're a good squad leader, College."

"Thanks, sir," Mike had replied politely, taking the cigarette. He had no intention of becoming a lifer. As soon as his tour of duty was over, he was going home. Back to Boston College, back to his guitar, back to the World. He'd reached into his pocket and felt for the tiny soldier. Still there. He'd touched its head and felt that familiar sensation wash over him: comfort. It had been passed on to him by his mother; it was the only remnant of her childhood at a Prague orphanage. Her good-luck charm; she'd kept it close during her escape from Czechoslovakia, where it had been a gift from the nuns. The little soldier was the only token Mike had brought with him to Vietnam. He was careful never to let the guys see it. What would they think of him, carrying around a stupid doll?

Boots was still complaining. "Three days, man. Three days! And I thought this was cherry, and it's grape. Which one of you jerks screwed me on the Kool-Aid?" He waved his canteen wildly, glowering.

"Shut up, will you!" Miles looked up from his can of peaches. His real name was Charles, but his surname was Davis and he was black; so they'd immediately christened him Miles—after the famous jazz musician Miles Davis—when he'd arrived four months ago. "All day long, you complaining. Here." He tossed his own canteen at Boots. "Choo-choo cherry. All yours, man."

"Thanks, man. I owe you one." Boots threw his canteen at Miles, who caught it without looking up, deep in concentration over his peaches.

The five of them were heading out again tonight. They

were lucky to have had any reprieve at all—platoons were known to spend weeks in the jungle now—but even during the two days back at camp, they had quickly become comfortable with the relative luxury of proper sleeping hooches and the occasional hot meal. No one was looking forward to moving out.

"The birds'll be in around nineteen hundred hours," Sarge had informed the troops earlier that day, referring to the helicopters that would drop them off in the wilds of the jungle. They'd known already—Fries, the radio operator, had given them the heads-up the night before—but hearing the details from Sarge forced the men to swallow the reality like the antimalarial tablets that yellowed their skin and gave them chronic diarrhea. "More instructions to follow. Any questions?"

Red had waved his hand.

"Red?"

"Yeah. What's the point of this damn war again, sir?"

Boots snorted. Sarge frowned. "Shut up, Red, or you're taking point."

"Yes, sir. No thank you, sir." Red's emphasis on the word *sir* bled with heavy sarcasm.

Sarge had shot him a warning glance, and they'd all dispersed.

"Fries, you know where we headed tonight?" Miles had finished his peaches. He was smoking now.

"Just the bush, dude." Fries—whose real name was David McDonald—shrugged. "Zippo mission, maybe. Search and destroy. Find 'em, kill 'em, run like hell."

"Another snafu in the making, then," said Red in a bitter voice.

Mike spoke up. As the squad leader, he was saddled with the responsibility of keeping the men in reasonably good spirits and from killing each other. It was difficult when he didn't feel all that gung-ho about a night in the jungle himself. "Take it easy, Red. No one is happy about it."

Red shook his head, disgusted. "It's this war, man. It's just useless. My old man, he was in France back in '44. They used to *do* stuff, you know? They used to take towns. Hills. We keep walking and walking, and we don't do nothing."

Mike sighed. They'd all heard the speech a hundred times, maybe more. Red was political: an angry, brooding sort of guy. On the back of his flak jacket, he'd sketched a peace sign underneath which he'd scratched the words *Ship my body to Nixon*. He also liked to quote Tolstoy.

Fries rolled his eyes. "You gonna start with the *Peace and War* again?"

Miles shot him a look. "It's *War and Peace*, man. Come on. Everyone knows *War and Peace*. Even you ain't that stupid."

Boots grinned. "He might be. He volunteered."

Ignoring them, Red continued. "You kill one Viet Cong soldier, maybe two, and they call in ten confirmed and the mission's a success. It's messed up, I tell you."

Fries shrugged. "We here to kill some commies. That's all I know."

"Commies." Boots laughed. "Communists, my foot. As if you can tell everybody apart. I wonder how many of the

guys we killed were probably on our side? It's a snafu all right,
College."

"Boots, man, shut it. You short. You going home, man.
What the hell you always complaining about?" Miles again.
He and Boots were tight, but neither Boots, a white south-
erner, nor Miles, from Chicago's south side, liked to admit
their bond. Racial politics ran deep in the corps, even out in
the bush.

"How long now, Boots?" asked Fries.

"Ninety-six days and one wake up, dude. Back to the
World, back to Becky."

"I thought she was with another guy now."

"Shut up, Red. That'll all fix itself when I get out of this
living hell."

Mike thought of Karen and felt awash with sympathy
for Boots. He wondered if Karen was seeing someone else.
Probably. She was a real catch, Karen. She'd have moved on.
She never responded to his letters, anyway, other than to send
newspaper clippings deriding the war.

"Screw her, Boots." Mike tossed some crackers at him.
"Here. I got spaghetti; I don't need 'em."

"Thanks, College." Boots gave him a grateful smile.

Mike nodded. "No problem." He settled with his back
against a tree and tried again to remember what color Karen's
eyes were and found he couldn't.

It had been less than a year ago that they'd started the draft.

"Man, French!" Muttering to himself in frustration, Mike

tossed his textbook aside with a groan and flopped back on his bed. Closing his eyes, he tried to remember what his professor had said about conjugating verbs, but couldn't. With a sigh, he leaned over toward his bedside table and flipped on his radio. Music blared loudly—the Rolling Stones. Mike hastily turned down the volume. He was a huge Stones fan, of course, but if his mom heard the music, she'd flip. She insisted he study in silence for two hours every day. He had tried to reason with her—"Ma, I'm a music major, the book-learning stuff isn't that important"—but he had been cut off with a look that would have caused a Rottweiler to pause in its tracks.

"Music," his mother sniffed. "You call what you do music? Mozart; that's music. Your music is more like noise. You will study your English and your math, Michael, because you are going to be a high school teacher!" And this was, of course, followed up with the usual "as long as you live under our roof" speech. He got that one so often, he knew it by heart.

Mike rolled his eyes just thinking about it. His mother had no understanding or appreciation of rock and roll. She wouldn't even listen to music if it had lyrics. His father was the same way. They would have never let him major in music if it had been up to them. Luckily, Boston College had come through with a full-tuition musical scholarship. His parents had then latched onto the idea that with a music degree he could teach and that, naturally, he would be a high school teacher. They were happy with this—teaching was a noble profession, in their opinion. His father, who had left Czechoslovakia shortly after the war, had never had the opportunity to attend college. He worked at a small grocery near the Common and swelled with pride at the idea of his son as a teacher.

"A teacher is a professional," he would say, patting Mike on the back. "It's a good, steady living. And important. Worthy of great respect."

And Mike would bite his lip in frustration, because he had no intention of ever setting foot in a classroom. Well, not as a teacher, anyway. It was a respectable job, fine, but it wasn't what he wanted to do. In fact, the thought filled him with dread. He could remember all too well how he and his friends had treated their high-school teachers: he recalled Miss Webb, who had fled the room in tears after Eddie O'Hara had put a scantily clad Miss November inside her history textbook, and Mrs. Andrew, who'd fainted in terror at the cockroaches Billy Gallagher had slipped into her lunchbox. But what could he say, really? He didn't want to hurt his parents, and he couldn't afford to move out and live on campus.

It seemed like everyone at BC had money but him. His family wasn't poor, not exactly, but they weren't rich, either. Certainly there was no money to spare for Mike to move only a few city blocks away. He sighed. Too bad it hadn't been a scholarship to a California school. Then he would have had no choice but to leave.

Mike grabbed a pillow and covered his face with it. It was depressing, really, living with your parents at eighteen. Besides the rules, there were other issues. Girls, for instance. The girls at college weren't like the girls he'd grown up with. What would he do—ask one back to watch TV at his parents' house and eat cabbage rolls? Just thinking about it made him cringe. Rolling over, he looked longingly at his guitar leaning against the bookcase. He was only allowed to practice once the two hours he was supposedly devoting to French were up.

"Michael?" His mother's voice called from downstairs. Panicked, Mike reached over and shut the radio off. How could she have heard it on such a low volume? The woman must have supersonic hearing! As a kid, he had believed it when she said she had eyes in the back of her head. For years, he hadn't wanted to touch her hair, convinced he'd find a watchful pair of eyeballs underneath, green and knowing.

"Michael." It was his mother again, this time just outside the door. She rapped on it lightly. Mike sat up hastily and pretended to be busy reading his French text. "Come in, Ma." He gave her a bright smile. "Just practicing my French."

"What?" His mother looked at him, distracted. "Michael, you have to come downstairs, to see the television. On the news, there is going to be a lottery for the draft, for the war..." her voice trailed off. She looked scared as she wove her fingers in and out of each other, the way she did when she was nervous.

Michael felt his heart skip. For months, he and his friends had worried about this possibility, discussing it in dorm rooms and cafés and bars around the city. He had tagged along to a couple of protests against the war, too—he just made sure to keep his attendance a secret from his parents. His father, who had escaped the communists in Czechoslovakia, supported America sending troops to intervene in Vietnam. His mother had escaped too, of course, but was silent on the controversial subject. She didn't sound happy now, though.

Mike looked up at his mother's anxious face. He stood up and hugged her awkwardly. "It's okay, Ma," he said. "Let's go see what they're saying."

Silent, his mother turned and headed back down the steps. The television had been left on in the living room, and Mike could see the reflection of the flashing images bouncing off the bay window at the back of the house. The CBS newsman looked serious as he discussed the draft lottery with another journalist.

"The draw will be done tomorrow, December first," the second man explained.

The anchor was nodding his head. "Please tell us again how it's going to work, Don." He made eye contact with the camera. "It's a bit confusing; I'm sure our viewers would appreciate another explanation."

The man nodded and launched into a complicated explanation involving birthdates and numbers and capsules. Mike's eyes glazed over like they did when he studied; he tried to follow, but found his mind wandering. What if he was drafted? He tried to picture Vietnam on the map. Was it next to China, or was that Japan? Next to French, geography had always been his worst subject.

On the television, the anchor was still bobbing his head. "I see," he said to the expert. His tone was grave. "And that's for all men born between 1944 and 1950, you said?"

The other man inclined his head in agreement. "That's

correct." He looked like he was about to say something else, but the anchor interrupted him to go to commercial.

Mike got up to shut off the television; he looked over at his mother, who was leaning against the doorway, tense and pale.

"You are included in this, then, Michael?" It was posed as a question, but he could tell she already knew the answer. She was a smart woman, and her English was better than she let on.

"Yes, Ma." He tried to smile. "Don't worry though. My birthday could be drawn last, right? The war could be over before my number is even called. If that jerk Nixon—"

His mother bristled at his words. "We do not refer to the president as a jerk," she said, her tone severe. "Even if you disagree with him, you must show some respect."

Mike bit his lip, exasperated. Good thing she hadn't seen the posters Scott had made for that protest over in Cambridge—she'd have had a heart attack, probably. They certainly didn't paint the president in a very flattering light. One had a maniacally grinning Nixon toting a rifle pointed at a group of cowering Vietnamese children.

"Mom, you're so old fashioned," he said instead, kissing the top of her head. His mother, though a formidable woman, was tiny and delicate, standing barely five-feet tall. He had grown taller than her well before his fourteenth birthday.

Mike dashed upstairs and grabbed his guitar, which he quickly zipped into its case and slung over his shoulder. He then hurried back downstairs. Opening the closet, he found his coat and hat. "I'm going to go see my friends about this, okay,

Ma?" he said, zipping up the front of his blue parka. "I'll be back in time for dinner, I promise." He pulled his homemade red hat down over his ears.

His mother frowned, disapproving. "What about your math?" She looked at her watch. "You should be doing your school work."

"Ma." Mike's voice was pleading. "This is important. I need to talk to people about the draft and get more information. I need to see Scott and Howard and the others. Come on. Please."

He didn't add what else he was thinking. "I'm an adult!" he wanted to shout. "I don't need your permission!" But he said nothing else; he loved his mother.

Her expression softened with understanding. "Go," she said. She reached up and touched his face quickly. "I know you're a good boy, Michael," she said. Her voice was quiet now, and more urgent. He looked at her, surprised. She noted his expression. "Your father may be in favor of this war and this draft," she said. "But I have only one child." Her voice caught, and she turned away quickly and hurried into the kitchen. Mike said nothing as he left, shutting the door quietly behind him.

It was the darkness that did it every time. Even the bravest of men cowered in the face of the unremitting blackness of the jungle at night.

"It's like being blind," Mike had said stupidly on his first night mission.

"You learn that in school, College?" Red had replied, his tone scathing. Mike had flushed, embarrassed. Thankfully, in the dark, his color went unnoticed.

Tonight was the same; the only thing that changed in the jungle was the season. It was the monsoon now, and together with the relentless blackness came with the unending downpour of rain.

Mike heard a noise in front of him. "Boots?" he tried to keep his voice to a whisper. "Everything okay?"

"Sorry, College. It's these damned malaria pills."

"So that's what that stink is." Fries said, laughing.

"No, that's Red. He's crapped in his pants, he's so scared."

"Shut up, Boots."

"All right, you guys. All of you shut it." Mike cut them off. If he had learned anything about Vietnam, it was not to let the darkness lull you into thinking you were alone. The enemy, when he came, came silently and without warning.

On little cat's feet, he'd thought to himself when he'd first experienced the feeling of being stalked. *Silent, like a cat hunting a mouse.* It was from a poem he'd read in high school, about fog, but it captured the anticipation of an enemy ambush. He'd known, once, who wrote the poem, but like many details from his old life, the memory had left him.

"Everyone awake?" The Lieutenant came up beside Mike, his voice quiet. They had been crouching in the same position for hours.

"Yes, sir." Mike's voice came out hoarse.

"We're going to move again, College."

"Yes, sir." Mike cleared his throat. "We're moving out," he hissed.

There were rustlings as the men struggled with their rifles and packs in the dark. Mike swung his own M16 over his shoulder and prepared to walk.

There was a lot of walking in Vietnam. Red liked to gripe that if you built a bridge across the ocean, you could walk back home from here, with all the walking they did. He probably wasn't entirely off base.

"Intel says there's VC about thirty klicks northwest of here," said the lieutenant.

"Thirty klicks?" Red's voice rose in indignation from the back of the line. "So we were dropped off five hours ago in the damned rain, nearly twenty miles away from where we have to be?"

"And there it is," said Fries. "At least it was only five hours. Remember Quang Tri? That was at least ten."

"What did I tell you? Snafu."

"Aw, shee-it, Red, just shut up. It's bad enough without your damned politics."

"It's not politics, Boots, it's common sense."

"You know what's common sense? Shutting your traps so we're not killed." Miles now, his low voice like thunder rumbling in the distance.

"Killed? Charlie ain't here, Miles. You heard the Lieutenant. They're thirty klicks away."

"Yeah? You want to end up like Pan?"

Instantly quiet, they all remembered Peter Berlin, a quiet

boy from Wisconsin who'd liked comic books. Pan had faced a tiger, and lost, in the blackness of the jungle. They'd had to bind the body together with field wire before they could carry it back to base. They hadn't been able to find all of it. His parents had been told he'd died for his country in battle, a hero.

"Right. So shut it."

They walked in silence.

Mike grabbed another slice of pepperoni and watched as Karen Markham, the de-facto leader of the campus anti-war movement, climbed up on a chair, ready to speak. She cleared her throat loudly and waved her arms to get their attention. Her dark hair was long and straight, and she was dressed in what his mother, frowning and shaking her head, would have referred to as "hippie wear": wide-cut, faded jeans, a frilly, lavender peasant blouse, and a thin white bandana tied neatly around her head.

"If I could get everyone's attention, please!" Karen clapped her hands and swung her long hair so that it tumbled down her back.

"She's a real looker," said Scott in a low voice.

Howard nodded in agreement. "Even if I was a gun-toting Republican, I'd be here."

Scott snorted with laughter and tapped his bottle of Coke with a spoon. "Hear, hear."

"Guys, sh." Mike's voice was disapproving. "It's rude."

Chastened, the others quieted and turned their attention to Karen.

"So," she said, looking out at her audience. "It's finally happened. The government is starting a draft. No choice, no freedom. If your number's called, off you go to Vietnam. To fight in an unjust war." Her expression hardened. "They might as well just spit on the Constitution of the United States of America!"

People cheered. Karen was a good speaker, the kind that drew people's attention immediately, a bit like a hypnotist at a magic show Mike's uncle had taken him to see as a child. She waited a moment, pausing for effect, then held her hand up to silence them. "What we need," she said, voice calm, "is a plan. A strategy. What should we do? Because—" her voice grew louder, "—there's no way all of you guys are going to Vietnam!" She swore loudly.

There was a buzz about the café. Did Karen have a strategy? What did people plan to do? Someone waved their hand and stood up.

"Steve?" Karen pointed to him. "You have any good ideas?"

Steve shrugged and fiddled with his baseball cap. "I heard that if you're in college, like us, you can use that as an excuse to get out of the draft. That's what my cousin said, anyway. That it can buy you some time at least." His voice was tentative.

"Steve Mason!" Karen's voice echoed loudly. She shook an admonishing finger at him as he slinked back into his seat looking mortified. "How can you even suggest such a thing? So you get a pass while your brothers who don't have the opportunity to attend college, who don't have rich parents—they should die in the jungle instead of you?"

A low hiss of disapproval sounded throughout the room. Mike glanced over at poor Steve, who looked now as if Vietnam might be a reasonable option, so long as it got him out of the café. He felt a pang of sympathy for the guy. He had been gutsy enough, at least, to vocalize what a lot of them had been thinking. But Karen was right. It wasn't fair. He thought of Buddy and Donny and Sam and all the guys he'd grown up with who hadn't gone off to college, who now worked construction or in the quarries or painted houses. Heck, he might have been doing that kind of work if he hadn't been offered the music scholarship.

"Mike?" Scott was looking at him. "Earth to Mike. Come in please." He grinned as Mike blinked and jumped slightly. "Where were you, buddy?" he asked, amused.

"Just thinking about the draft. I don't know...I don't know what I would do if my birthday came up."

Scott looked at him queerly. "What do you mean? You wouldn't go, would you?"

"I *said* I don't know." He felt uncomfortable. "Why, what would you guys do? The college thing?"

"No, you heard the lady. That's wrong." Scott grinned, mocking. "I was actually thinking about some kind of medical exemption. Like if you have asthma."

"You don't have asthma, though."

"Not yet."

Mike felt surprised at his friend's reaction. He turned to Howard. "What would you do?"

Howard shrugged. "Canada, maybe," he said tentatively.

"My family all live in Detroit. It's right on the Canadian border, and they could come and visit. You do what you have to do, right?"

"I guess." Mike thought about his parents. They didn't live near the Canadian border, and they didn't have a lot of money to travel, either. Not to mention that his father would probably disown him if he was called to war and fled to another country. He sighed; it was a lot to think about.

"You could go to Canada too," Scott suggested.

"I don't think I could." Mike tried to vocalize what he was feeling. "It's like Karen said. Why should I be able to use college as an excuse when others can't?"

"Because it's a stupid war? Because we shouldn't even be in Vietnam?" Scott's eyes were hard and cold, like the ice that had begun to form on the Charles River. "We shouldn't be fighting the communists. We should be joining them, man."

Mike frowned. "I don't know about that," he said. "Maybe we shouldn't be in Vietnam, but I don't know about the communists. Like, think about my parents—the communists were pretty bad in Prague."

"What are you, some kind of fascist?"

"Go to hell." Mike jumped up. "You have no idea what you're talking about. You want to talk about fascists? You remember a guy called Stalin? In charge of a big communist country called the Soviet Union?" He gripped the edge of the chipped table to control himself from lashing out at Scott.

Scott stared at him. "Are you going to *hit* me, Stepanek? At ease, soldier."

Mike took a deep breath. He wouldn't lose his temper, not so that they could all dismiss him as another violent Southie, a bad boy from the wrong side of town. He picked up his guitar. "I'm leaving," he said. His voice was calm now.

Howard tried to interject. "Come on, guys. Forget it."

"I'll see you later, How," said Mike. He ignored Scott and quickly left the café.

Outside, he felt immediately better, the cold air penetrating his lungs, slowing down his racing heart. He walked quickly, feeling the tension decrease as he breathed in the night air. He clenched and unclenched his fists thinking of Scott and his arrogance and the draft and the war. It was snowing now. He watched as the snowflakes landed on his guitar case and then succumbed, melting.

It was cold, but Mike had grown up with the cold, and it was in his blood; it didn't bother him. He settled down on a bench that had been forest green, once, but a succession of winters had worn it down, chipping away at its paint to reveal the weathered wood underneath. He took out his guitar and began to play, letting himself become consumed by the music.

As often happened, other thoughts left his mind, and he forgot where he was. Nothing mattered but the song. He closed his eyes and let himself be completely absorbed by the melody and rhythm of his fingers.

Mike opened his eyes and found himself staring into the eyes of Karen Markham: bright green, like a cat's.

"That was groovy," she said. She twisted a lock of long

dark hair around her index finger. She was wearing a hat now, a little white one. It was covered with a fine dust of snow. "Did you write that yourself?"

"Yeah." Mike felt his cheeks go red despite the cold. He offered her his hand. "Mike Stepanek," he said. "I'm a music major."

"Karen Markham." She shook his hand. "I'm pre-law."

"That's cool." Mike was impressed.

Karen nodded. "Thanks." She settled down next to him on the bench. "I noticed you with your friends at the café."

"Yeah."

"They were still there when you left."

"Uh-huh." Mike changed the subject. "I agree with you that you shouldn't use college as an excuse," he said firmly. There was noise behind them: students, heading back to campus from a nearby subway stop. He turned and watched them. They were carrying posters.

"I know." Karen's voice was full of passion. "It's just so unfair. But I bet a lot of people here end up doing that."

"I could never do that." He turned back to Karen. "My friends from high school, right? I was pretty much the only one to go to college. I could never take a pass while all those guys were shipped out. You know?"

"Absolutely." She was gazing at him with admiration. There was a pause, and they both laughed, a nervous sort of laughter.

Karen stood up. "I should get going." She brushed the snow off her jeans. "Lots of poli-sci work."

"Sure." Mike watched a snowflake land on the tip of her nose and felt his heart speed up for the second time that night. "Say, do you want to maybe grab some coffee or something sometime?" It came out as a rush of words, and Mike mentally flogged himself for sounding overeager.

Karen smiled easily. "I'd like that." She took out a notebook and scribbled something. "My phone number," she said, tearing out the page and handing it to him.

"Thanks," he croaked. "I'll call you tomorrow."

Karen swung her book bag over her shoulder and turned to leave. "Great!" she said. Her eyes twinkled and looked very green. "See you, Mike." She waved and swept through the park toward the subway station, her hair flapping behind her like leaves dancing in the wind.

"I'm gonna die." Boots was panting. Mike could feel him about five paces in front. He was whispering, but in the relative quiet of the bush, his voice was like an exotic shrieking parrot.

"Sh." Mike swung his rifle nervously from side to side. There was a rustling off somewhere to the left. He held his breath, waiting, but nothing happened. An animal of some kind, no doubt. He shuddered.

"Course you're gonna die." Red now. "Do you know what the average lifespan of a 'Nam trooper is? Twelve days."

"Why you still alive, then?" Miles now, from the front of the line. He was on point.

"Luck. I don't expect to make it back to LA, unless it's in a rubber bag."

"LA? Aren't we shipping your sorry ass back to the president?"

"I wish. That useless dumbass."

"You voted for LBJ?" Fries asked.

"I didn't vote."

"You didn't vote?"

"I'm an anarchist."

"You like pain?" Miles, sounding baffled.

"That's a masochist. An anarchist doesn't believe in government."

"That's a lost cause, man. You believe in them or not, they gonna screw your ass."

"Government is like slavery. It's violent. It's—"

"He's off again, with the Tolstov."

"It's Tolstoy, you dolt."

"Who gives a rat's—"

An explosion. Like the Fourth of July, only with less of the spectacle and none of the joy. Mike dove for cover, terror and dread competing for his attention. A booby trap or a mine. Damn it. He braced himself. "Who was it?"

"Me, College." Red. His voice was quiet now, with none of the earlier bravado. "Booby trap."

"You hurt?"

"You might say that."

Mike scrambled for his flashlight. He didn't like to use it, in case the enemy was nearby, but he had little choice now. He crawled back to Red and shone the light over him.

It was difficult to tell what had happened. The darkness

and the mud made it hard to see the blood, but the spatter-
ing on the tree behind Red suggested it was more than a flesh
wound. Mike waved his flashlight up and down Red, searching. Where was the injury?

Then he saw it.

"Can you give me a hand, College?"Red smiled weakly.
"I seem to have misplaced mine."

In place of where Red's left arm had been was now a gaping hole. Blood gushed out on the ground beside him.

"Boots." Mike called him over. "Apply pressure to Red's
arm."

Boots nodded automatically, in shock. He pressed against
the wound to staunch the bleeding. His eyes met Mike's, but
neither of them spoke.

Choking back vomit, Mike shone the flashlight over
Fries. "Get Doc over here. And we need a Medevac. Now!"
He turned back to Red. "You're getting out of here," he said.
He gave him a wan smile. "Home, man. Back to the World."

"Right." Red was staring at the hole where his arm had
recently been.

"Back to LA. No bag."

"Right," he said again absently. His eyes were unfocused.
"Do you think it's hard to switch hands?"

"Sorry?"

"I'm left handed. Was."

"Oh." Mike tried to think of a reply, but couldn't. "Doc'll
be here any second."

It was hours before they heard the rhythmic drum of the chopper.

"You can't go. I forbid it."

Karen was wrapped in a white sheet. She was sitting up now and had turned to face him. Her teeth were slightly bared, the way they always got when she was angry. She looked fierce.

"I haven't got a choice, Karen. I've been drafted." Mike was still lying down. He'd waited until after they'd made love to tell her; he was worried she wouldn't want to once she knew.

"You have a choice. Everyone has a choice. You could go to Canada."

"I don't want to be a fugitive."

"You want to go kill little kids?"

"I'm not even going to answer that." Mike turned away and looked instead at the wall. A map of the world hung there haphazardly. It was an older map; instead of Vietnam, the country was labeled "Indochina." Mike stared at it, then searched for Boston.

"Well, that's what's going on over there. US soldiers killing women and children while the people of the Republic of Vietnam fight for equality—"

"Cut the republic and equality crap, will you, Karen?" He turned back to her and scowled. "My family escaped Czechoslovakia on foot to get away from the communists there. You don't know what you're talking about." He stared again across the room, where he caught sight of the little soldier doll. It had escaped communism, too, had been witness to the violence of war. Silently it watched them now, debating the merits of another war in another place.

"And you do," she shot back.

"Maybe I don't, but I don't think it's so black-and-white as you make it out to be."

"You just don't want to admit you're going off and being forced kill innocent people in another country's war. You don't want—"

"Enough." He sat up now and grabbed her arm. "Stop it. Please. You think this is easy for me? You think I want to go off to some jungle in the middle of nowhere?"

Karen pounded the bed with her fist. The cheap dormitory mattress groaned and squawked. Mike wondered briefly if it might split open.

"So don't go! Go to Canada! We could go together, maybe. We could go to a school there, and—"

"No. We've gone over this. My dad would kill me. And it would be…" Mike's voice trailed off. He clenched his fists and looked up at the ceiling, searching for the right word.

"What? It would be what?" asked Karen, exasperated. Her hands were on her hips.

He shrugged. "I don't know. Kind of…dishonorable."

"You've got to be kidding me, Mike. *Dishonorable?*" She stared at him in disbelief.

"Yeah. I'm not a coward." Mike met her eyes.

Karen kicked her feet in frustration. "What is this? Some kind of macho thing?"

"I just couldn't face the guys in the neighborhood. Like

this guy, Buddy O'Brien. He was my best friend growing up. He's an apprentice plumber. You think he could get a deferment for that?"

"Was he drafted?" Karen demanded.

"No, but—"

"He hasn't even been drafted! So what are you talking about?"

"You don't get it. It's an honor thing." Mike shook his head.

"You'd rather go get killed in Vietnam."

"You just can't understand it, Karen."

"Obviously."

They sat in silence for a moment. Karen wrapped the sheet around herself tighter. "When?" Her voice was quieter, with a hint of resignation.

"I have to check in Thursday."

"Thursday."

"Yeah. After that there's training and stuff, I think, out in California."

"California," Karen said dully.

"Yeah."

Mike reached for her. She didn't pull away, but she didn't respond either. She felt cold.

"It's only a year."

Karen made a noise.

"I'll write you."

"Mmmm."

"Please, Karen."

"What do you want me to say?" She looked at him, her arms spread out helplessly, and the sheet fell. She grabbed it to cover herself back up. Mike watched as she struggled with the bedding and knew what was coming.

"Will you at least write?" His voice was quiet now.

"I guess."

"Will you wait for me?" He caught the note of pleading in his own voice and cursed himself for his desperation.

Karen didn't answer. She turned away and looked at the map. He watched her eyes travel to Asia. After a while, she spoke up. "I don't think so, Mike." She looked at him. "I'm sorry."

"Right." Carefully avoiding eye contact, he reached for his jeans. He turned away as he dressed, suddenly embarrassed at his nakedness. He gritted his teeth until his temples throbbed; he wouldn't cry in front of a girl.

"I do love you, Mike." Karen was crying as he made for the door.

"You have a funny way of showing it."

He didn't see her again.

The sun was hot. As it beat down against his back, Mike contemplated how that fiery orb was in fact a star millions of miles away. In another universe. Or was it a galaxy? He couldn't recall; his brain felt cooked, as if it had been doused in oil and set ablaze. Dazed, he shifted his pack and wiped away a pool of sweat that had accumulated on his upper lip. He caught a taste of salt, and his hand drifted toward his canteen.

"Don't do it, College," warned Miles. He was about five paces behind Mike. "Not yet."

Mike willed his hand away, letting it drop back to his side. Miles was right. He should save his water. If he started now, he wouldn't be able to stop. That first taste, that first trickle that you could feel right down to the base of your spine, it was like a drug. It made you want more, until your canteen was empty and you were left to swelter in the furnace of the jungle without water. When that happened, you got crazy. He'd watched guys—guys who were ordinarily sensible—plunge face-first into rice paddies or streams without thinking, gulping down the untreated water with gusto. Spaceman had done it. He'd ended up in Okinawa where the docs had yanked out a white worm roughly the length of the Mississippi River from deep inside his guts.

"Where we going again?" Boots was on point. He turned back to look at Mike, his voice taking on its now-characteristic whine.

"What does it matter?" An irritated Fries shifted the radio equipment to his left shoulder and made a face at Boots's back. "Who cares?"

"What do you mean?"

"I mean we're not headed to New York City. They're all the same, these villages. What does it matter?"

"I want to know."

Mike spoke up. "Phu Phom Four," he said calmly.

"Four?" A voice behind Mike spoke up, amused. "Where are one, two, and three?"

"Probably napalmed, burned to ashes, Newguy." Fries didn't bother turning around.

"Stop calling me that. My name is Newton."

"Relax, Newguy."

"Will you keep calling me that when the next guy joins the squad?"

"If he replaces you? Sure."

Newguy quieted down, silenced by the suggestion of his own impending demise.

They walked. Mike thought of Red, who had sent them a postcard from Okinawa. It had been three weeks since he'd left and two weeks since Newton had joined the squad. The note had Red's words, but was in the neat handwriting of one of his nurses. He was being shipped back to the World, where he would see a specialist about an artificial arm. Mike pictured a hook like a pirate's and shuddered involuntarily.

"How much farther?" Boots again. Mike gritted his teeth in an effort not to snap back at his friend. The heat was making them all irritable.

"Not too far now, Boots."

"Boots, man, you need to get your act together. You sound like a toddler." Fries was adjusting the radio again. Mike thought of carrying an extra heavy load of radio equipment and felt a wave of sympathy. He wasn't surprised Fries sounded on the verge of losing his temper.

"Stop giving me shit, Fries."

"When you stop acting like a damned two-year-old, I'll stop."

"I'm not—"

"Shut up." Miles's voice was low and threatening, a bit like the sound of far-off mortar shelling.

"Sorry, Miles."

"Just shut it, Boots. It's too damn hot for this right now."

They reached the village around high noon. Mike stared at the now-familiar scene: the squalid huts cobbled together from C-Ration tins or cardboard, the vacant-looking elders, the children covered in sores. He felt the rush of pity and revulsion that never failed to overtake him on these missions. The other guys seemed to have built up an immunity to the poverty and suffering, vaccinated against it by constant exposure, but for Mike, the sight of each village was always fresh.

"What now, College?" Boots turned and gave him an expectant look.

"We're supposed to interrogate them about supply chains."

"I'll do it," said Newguy with bravado. He marched over to a stooped, disheveled-looking man with gray hair. The man's eyes were dull. He looked about eighty, but Mike knew from experience he was probably younger than his own parents.

"You," said Newguy. He jammed the butt of his rifle against the man's chest. "You VC? You give supplies to VC?"

The man stared at him. "*Tôik hông hiểu,*" he said calmly.

Newguy spoke louder. "Supplies? Food? Weapons?" He gestured to his own rifle. "To VC?"

"*Tôik hông hiểu.*"

"He's saying he don't understand, dude." Miles raised his

eyebrows at Newguy. "Yelling at him ain't gonna make him speak English."

Newguy turned red. "Right," he muttered. He took a few steps back and scuffed his foot into the dust.

Miles sighed. "*Homdan?*" he asked the man, in a kinder voice. "VC?" Miles had a knack for picking up words and phrases in Vietnamese, a talent he didn't particularly enjoy exploiting.

"No, no VC." The man shook his head. "No *homdan.*"

"What's he saying, Miles?"

"He saying he's not VC, and they got no ammo here."

"Bull." Fries spat at the ground. He was covered in sweat. His arms shook as he shifted the radio pack again. "They're all VC."

They searched the huts. They turned over the meager belongings of the villagers while the people watched them passively from doorways. They said nothing, standing stoically as what little they had was tossed around in the manner of bears scavenging a dump. Mike looked around at the chaos, feeling hot with shame. He watched a woman rush for a worn-out pot once Miles had finished looking inside. She clutched it protectively against her chest. Mike's stomach turned.

"There's nothing here," said Boots. He yawned. None of them had slept the previous two nights for more than an hour at a time.

"Bull," said Fries again. He grasped an older man by a graying ponytail. "Where is it? Where's the ammo?"

The man said nothing. He stared at Fries blankly.

"Say something! Something! What is wrong with you people? Do something!" Fries's eyes were wild. He pulled harder at the ponytail. The man had no reaction, allowing himself to be pulled to the ground like a marionette.

"Forget it." Mike put his hand on Fries's arm. "Fries, come on."

Fries met Mike's eyes. They stared at one another. Slowly, Fries relaxed, the release of tension evident from the slump of his shoulders. He shook his head and waved his hands slightly, as if to push away the demons that had momentarily overtaken him.

"Sorry, College." His voice was soft now.

Mike didn't say anything. They stood quietly for a moment, looking at each other.

"GI?" A girl about twelve. She was at his side, barely taller than his waist. She put out her hand, hopefully. "Food, GI?" He looked down at the top of her head, which he noted was covered in sores.

Mike ruffled through his pockets. He usually carried a bar of chocolate, but he hadn't remembered to pack one today. Then, he felt a little wooden foot. He looked again at the girl, her eyes alive with hope.

"Here," he said, before he could change his mind. He thrust the soldier doll at the girl, who took it, surprised.

The girl looked at the doll, then back at Mike. She nodded. "Thank you, GI," she said softly. She brought the doll to her chest in a quick embrace, like a small child.

The others watched but said nothing. The girl, still cradling the doll, slipped away, invisible.

"Let's move out." Mike's voice was short. No one questioned him. They gathered their things in silence and made once again for the darkness of the jungle.

CHAPTER 10
Toronto, Canada
2007

"Liz?" Elizabeth can hear her mother calling and groans. She's cross-legged on her bed, absorbed in a novel she found at Evan's shop. She knows her mom's been unpacking the basement all day and has been strenuously avoiding having to partake at all. She pretends she doesn't hear; she's wearing her iPod, after all. At the sound of her mother's footsteps on the stairs, she turns up the music to assuage her guilt: If she really can't hear her, it's not technically ignoring, is it? She turns away from the door, pretending again not to hear the knock. Humming to herself, she turns a page.

"Liz!" Her mother approaches from behind, waving her hand in front of her daughter's face. "Hello!"

Elizabeth sighs, resigned. She pulls out her earphones and

raises her eyebrows at her mother, questioning. "What is it?" She motions toward the book. "I'm trying to read here, Mom. Educating myself."

Her mom looks at the cover. "*The Haunted Diner*? Is that what passes for education these days?"

"It has a lot of big words."

"I'm sure."

"And an important message."

"Right. Don't order your eggs with a side of poltergeist."

"We can't all be literary snobs like you, Mom. How's that one you're reading—*Violent Vaccines*?"

"*Venomous Vaccines*, actually."

"Hemingway, right?"

"You know what? I'm going to leave, and I'm going to take this letter with me." She waves an envelope enticingly in front of Elizabeth's face.

Elizabeth looks confused. "What—oh!" Her face lights up in comprehension. She eyes the envelope. "Is that—?"

"Yup." Enthused, her mother cuts her off. "Look at the back!" She tosses the envelope on the bed. Elizabeth picks it up and feels a wave of excitement: it has a London return address.

"I was starting to think she'd never write back," says Elizabeth, turning it over in her hands. She had written Ms. Merriweather over a month ago. She'd described how she had found the doll, then taken it to the University to try to verify that it was the real thing. She had written the letter very carefully so that it sounded grown-up, with proper grammar. Her parents had both proofread it for her. Then she had mailed it to the publisher's address she'd found online with Evan. Her dad had even paid for it to go express. Then they waited. And waited. And waited.

"Why couldn't she just have an e-mail address, like any normal person?" Elizabeth had grumbled over dinner, frustrated, after two weeks had gone by without any reply. She wasn't used to sending letters in the mail. It just took so long.

He dad had chuckled and explained to her that Ms. Merriweather, who was very old, may not even have a computer. Elizabeth didn't believe him. "Granny has a computer," she pointed out. "She e-mails all the time. Everyone has an e-mail address." Her parents had looked at each other and laughed.

Elizabeth had felt annoyed. "Stop laughing at me!"

"We just feel old. We remember when there was no e-mail. Or texting."

"Or iPods."

"Or even CDs."

"Microwaves!"

"Microwaves?" Elizabeth looked aghast. "How old are you two anyway?"

"Old enough to remember life before e-mail."

"Well," said Elizabeth fairly, "I guess not everyone has e-mail. There's that tribe in the Amazon that has no contact with the outside world. Probably they don't have it."

"Probably not even microwaves," added her mother dryly.

"Where do they heat up their takeout?" Elizabeth smirked at her parents.

Her mom suggested that while Ms. Merriweather might indeed have a computer, she could be a very private person and not want her e-mail address publicly available. Elizabeth knew her mother was probably right—she and Evan had come to that conclusion too—but still felt that the whole process was being unnecessarily slowed down by having to rely on sending the letter the old-fashioned way.

But now the wait is over. Elizabeth stares at the envelope. "I'm going to open it," she declares.

"Not so fast." Her mother snatches it back. "We should wait for Dad. He'll be home any minute. It wouldn't be fair to open it without him: you know how excited he is about all of this." She tucks the letter in her belt. "Think about how you'd feel if we opened the letter before you got home."

Elizabeth sighs. She wonders how her father would feel if she went to Afghanistan for a year. She doesn't say that, though. "Fine," she replies instead. "You're right. It would be uncomfortable for everyone to watch him cry." She picks up her book, but eyeballs the letter again. How does her mom have such restraint? Elizabeth would have opened the envelope even before she made it through the front door.

Noting her daughter's expression, her mother backs out of the room. "Don't even think about it." Her tone is cheerful. "I'm going to hide it."

When her father finally gets home, he practically jumps up and down at the news. "She wrote back!" He is almost squealing, like a little kid on Christmas morning. Elizabeth cringes slightly. *Does he have to act so weird?* Her dad doesn't notice. He takes the letter from his wife and stares at it. "I was starting to think she would never reply, you know. That she doesn't regularly check her mail, or that maybe she's even too old to read, to see the letters on the page. I thought maybe we'd never even hear back and that we'd never know and that the whole thing—"

"Dad!" Elizabeth reaches over and grabs the letter from her father. "You're rambling. I'm opening it." She tears at the envelope and removes the letter from inside. It's handwritten on thick, creamy white stationery with the initials *M.M.* in black script at the top. She begins to read:

Dear Elizabeth,

Thank you so much for your letter. I have, over the years, received a great many letters from people claiming to have found the soldier doll. Each one ended in disappointment for me, as none was ever my doll. Worse, some were faked, which was disheartening as well as disappointing.

However, from your description, photograph, and laboratory tests, it would seem that the doll you have found is almost certainly my own soldier doll! His uniform is a different colour than I painted it all those years back, but obviously it is natural that people would have fixed him up as the years went by. I can scarcely believe that after all this time, I may see the doll again.

Because of my advanced age, I regret that I cannot travel to Canada to see the doll in person. Your suggestion of coming to see me in London, therefore, is very kind, and I do heartily accept the invitation to meet. I would be happy to host your family for tea at any time.

I look forward to your reply and anticipate your arrival in London in the near future.

Yours truly,
Meg

P.S. I look forward to future correspondence with you. For your convenience, my e-mail address is Meg_m@ quickmail.com.

Elizabeth looks up, smug. "See?" she says. "She has an e-mail address, Dad. I told you. Everyone has an e-mail address."

He mother grins. "What about the pygmies?"

"Right, except for them."

"Well now, how can we be sure?"

Elizabeth snorts and picks up the letter. "So, Margaret Merriweather thinks it's the real thing! And she's invited us to London."

Her mom nods. "It's very exciting."

"Absolutely," agrees her father. "But we can't go right away. There isn't time now. It will have to be after I head out. When I have some leave time. I'll have to meet you there. And then there's the question of money…" Her dad frowns, whipping out some paper and a pen. Muttering to himself, he starts scratching down figures.

"Calm down, Dad." Elizabeth takes the letter back from him. "You're freaking out. Can't we just relax here for a minute and be happy about the doll?"

"She's right, John. We haven't been to London in years." Her mother has a dreamy look in her eyes.

"That's true, hon. How many years has it been?"

She looks at Elizabeth. "Well, Elizabeth is fifteen, so it was about sixteen years ago now, I guess. She was born about nine months after we got back." She winks at her husband, who's smiling nostalgically. He takes the letter back again.

Elizabeth catches the wink. "Ew," she says, groaning. "Gross. Gross! Why do you do this to me?"

"Do what?"

"You know. Talk about how I was born nine months later. Yuck!"

"Why is that upsetting? Nine months later, the stork brought you, in a neat little bundle—"

"*Uch*, just stop it." Elizabeth is blushing now.

Her mother pats her hand. "Relax," she says. "You should feel lucky we're so open with you."

"I think we could be a little more closed."

"It's just a stork."

"Funny."

Her dad looks up. He's been concentrating on some arithmetic. "Sorry," he says. "What are you two talking about?"

"Birds," says her mom. "Liz doesn't like them."

"Well, she's never been very outdoorsy," he says, oblivious.

Elizabeth coughs, trying not to laugh.

He rubs his hands together. "It will be expensive," he says, looking up from his calculations. "But I think we can manage a trip to England in the fall."

"Yay!" cheers Elizabeth. Mentally, she starts packing. *What's the weather like in England in autumn?*

"You're sure, John? We can afford to go to London, the three of us?" Her mother looks worried now.

Her father looks down at the paper in front of him. "I think so," he says. "We haven't had a family vacation in over a year. It would mean dipping into our savings a bit, but I think it's worth it. Especially now."

The unspoken words hang in the air. He's shipping out in less than a month. Elizabeth pushes the thought out of her mind.

"I need to go tell Evan," she says, standing up. She'd think more about tracking people down later. Right now, she wanted to share her news. She had promised she'd let Evan know as soon as she'd had word from Ms. Merriweather.

Elizabeth logs on to Facebook and sends off a message to Evan. She balances the computer on her lap and leans back against her yellow tufted headboard, bare feet stretched out toward the end of the bed. She examines her toes critically. The purple nail polish is chipping; she'll have to fix it later. She picks at the lint on her duvet cover impatiently, staring at the floral pattern until it's a pastel blur. He usually responds right away.

Waiting, she checks her friends' pages, looking at their recently posted pictures. They'd all gone sailing last weekend, by the looks of it. Katie's parents have a boat they keep at the marina. There is a photo of Jamie Sullivan and Elise, with Jamie's arm around her. They're wearing bathing suits and laughing. Jamie's hair is wet and sticking up in different directions, like Evan's. Elizabeth is surprised and relieved that looking at him now, she feels nothing.

She remembers the day she'd found out about him and Elise. She'd been at her locker. The stupid thing had never opened properly, and she'd been pulling at it for at least five minutes, trying to unstick the door.

"Liz!" Elise had sidled up next to her. Her eyes were shining with excitement. "Guess what just happened!"

"What?" Elizabeth had tried to sound interested. Elise always acted as if the slightest thing was a major event. She was the kind of girl who threw birthday parties for her cats.

Elise had proceeded to show her a text from Jamie asking her to go for coffee. Elizabeth remembers how she'd felt her heart pound, her stomach turn, and her cheeks flush, as if she had taken a swig of spoiled milk. How she'd had to pretend to be excited for Elise, when all she really wanted to do was pull her hair.

How could this have happened? she'd thought at the time, agonized. Jamie was supposed to like *her*. Just the day before, he'd asked her to be his lab partner and suggested they write up their reports together. She had realized then, with a sickening lurch, that he had probably just acted that way to get closer to

Elise. She'd felt almost dizzy with humiliation. Thank goodness no one had known she liked him. The feeling of embarrassment surges through her again now, and she shudders. She recalls how, for months, whenever she saw or even thought of Jamie, she felt as if she'd been punched in the gut.

Looking at the screen now, Elizabeth feels embarrassment but none of that awful, hurt feeling. *How wonderful to be free of it!* Then a message pops up from Evan, and she feels a small thrill of excitement.

She and Evan talk almost every day now on Facebook. Mostly about the soldier doll and the bookstore, but sometimes about other stuff too. Elizabeth has even confided to him how worried she is about her dad shipping out to Afghanistan. They've also been out together a couple of times. Not on a date or anything like that, but she'd met up with him at a few parties he'd told her about. And, she had even made friends with two girls in her grade at school: Emily and Annie had been impressed by the strappy, high-heeled silver sandals she'd worn to a party at Evan's cousin's; the shoes had been her mom's from back in the eighties. They'd struck up a conversation about fashion, and she now chatted with them on Facebook too. This weekend the three of them had plans to check out some of the vintage clothing shops downtown. She was looking forward to it.

Emily and Annie both teased her about Evan. "He likes you," insisted Annie, two nights ago over coffee. She looked at Elizabeth with earnest eyes from beneath her dark brown bangs. She sighed. "It's so romantic."

Elizabeth blushed and shook her head furiously. "No." Her voice was firm. "We're just friends. We're both doing that soldier doll thing I told you about. He's just nice."

Emily shook her head, her wavy, red hair falling into her eyes. "He wouldn't bother talking to you all the time if he didn't like you." She spoke with authority. "Trust me. I know these things."

Elizabeth raised her eyebrows. "How do you know?"

Emily sipped her iced coffee. "I have an older sister," she said airily. "She's twenty."

Annie rolled her eyes and leaned conspiratorially in toward Elizabeth. "That's her answer for everything," she whispered loudly.

Emily glared at her, miffed, and stuck out her tongue. "It's true, though," she said. "Carrie is a very valuable source of information. She's already in university." She said the last word reverentially.

Elizabeth stirred her own iced coffee absently. "He doesn't like me," she said again. "He's never asked me to get together alone or anything."

Annie frowned. "That is weird."

But Emily shook her head. "There must be some reason for that," she said. She picked a sugar packet off the table and fiddled with it.

"Yeah, the reason is that he only likes me as a friend!" Elizabeth said good-naturedly. She changed the subject to some new music she'd downloaded, and they hadn't discussed it again.

Now, though, she feels a familiar sensation in the pit of her stomach as she messages back and forth with Evan:

> Gr8 news! So you're going to London??

> I think so, yeah!! In the fall.

> Wow, lucky. London AND you'll probably miss school.

> Ooh, hadn't thought of that! You're right!

> Don't know which I'm more jealous of. How come you haven't friended Boris, by the way?

Elizabeth blinks, rereading the words on the screen.

> Boris has his own Facebook page??

> Sure. He's a popular guy.

> I should have realized. OK, doing it now.

> We should celebrate this new development. You busy? We could go grab something. My night off.

Elizabeth stares at the laptop. She reads the message again to make sure she's read it correctly. Then she reads it five more times, trying to think of a clever response.

> Sure.

She winces, waiting. *Sure?* Why did her sense of humor always seem to evaporate at the most inopportune moments? She liked to think of herself as witty. *Sure* wasn't witty. It wasn't anything.

> How about some ice cream? Sick of coffee. Had 6 cups today at work.

> 6? How do you sleep?

> Tax law.

> ???

> An old book I found in the store. Works every time.

Elizabeth laughs. She thinks he's probably telling the truth.

> Which ice-cream place?

> Near the bookstore. Do you know it?

> Ya, of course.

> Meet at 8?

> Sure.

> K, c u soon.

Elizabeth's fingers tremble slightly as she logs off. She goes to her closet and rummages through it, frantic. Why doesn't she have any nice clothes? Everything suddenly looks worn and ugly. She pulls out a few things, but none of them are right. Yanking a fifties-style, yellow sundress off a hanger, she glares at it. She tosses it on top of a growing pile of discarded choices.

"What's going on here?" Her mother sticks her head in the doorway. She notices the pile of clothes on the floor. "If you get rid of all that, you won't have much left to wear."

Elizabeth pauses and looks over at her mother. She blushes slightly. "I'm trying to find the right thing to wear," she mutters, turning back to her closet.

"For what?" Her mom looks at her, curious, and her eyes light up. "Did he finally ask you out? Evan?"

Elizabeth cringes. *Ask me out? No one talks like that anymore.* "We're just going for ice cream." She feels embarrassed. "People don't ask each other out, Mom. He's not coming with flowers."

It's her mother's turn to roll her eyes. "Who suggested it?" she demands.

Elizabeth goes redder. "He did." She picks up a lavender tank top and looks at it, considering.

Her mom smirks at her. "Then he asked you out, did he not? I win." She puts her hands on her hips.

Elizabeth sighs. "It's not like that." She pulls on a pair of skinny jeans with the lavender shirt.

"That looks great." Her mother smiles. "Have fun. When are you going?"

"Eight." Elizabeth brushes her hair vigorously.

"Careful with that thing." She nods at the hairbrush. "It's not a weapon." She turns to leave, but first smiles and gives her the once-over. "You look great, Liz. Seriously."

"Thanks." Elizabeth feels nervous. "I won't be home late."

"Just text me if you're going to be later than ten-thirty. I worry. I can't help it." She smiles again and ducks out of the room.

It's still light out when Elizabeth reaches the ice-cream parlor. Evan isn't there when she arrives, and she stands outside, feeling awkward. Mesmerized, she watches a green electric sign across the street flicker on and off. Where was he? She feels like everyone is looking at her. She gets out her phone and pretends to be absorbed by the screen.

"Sorry!" Evan appears next to her, out of breath. He's wearing the "Satan" shirt again. His jeans are torn at the knees, and Elizabeth wonders briefly if he tore them on purpose. "I was halfway here and had to run back to get my wallet. It's been a long day." He gestures toward the door. "Should we get in line?" The line is long, winding around the inside of the shop. Children weave in and out of it, going back and forth to the counter to press their faces against the glass to try to decide on a flavor.

Evan gets her a raspberry waffle cone and insists on paying. *Does that make it a date?* she wonders. She isn't sure. They sit down together at one of the outside tables. It's getting dark now, but it's still hot; the patio is packed. Next to them, a small girl drops her cone and wails loudly. Elizabeth takes a tiny bite of her ice cream and wipes her mouth delicately with a napkin. She watches the girl's father get back in line; he looks tired.

Evan has opted for peach, in a cup. He offers her a spoonful. "Mmmm," she says, tasting it. It's delicious: cool and refreshing. "I'll have to get that next time."

Their eyes meet, and there is an awkward pause in the conversation. Elizabeth notes that Evan's cheeks are slightly pink as he quickly launches into a story about his day at the bookstore.

"So this guy comes in," he says, lowering his voice, "with a box. So I know already it's going to be a bad day."

"Like I did?" Elizabeth smiles, a teasing expression on her face.

"Not exactly. The contents were…unusual."

"Unusual?"

"Yeah." Evan is blushing now.

"What was in the box?"

"A bunch of…um, I guess there's no other way to say this. Sex books."

"Sex books?" Elizabeth feels her own cheeks go red.

"Yeah. Like, instruction manuals…"

"A bunch of them?"

"I know, right? Like, why would you need so many? You'd think one would be enough."

Elizabeth snorts with laughter into her ice cream. She feels some on her nose and hastily wipes it away.

"Wait, I haven't told you the best part." Evan is grinning.

"It gets better?"

"Way better. This guy, he's a teacher at our school. He teaches biology."

"Biology!" They are both laughing now.

"So he recognizes me, right? And he starts muttering something about research."

"Research? Like for class?" Elizabeth guffaws.

"I guess. It was so embarrassing. We were both totally humiliated. I gave him twenty bucks just to get him out of there. Sam is going to kill me. We don't even have, like, a sex section."

"You can put them in science," suggests Elizabeth, feeling witty.

"Ha. I'm for sure going to get him next year for biology now, and the whole year is going to be, like, beyond awkward. It will be, like—" he stops suddenly.

Elizabeth waits for him to continue, but he doesn't. "What is it?" she asks. She notices him staring at something over her shoulder. She turns her head to see what he's looking at.

It's a girl. "Evan!" The girl waves and makes her way over to the table. She sees Elizabeth and raises her eyebrows. "Aren't you going to introduce me?"

"This is Elizabeth." Evan's expression is wary. "Elizabeth, this is Trish."

Trish looks at Elizabeth, sizing her up. "You dripped ice cream on your shirt," she says rudely. Elizabeth looks down in horror and grabs a napkin, then starts dabbing at it.

Trish turns back to Evan. "Ashley's getting back tomorrow!" She gives him a bright smile. "You must be so excited."

Elizabeth looks up sharply. *Ashley?*

Evan pales. "Right." His voice is neutral.

"You guys were so adorable at that party, before she left," Trish says sweetly. She turns to Elizabeth. "Ashley and Ev are the cutest couple."

Elizabeth stares blankly at her. She looks at the cone in her hand and feels nauseated. She needs to get rid of it. *Where is the trash can?* She looks around, feeling panicked. *Why couldn't I have just ordered a cup, so I could leave it on the table? Why am I such an idiot!*

Elizabeth stands up, still holding the cone. "You know," she says hurriedly. "I really need to get going."

Evan jumps up. "No, wait." He reaches out to take her arm.

Elizabeth wrestles her arm away from him. The ice cream has dripped everywhere now. It's all over her hands, her jeans. The floor.

"You're making a real mess with that." Trish stares at her in amusement. Elizabeth makes a small noise and turns away, moving quickly toward the street. "Who is she, anyway?" she hears Trish ask.

Evan ignores her. "Liz!" He rushes after Elizabeth.

She is on the sidewalk now, breathing heavily. She glares at Evan. "What do you want?" she says. Her voice catches. She looks around and notices a trash can, finally. *Thank God.* She turns her back to Evan and heaves the melted cone inside. Her hands are a sticky mess. She wipes them on her jeans; it doesn't matter how she looks now.

"Liz." His voice is desperate. "I'm sorry. I can explain."

"There's nothing to explain." Elizabeth takes a step back from him. "Ashley's your girlfriend?"

"I can explain," he says again. "It's complicated. We broke up before the summer. Trish is Ashley's best friend. She can be kind of a…" His voice trails off.

"Yes, I can see that." Her voice is as cold as the ice cream they nearly finished eating.

They stand facing one another. Elizabeth folds her arms protectively across her chest and glowers at him.

"I'm sorry," he says again. "I really—"

She cuts him off. "You should get home," she says brusquely. "Ashley's getting back tomorrow." She turns and begins walking quickly. She feels her left foot scrape against the inside of her shoe and winces.

"Elizabeth! Wait. Come on—*please*." Evan's voice is pleading now.

She walks even faster, gritting her teeth. Her left foot drags slightly. She notices some blood on the satin fabric and feels the tears prick at her eyes. Her cheeks are hot and wet.

"Liz!" She hears his voice again, but doesn't turn back.

CHAPTER 11

Toronto, Canada
2007

"Liz?" Her mother is hovering outside her door. "Can I come in?"

"Whatever." Elizabeth's voice is listless. "I don't care."

Her mom enters the room and sits down on the bed, careful not to sit on a pile of old T-shirts Elizabeth was sorting through for a clothing drive—before she lost interest. She's at her desk now, her laptop open in front of her. On the screen is a vintage clothing website. She scrolls down the page, only half looking at it.

"Evan keeps calling here." Her mother looks at her, questioning. She pauses. "What, exactly, happened?" It has been two weeks since the date with Evan. It isn't the first time her mom has asked this question, nor is it the first time Elizabeth has ignored it.

Elizabeth shakes her head. "I don't want to talk about it," she says again. Then she looks over at her mother in surprise. "He's calling—really? Like, on the phone?"

"Yes." Her mom raises her eyebrows. "I know you guys pretty much consider the landline to have gone the way of the phonograph, so I think he must really want to talk to you."

Elizabeth shakes her head again. "He's a total jerk." She gives her mother a sidelong glance. "What's a phonograph?"

"An old record player."

Elizabeth smiles slyly. "What's a record player?"

"Right." Her mom tosses a pillow at her. "Very funny." She pauses again tentatively. "You can tell me what happened, you know. It may be hard to believe, but I was once a teenage girl too. What was it? He gave you the just-want-to-be-friends speech?"

Elizabeth is quiet for a minute. "He has a girlfriend. She was away for the summer." Her cheeks flush as she relives the humiliation of the evening. It feels good to talk about it, to finally get it out. She hasn't told anyone, not Emily or Anna. Not even Katie back home.

"Ah." Her mother nods sagely. "The on-again, off-again girlfriend."

"This girl showed up." Elizabeth turns her chair around fully, so she can face her mom. The words are coming easier now; the more she speaks, the better she feels. "The girlfriend's best friend. She was a total—well. You know."

"I think I do." Her mom's voice is sympathetic. "Girls can be so mean."

"Not fair to totally blame her though," Elizabeth says, angry again. "Why did he act as if he liked me if he had a girlfriend?"

"Well," her mother's voice is cautious, "How do you know he *doesn't* like you? Maybe he was planning to break it off with this other girl. What did he say?"

"I don't know," Elizabeth admits. "I wouldn't let him talk. I just left." She gives her mother a helpless look as she picks up a T-shirt and absently fiddles with the collar. "It was so embarrassing and horrible."

"I'm sure it was." Her mom reaches over and puts a hand on Elizabeth's knee. "Have you thought, though, that maybe he feels just as bad as you? He seems pretty desperate to talk."

Elizabeth shrugs. "I don't know," she mumbles. "I wouldn't know what to say."

"You might be missing out here, Liz." Her mother's voice is gentle. "You're not punishing anyone but yourself."

Elizabeth sighs. She looks at her mother, considering. "Maybe you're right." She sounds reluctant.

Her mom smiles. "I'll bet that was painful."

"I only said *maybe*," pouts Elizabeth. She brings her knees to her chest, hugging them.

"Fair point. You're right, it may be way better to spend the rest of your summer sulking indoors," says her mother. She takes the T-shirt Elizabeth has been playing with and folds it neatly, placing it back on the bed.

"That's not fair. I spent at least two hours sulking in the backyard yesterday." Elizabeth gives her mother a little half-grin.

"I stand corrected. So, are you going to call him back?"

"No."

"Really? No?"

"I'm not going to call him." Elizabeth gives her mother a sly glance. "I might send him a text or something though. The phone is for old people."

"Right. You must be feeling better. You're acting like your charming self again."

"I try." Elizabeth turns back to her computer and pulls up her Facebook page and stares at it. Should she send Evan a message? What should she say?

"Huh?" She looks up, realizing her mother has been speaking.

"The door."

"What door?"

"The front door." Her mother gives her an odd look.

"What about it?" Elizabeth asks impatiently. She's mentally composing and editing a message to Evan, but can't get it right.

"It just opened, space cadet. Dad's home. Suppertime. Go wash up and come downstairs." Her mother reaches over to ruffle her hair, briefly, before Elizabeth can protest, then leaves the room.

Elizabeth glances at the clock and blinks in surprise. How is it six o'clock already? Looking at the screen, she notes Evan's photo—he's changed it to one of himself holding Boris up on top of his head. Her eyes linger on the picture for a moment, smiling. She'll send him a message later, she resolves. Feeling more cheerful than she has in days, she puts down her pen and snaps her laptop shut.

Should she message Evan? Maybe texting would be better. Or an e-mail. Back at her computer, Elizabeth drums her fingers on the keyboard. She's still a bit angry—ice cream for dessert at dinner reminded her again of the ice-cream parlor—but it does seem he has made a rather valiant effort to get in touch with her. She can't even imagine calling someone's house and having their parents answer. Decisively, she pulls up her Facebook page again, but then frowns. What should she say? She takes a deep breath and stares at the screen. Finally, she types:

> Hi.

He responds almost immediately.

> Hey. FINALLY. I need to talk to you. Can we get together?

Elizabeth taps her fingers again, thinking. How to respond? She isn't sure she's ready to see him.

> Kind of busy. What's going on? My mom said you are call-ing??? On the phone???

> Yeah. You won't respond to my messages or texts. I need to explain about Ashley.

> You're engaged?

> Funny. Listen. I broke up with Ashley.

> Trish said you're the cutest couple.

> Trish is an idiot. Anyway, Ashley and I are done. She met someone else anyway. At her camp.

> I'm sorry. You must be heartbroken.

> Wrong again. Please Liz? I really like you. OK? (That was hard to write.)

Elizabeth stares at the screen. *I really like you.* Her heart beats faster, but she still feels unsure. She recalls the humiliation of their failed date and pauses. She doesn't want to get hurt again.

> It's really over with A?

> YES. I swear.

> You were a jerk.

> I was. I'm really sorry.

> Are you?

> I am throwing myself at your feet, begging for forgiveness.

Elizabeth laughs. She feels a bit better.

> I'll think about it.

> Progress! Come on, can we go out again? I miss you.

Elizabeth feels her cheeks flame as the last of her anger melts away.

> Well...OK.

> I'm coming by at 8.

> Not the ice-cream place.

> Are you crazy? We'll go somewhere else. Maybe just a walk.

> OK. See you soon.

Elizabeth logs off and looks around her room. What should she wear? She eyes the pile of discarded T-shirts on the bed. Maybe she has been too hasty, planning to give these all away. She fishes out a mint tank top and stares at it for a moment before tossing it back down. *Maybe I'd better go through these again. Just to be sure.* She picks up a blue halter and tries it on.

CHAPTER 12
Toronto, Canada
2001

"Dad?" Alex Cameron called out for his father, his voice shaking slightly. When there was no reply, he tried again, this time injecting the call with the urgency he felt appropriate given the circumstances. "Dad!"

"What is it, Alex? Are you going to be sick again?" His father, dressed in an orange bathrobe, stuck his head around the living-room doorway, his face betraying concern mixed with modest irritation. Alex was home sick from school with either a stomach bug or the after effects of last night's supper of week-old pizza. His dad was supposedly caring for him, but that had so far consisted mainly of turning on the TV and handing Alex a wastebasket while he worked in the other room. He was chewing a piece of red licorice; he went through bags of it when he was writing, and now a strand dangled from between his teeth like a cartoon cigar in a comic strip. He'd already gone through half a bag, and it was only just past nine in the morning.

Alex stood in the center of the room, gesturing helplessly at the television. "Look," he said. His voice sounded strangled, as if something were caught in the back of his throat. "Look at what happened. That plane. That plane, it…" His voice trailed off, trying to explain.

The two turned toward the screen and watched the chaos unfold before them, live on TV. There was footage being replayed of an airplane crashing into what appeared to be one of the World Trade Center towers in New York City.

"My God," his father said. As he spoke, the licorice fell to the ground; neither bothered to pick it up. "That doesn't look like a small plane; it looks like a jet. How did the pilot miss—"

He stopped abruptly and looked closer at the screen. "Wait—what happened to the other tower?"

Alex looked at him grimly. "It was hit just before this one."

"Hit?" His dad's expression was blank. He glanced back at the television where ashen-faced reporters were abuzz with snatches of information regarding the catastrophe. He looked at his son. "Wait," he said, realization dawning on his face. "You mean…another plane? Two planes hit the World Trade Center? On purpose?"

"That's what it looks like." Alex sank down on the worn leather sofa and drew his knees to his chest, hugging them tightly. "They're saying it was a terrorist attack. They think, anyway."

His father sat down next to him, his robe flapping open as he did so. Alex cringed but said nothing; it wasn't really the time, though he did wish his dad would put some boxers on when he wore that thing.

"It's just in New York?" His dad turned to him.

"What do you mean?"

"Just New York? The planes that hit?"

"Yeah—why?"

"No, nothing." His father turned back to the TV, but Alex could tell he was anxious: he was shaking his foot compulsively and drumming his fingers on his knee.

"Why are you doing that?"

"Doing what?"

"You know, that shaking thing."

"I don't know, nervous tic. Why are you hugging your legs?"

They turned their attention back to the news just as the shocked anchor cut off her colleague who was on the street in New York.

"Just a second, Jessica, sorry," she announced, visibly shaken. "We've just had word that a plane has hit the Pentagon in Washington, DC."

His dad jumped up. "Good Lord," he whispered. "It's the end of the world."

"Dad?" Alex looked at him, frightened.

His father blinked at Alex, then reddened, as if remembering that, as a parent, he had a duty to make things seem okay, even when they clearly were not. He reached over and patted his son awkwardly on the back. "It'll be all right," he said unconvincingly.

"You'd think there would be, like, a force field or something around the Pentagon," said Alex. "Like, you couldn't crash into it; the plane would blow up or something."

His father said nothing, standing frozen next to the couch. "Dad?"

There was no response. His father was moving again, this time to the phone.

"I'm going to try to get in touch with Mom."

"Try?" Alex frowned.

His dad turned away. "She's flying today." He was trying to sound casual, but Alex caught the edge of fear in his voice.

"She is? I thought that was tomorrow!" Panicked, Alex's voice rose. His mother traveled weekly for her work as a consultant, and it was often difficult to keep track of her busy schedule.

"She had a seven-thirty flight to Kansas City." His father was fiddling with the phone.

"Is she there? Is she answering?"

"No." He watched his dad's shoulders slump. "It was a long shot." He clutched the phone to him and stared at it, willing it to ring.

"Where exactly is Kansas City? What if it's next?" Alex's voice was high pitched and caught as he tried to choke back his tears. He felt hot and cold at the same time and a bit lightheaded, as if he were watching himself from a vantage point somewhere near the ceiling.

"Don't worry." His father came over and hugged him. "There are no tall buildings, really, in Kansas City."

"The Pentagon isn't a tall building!"

"It's important though, the Pentagon. It's a symbol. Kansas City—it's not even in Kansas."

"Huh?"

"Well, actually, there is one in Kansas, but she was going to Missouri."

His dad was rambling now, even more than usual. Alex felt dizzy and sat back down, trying to regulate his breathing, which had become increasingly quick and shallow.

Suddenly, the scene before them on the screen changed; it was back to New York, where people were running frantically. A few stopped to look back as they ran, screams and moans erupting from the frenzied crowd. Alex stopped and stared; the scene reminded him of images from old movies like *King Kong* and *Godzilla* that looked as if they'd been filmed in a shadow box with a single camera.

"What the—" He stopped in mid-sentence as he realized what was happening. In stunned silence, he watched replays of the twin World Trade Center towers crumbling to the ground like sandcastles, decimated by the tide on the beach.

"Oh, my God," said his father, his voice full of horror. "Oh, my God."

It took only minutes for the towers to fall, but to Alex it felt like hours. There was something riveting about watching those two tall towers buckle to the earth again and again. How could they just fall like that? And so quickly? If it had been in a movie, it would have taken longer. And then, before he could even digest the enormity of the event, the news anchor was back with more bad news: another plane had crashed in a field somewhere in Pennsylvania.

Alex looked over at his father, who sat next to him with his head in his hands, rocking back and forth ever so slightly, as if propelled by a slowly unwinding spring. "Dad?"

"It's okay," he replied automatically. "There are so many flights every day. Do you know how many? Thousands. These are only four."

"What are you talking about?"

"Only four flights. The odds of something happening to her plane are very low."

"The odds were low for all the people who died on the other planes too." Alex's voice was louder now. "I can't even imagine the probability for something like this. This isn't a rational, logical thing, Dad. This is chaos. And don't pretend you're good at math." Alex himself was going off to university next week as a math major. Even as a child, he'd amused himself with numbers, manipulating them the way the other kids did puzzles and blocks.

His father clutched at his neck. When he pulled his hands away, there were deep red marks from where his nails had dug in. "Don't get angry with me!" he said. "I'm just trying to hold it together here."

Alex felt bad; his quick temper was legendary among family and friends, though he tried hard not to let it dominate him. "Sorry, Dad." He put a hand on his father's arm. "I'm just scared."

The phone rang, startling both of them. His father, who was still clasping the receiver tightly in his left hand, stared at it as if it were an unidentifiable object.

It rang again. "Dad?" Alex pointed at the ringing phone. "The phone!"

His father shook his head quickly, as if trying to clear the dust from his brain. He pressed the green button and took a deep breath. "Hello?"

Alex didn't breathe as he waited for his father's next words. He felt the blood rush in his ears and a wave of dizziness overtake him. He sat down again and put his head between his legs.

"Thuy."

Alex's entire body relaxed as he heard his father utter his mother's name. He'd always liked it—when people misspelled it "Twee," he was reminded of birds singing, which was the way his mother sounded to him when she spoke.

Alex grabbed for the phone.

"She's okay. I'm putting it on speaker."

Alex could see the tension slowly releasing from his father's body; he was less rigid now and sank down onto the couch.

"Mom?" Alex took the phone and held it gently in his lap.

"Hi, sweetheart. Are you okay?"

"Mom, it's awful." Alex felt himself tear up at the soothing melody of his mother's voice, still with the trace of an accent despite over twenty-five years in Canada.

"I know. We just heard here," she said soothingly.

"Are you in Kansas City?" asked Alex's dad.

"No. All flights have been grounded, apparently. We landed in Chicago."

"When are you coming home?" Alex blurted out. He hugged his arms around himself.

"As soon as I can," she replied. Alex could hear shouting in the background and felt frightened.

"You're not going to fly?" he asked, his voice small.

"I'm going to look into renting a car," she replied quickly.

"You could try the train." His father now, leaning toward the phone.

"No!" Alex's voice was sharp.

His dad looked at him, surprised.

"I just think it's safer to drive your own car." Alex felt silly trying to explain, but he felt strongly his mother shouldn't take the train. "What if they blow up trains next or something?"

"Don't worry." His mother sounded concerned. "I'll be fine. It's easier to just drive, anyway."

There was the crackle of static as his mother said something further that he couldn't make out. "What?" Alex shook the phone in frustration.

"I said I love you and I'll call again soon. I see an Avis counter; I'm going to go talk to them."

Alex nodded at the handset. "I love you too."

"Bye, hon. Put your dad on for a sec."

Alex handed the phone back to his father, who turned off the speaker function and had a brief exchange with his mother in hushed tones. Alex wondered what they were saying, if they were hiding something important from him. He felt his fear, which had slowly ebbed away at his mother's reassuring words, slowly turn to irritation and anger. He was eighteen now, a real adult. What was it they couldn't say in front of him?

Alex turned back to the television, where the anchor was interviewing a woman by phone. Apparently, her husband had been on the plane that crashed in Pennsylvania.

"What did he say?" The anchor's tone was gentle but urgent.

"He said…he said the plane had been hijacked." The woman's voice was soft. There was an air of disbelief to it.

"And?"

"And that they weren't going to let them do what they did in New York. They were going to take back the plane." Her voice choked.

"And then what happened?" Alex found himself glaring at the anchor. She was being a bit pushy now, given the gravity of this woman's testimony and all that had just happened.

"He said good-bye." The woman's voice broke. "That's all."

"People are saying the plane was headed to the White House." The anchor was speaking again.

"I don't know." The woman sounded faint. "I don't know anything about it."

"Thank you for speaking with us." The call ended, and the anchor switched back to an on-the-scene report from the Pentagon.

Alex had seen enough. He turned off the television and headed to his room. Falling on his bed, he thought of the people who would have been on those planes. People like his mom, heading to a meeting. Or families with kids heading off on vacation. He recalled his last flight: he'd been seated behind a couple and their lively toddler, who intermittently poked her head around the seat to stare at him in a one-sided game of peek-a-boo. She'd had pigtails on either side of her head fastened with little rainbow barrettes. He imagined her incomprehension as the adults around her wailed and clutched at each other in a frenzy of fear while the plane disappeared in a burst of fire and cloud of smoke. The terror of the other passengers, of parents who'd have realized they'd never see their kids again, of business travelers facing the prospect of a terrifying death all alone. He wondered, if he were alone on a plane that was about to crash, would he hold the hand of the person next to him, even if he didn't know them? He thought he probably would.

Alex surveyed his room. There was still so much packing to do before he left for university. He had left it all to the last minute, figuring it wouldn't take that long. Clearly, he realized now, he had miscalculated. His clothes were heaped in piles on the floor, only vaguely grouped into any kind of classification system. He had tried to separate the room into summer versus winter clothes, but at some point, the T-shirts and sweaters had intermingled into a single giant "shirts pile" in the center of the rug. He looked at his bookcases, which were nearly empty now. He noticed an old calculator on one shelf and frowned, wondering if he should take it as a backup. Had he remembered his graphing calculator? Leaning over, he ruffled through one of the boxes on his desk but didn't see it. He pulled out an old Gumby toy and stared into its vacant eyes. Did he need to take Gumby? He wavered, debating. Then he shrugged. *Why not?* Gumby went back in the bag.

In pursuit of his graphing calculator—it had cost his parents over a hundred bucks; they'd for sure kill him if he lost it—he reached for his desk drawer and yanked it open. Pens, pencils, scented markers, a broken geometry set, a crappy macramé bracelet from Katie Kastner before she'd decided she'd rather go out with one of the soccer guys, Disney Band-Aids, used tissues. *Damn. Where was it?* Alex rummaged through the back of the drawer.

There it was. Relieved, Alex tossed the device into the box along with a couple more pens. *You could never really have enough pens*, he reasoned to himself. He aimed his pens at the cardboard box labeled "desk crap" and lobbed them inside.

"Shoot," he said, irritated, as one fell behind the desk. Sighing, he bent down to look for it. Reaching behind the desk, he felt for it with his hand and encountered a larger, odd-shaped object.

Alex pulled at it and retrieved it from its hiding place.

"Oh, you." Alex stared at the soldier doll, feeling guilty. He was glad he'd found it before his mother had. It was lodged behind his desk between the computer and the wall. She'd have been furious with him. She'd only reluctantly handed it over to him after he'd begged for it as a plaything years ago. For a long time, it had sat perched on the corner of one of his bookshelves. He wondered when it had fallen.

"From an American soldier," his mother had said briefly, when he asked where she'd got it. "They sometimes gave out toys or candy to orphans in the anti-communist villages."

His father had been curious, too. "It looks older, though," he'd said once, examining it. "Like an antique."

"I doubt it's valuable," his mother had said dismissively. "I'm sure he wouldn't have given it away if it were."

His mom didn't like to talk about the war. She'd immigrated to Canada in 1975 with a distant relative, a third cousin she'd called Auntie, who would beat her regularly for transgressions as minor as not buttoning a shirt properly, she'd told Alex. Alex had only a vague memory of the woman, who had died when he was four. When asked about the war, his mother would simply say, "it was a terrible time." She didn't elaborate, and his father warned him not to push her.

"Don't pester your mom about the war," he'd say. "It was a very traumatic time." He'd follow with his own lectures about the war, which, to Alex, were less history lessons and more political diatribes against various governments and someone named Nixon. Once he'd crept quietly out of the room, unnoticed, as his father railed against politicians who were no longer in power and, frequently, dead.

His father was what people still referred to occasionally as a draft dodger. When his number had come up for the draft, he'd headed for the Canadian border rather than compromise his principles and fight in a war he opposed. He'd lived for a couple of years in Montreal before settling in Toronto, where he worked as a writer and occasional teacher. He'd met Alex's mom sometime in the eighties at a reading, where she'd been impressed by his emotional deliverance and creativity. What his mother did, he was never quite sure; he knew she was a consultant, but what that meant baffled him. What he did know was that it paid well.

He was an only child. His mother had been told she might never have children—years of poor health and hunger during the war had taken a toll on her body—but he had been a welcome surprise several years into his parents' marriage. As a kid, he'd longed for a sibling: someone with whom to share the strangeness of being sort of Vietnamese and sort of not. When he was younger, he'd found it tougher. The other Vietnamese kids—not that there were that many at his school—all spoke fluent Vietnamese and brought dishes like *pho* and *bun* to school in their lunch boxes. His mother refused to speak Vietnamese, let alone teach it to him, and she didn't cook any Vietnamese food, despite his dad's fondness for rice noodles in chicken broth. The first time Alex had tried *pho* was with his father. "Don't tell your mother," he'd said, offering Alex a plateful of the best spring rolls he'd ever tasted.

Alex turned the carved wooden doll over in his hands. There was talk in the papers of war as retaliation for the attacks. Fingers pointed at Osama bin Laden. He was believed to be hiding out in Afghanistan, a country Alex only vaguely recalled hearing of before September 11, 2001.

"It's near Russia, right?" He'd been at the dinner table with his parents discussing the latest news on the terrorist attacks and the impending war.

His father looked impressed. "That's right," he'd replied. He'd given his mother a smug look. "See? We didn't need to send him to a private school."

"Actually, I know that from this video game on the PlayStation. It's called—"

His mother cut him off and looked at his father with raised eyebrows. "You were saying, Don?"

"Never mind."

His parents were at odds about the possibility of war. They'd argued over it again this morning at breakfast.

"War is never the answer," his father passionately declared. "It's never the reasonable path."

His mother was more philosophical. "No one ever wants to go to war," she said, calmly taking a bite of her toast. "But sometimes you have no choice. Sometimes you have to fight evil with a little bit of evil."

"I'm surprised at you, Thuy," said his dad, shaking his head. "After living through war, seeing what it does to people."

"Not every war is the same," she countered. "What if the Americans hadn't fought the Nazis in World War II?"

Alex sighed. He wondered how they could endure having the same conversation over and over. They'd go back and forth like that every day, neither of them ever budging. What was the point?

Alex stayed out of these debates. He wasn't sure how he felt about a war. On the one hand, if there were a war, lots of people would die. On the other hand, it seemed like the Americans were pretty justified in getting some kind of revenge against this bin Laden guy who supposedly planned the attacks. Alex wasn't exactly sure how invading a whole country to find one guy worked, but he'd also read online that the people who ruled Afghanistan, the Taliban, were a pretty nasty group who wouldn't let girls go to school and held massive public executions. Overthrowing them didn't sound like such a bad idea. Still, he stayed out of it.

Now, Alex looked at the small figure and turned it over in his hands. He'd loved it as a kid; its history was exciting to him. It represented mysterious faraway places and was the only tangible proof he had of his mother's past in Vietnam. Should he take it with him to school? His hand hovered over the box, ready to drop it in, but he decided against it. Standing up, he went back and placed the toy figure on the top shelf of his bookcase. *It'll be safer here*, he told himself. *If anything happened to it at school, Mom would kill me.*

Alex stared at the soldier doll a moment longer, then turned his attention to the pile of books stacked precariously on his desk. He picked up the first book—a biology text. *Will I need bio there?* he wondered. *Probably not.* There were no required bio courses in the math program. He was about to toss it onto the "stay pile" when he reconsidered. *I might take it as an elective.* He dropped it into a box marked "for school." He picked up the next book, a copy of *The Catcher in the Rye*. It was his favorite novel.

I've already read it, he reasoned, leaning toward the "stay" pile.

But you might want to read it again! A little voice in the back of his head challenged him, and his hand froze as he reconsidered.

Alex tossed the book in the "school box" and regarded the stack still in front of him: it was going to be a long day.

"You coming, dude?"

"Coming where?" Alex looked at his new friend. It was the end of the day; classes were finally over. Alex was looking forward to collapsing on his bed for a nice nap before hitting the dining hall and puzzling over his geometry text. He hadn't understood a word the professor had said in class this week and was worried. It had come to a point where the mere mention of the word geometry made him break into a sweat. Last night he'd awoken, heart pounding at three in the morning, muttering "Cosine! Cosine!" He couldn't remember the details, but nightmare hadn't been good. He'd never had any problems with geometry in high school, but in the three months since he'd started higher education, it had become the bane of his existence.

"The meeting." Benji looked surprised. "You haven't heard?"

"No." Alex felt embarrassed. He hated being left out of things, and his new buddies, Benji and Steve and Teddy, always seemed to know about parties and meetings and groups and stuff. He never did, and it sometimes felt like he was tagging along.

"Some army thing. Off campus—at the pizza place."

"*Army* thing?" Alex looked at his friend in disbelief. Benji had never shown any interest in politics. He didn't even read the newspaper, dismissing it as "a waste of time that could be spent on calculus."

"Free pizza," said Benji with a shrug. He lowered his voice. "Teddy said he heard there may also be free booze."

"Free booze? From the *military?*" Alex looked at his friend incredulously. "Doesn't that seem a little unlikely to you?"

"Dunno. Maybe it's not official army, like? Maybe just some army guys?"

"Benji, man, what the hell are you talking about?" Alex shook his head. "You're not making any sense."

"Trust me." Benji put his hand on his friend's backpack. "Free pizza, maybe free booze, and all you gotta do is pretend to care about the Caliban."

"Taliban."

"Whatever."

Alex didn't say anything. While his friends were decidedly apolitical, Alex found himself spending more and more of his spare time engrossed in newspapers and online magazines, reading about terrorism, the war in Afghanistan, and the situation in the Middle East. He'd even signed up for a class next semester called *The Middle East since World War II*. He hadn't told his friends, who assumed he'd signed up for the same music appreciation course all the math majors opted for.

"So, you in?" Benji waited for an answer.

"I guess." Alex thought of his geometry book and felt his stomach turn; he pushed all thoughts of angles and mathematical proofs out of his head and tried to focus on pizza.

"Great." Benji slapped him on the back. Alex winced;

Benji was a huge guy who didn't realize that his playful slaps had the approximate force of a sledgehammer.

"Go drop off your crap; I told the others we'd meet them outside the physics building at five."

"Okay." Alex trudged backed to his room, where he happily dumped his textbook-laden backpack on the ground.

"Where are you off to?" His roommate, Jonathan, looked up at him from his laptop.

"Some, um, army thing." Alex felt embarrassed. "There's free pizza," he added feebly.

"You're going to an army recruiting event for the pizza?"

"My friends are dragging me," Alex mumbled.

Jonathan shook his head. "You math guys," he said. "They should force you to take some history and poli-sci." Jonathan hadn't yet declared a major, but he told anyone who would listen that he was pre-law.

"I know history," retorted Alex.

"Relax, Cameron. I was only kidding." Jonathan made a face and went back to his computer.

Alex grabbed his coat and headed for the physics building. Jonathan was wrong; he wasn't ignorant. Just because he was a "math guy" didn't mean he didn't understand politics and current events. He was sure he knew more about the Taliban than Jonathan did about logarithms. Angrily, he kicked a stone and watched it bounce along the dusty road.

There was no free beer. They were real army guys, and they weren't about to risk buying booze for a bunch of underage kids. Benji and the others were disappointed, but were soon consoled with unlimited slices of free pizza.

"This is great pie," said Teddy, taking a third slice of pepperoni.

"It was worth coming for," agreed Steve.

Alex said nothing. He had eaten his two slices of pizza quietly, not really talking to the recruiters who were trying too hard to be friendly with the kids around the table. His friends had chatted freely with the guys, not realizing or caring that they were being manipulated.

"Hi there." One of the military guys sat down next to Alex and gave him a big smile. Alex felt himself cringe. "Hey," he muttered.

"What's your major? I'm Rory, by the way."

"Alex. I'm in math."

"That's great." Rory gave him another phony smile. "I did chemistry."

"You went to university?" Alex looked at him, surprised.

"Of course I did," said Rory. "And the army paid for it."

"Really?" said Alex. He currently had a scholarship, but he had a to maintain an A average to keep it and stay in the Honors Math program: an average that was seeming less and less likely given the current geometry situation.

"Yup. And I had a guaranteed job once I'd finished school, too."

"Huh," said Alex. "With the army?"

"Yes. A great job, in chemistry, with benefits and a great salary."

A guaranteed job in his field. Right after graduation. Alex pondered this.

"I don't think I'm really the army type," he said to Rory cautiously. "I'm not sure how I feel about the war in Afghanistan."

"I used to feel the same way," said Rory. "I thought, do we really have the right to be involved in a country so far away? Is it any of our business?"

Alex nodded; this meddling concerned him. It made him think of Vietnam.

"But," Rory went on, "I did some more reading. And you know what? I realized it's more immoral *not* to do something."

"You think so?" asked Alex. "Because they don't let girls go to school and stuff?"

Rory banged his fist on the table. "They don't just not let them go to school, Alex," he said. "They make them cover themselves from head to toe. They are not allowed to drive. They aren't allowed to do anything, and if they do, they're punished by *law*. And these aren't laws like we have here in Canada. Oh no! They can be beaten or stoned for something as small as trying to buy food for their children." Rory paused dramatically and shook his head.

Alex found himself nodding. He thought about what his mother had said, about it sometimes being necessary to fight evil with a little evil. Maybe she was right.

"Here's my card," said Rory. He handed Alex a little Armed Forces business card. Alex took it, surprised. He hadn't realized that soldiers carried cards like lawyers or bankers or whatever.

"Call me if you're interested. There are lots of opportunities for someone like you. We're always looking for math guys, people to work in encryption. Code breaking, stuff like that."

"Thanks," Alex replied automatically. He watched Rory's back as he turned to talk to another student. Alex thought about what he'd said. He pictured the burkas he'd seen on television, the long tent-like garments that women in Afghanistan were forced to wear. All they had was some netting at the eye area so the women could see. It wasn't at all clear to him how they could breathe in those things, and he was pretty sure Afghanistan was hot. It looked hot, anyway, on TV. He also remembered that big public execution he'd heard about, the one they'd held in, like, a soccer stadium so everyone could watch, like it was some big game.

"So, did you enjoy your free pizza?" Jonathan was still awake and working at his laptop when Alex got back. Jonathan shunned his desk in favor of his bed; he liked to spread his books around him like pillows and work in a slumped over, half-reclining position. Alex couldn't understand how he got any work done like that. If he laid down on his bed to work, he'd be asleep in under five minutes.

"It was fine," said Alex neutrally. He sat down at his desk chair and unlaced his boots.

"Was there booze?" Jonathan asked.

"No." Alex kicked off his boots. "They were real army guys. They weren't about to buy booze for us."

"Right," said Jonathan. "Because the army has never done

anything wrong or illegal before." He smirked, tapping on his keyboard.

"What do you mean?"

Jonathan snorted. "The military does all kinds of bad stuff. Didn't your mom teach you anything about the Vietnam War? You think we should be in Afghanistan?"

"I don't think they're at all the same, actually," retorted Alex. "What about women's rights? You support the Taliban?"

Jonathan laughed. "You think the war is about the Taliban? It's about *oil*."

"So you don't think there's any good in getting rid of a violent and…" Alex searched frantically for the right word. "*Oppressive* government?"

"Oooh. Ten points for that one, math genius." Jonathan grinned.

"Shut up."

"You're so naive. The Americans are over there protecting their own interests. They don't care about the people of Afghanistan."

"And the Canadians?"

"The Canadians are little puppets of the Americans." Jonathan waved his hand dismissively. "They really don't matter."

Alex was reminded of his father. "So what would be a justifiable reason to go to war?" He challenged his roommate. "What would make it okay?"

"I don't think war is ever okay," said Jonathan matter-of-factly. "There is always an alternative, a way to engage in peaceful negotiations."

"I don't agree." Alex was surprised at his own words, but the more he thought about it, the more he felt convinced he was right.

"Do me a favor, math genius. Go back to your trigonometry."

"You're an arrogant jerk." Alex clenched his fists, infuriated by Jonathan's patronizing tone.

"And you're being ridiculous. What are you going to do—join the army?"

"Maybe I will." Alex stood up. "Maybe I will. You know they pay for your school? And they give you a job after graduation and everything."

"Alex." Jonathan looked at him seriously. "You're talking about the army. Are. You. Insane? They'll send you to *Afghanistan*." His expression was incredulous: his eyes were wide and his mouth hanging half open.

"Well, I'm not you. Maybe that doesn't bother me." Alex pictured himself decked out in army fatigues, running through the desert with a giant gun. Could he really do that? But Rory had said there were other opportunities for people like him. Math stuff. Code breaking. "I could work in encryption," he added.

"Do you speak Arabic?"

"No."

Jonathan gave him a pointed glance but said nothing.

"I might do it." Alex threw his roommate a contemptuous look. "Not all of us are jaded about those poor girls in burkas."

Jonathan shook his head. "Do whatever you want," he

said, shrugging. "I'm just saying, it's not as simple as you think it is. It isn't all about being a hero and rescuing the good and innocent people of Afghanistan."

"No? Well, it's not just about oil, either," shot back Alex.

Jonathan didn't reply. "I'm going to hit the hay."

Alex watched, horrified, as he swept all his papers and books to the carpeted floor with a single arm motion. *How could someone stand to live in such a mess?* Alex backed away, as if the disorder was contagious. He thought he was messy, but Jonathan made him feel like his neat-freak mother.

"Goodnight, then." Alex turned away from his roommate and sat down at his own desk. He logged on to the Internet and browsed articles on the Taliban. He also read more about Osama bin Laden, whom the Taliban were hiding away somewhere. *Could I really join the army? What would my parents say?* He still wasn't sure.

"See ya, Benji." Alex waved and quickly rolled the window back up. It was freezing. Even with the heat going at full blast he could still see his breath. He rubbed his hands together for warmth—he had never been able to drive with gloves on—and placed his chapped hands back on the steering wheel.

Exams were done, and like pretty much everyone else on campus, Alex was headed home for the holidays. He was the only one with a car (a beat-up 1990 Ford with a large dent in the side), and he had offered his friends a ride so they could avoid the bus. Benji lived the closest to him and was the last one to be dropped off. Alex turned up the radio for the final few blocks of the drive and groaned: more Nickelback. Were they ever *not* on?

Alex had been home twice since leaving for school—once for his mother's birthday and then again at Thanksgiving. Both times he had expected home to feel different when he came back. He'd hoped that his parents would see him as an adult. Both times, though, he was surprised to find that it didn't feel that way at all. As soon as he was home, it was as if he'd never left. On some levels it was nice—he liked not having to do his own laundry, for example—but on others, he felt disappointed: he'd hoped going away to school would have elevated him somehow in his parents' eyes, made them realize he wasn't a kid anymore, and forced them to treat him more like an adult. But nothing had changed in the Cameron house, where his mother still sighed behind the bathrobe-clad back of his father, while he alternately lashed out at the morning newspaper and lectured Alex on current events.

Alex thought of how his father would react when presented with the news that his son was joining the army. He couldn't help but feel a small twinge of satisfaction as he imagined the horror and outrage on his face, his eyes bulging, nostrils flaring, and cheeks turning bright purple. *He's always so sure he's right*, thought Alex, digging his hands into the steering wheel. *Just like Jonathan.*

Since meeting Rory that first time, he'd met him twice more to discuss opportunities in the military. He'd also started attending debates on campus about the war in Afghanistan. He hadn't told the guys; they thought he was studying geometry in the library. He was still ambivalent about the war, but thought that if he joined the army, he would have a chance to do some good. He imagined himself handing out candy to barefoot kids and rescuing grateful women. Rory encouraged this. "It would be great to have someone like you in Afghanistan," he enthused. "Someone who's both gifted academically *and* motivated by the desire for positive change. You have real leadership potential, Alex."

The only person who was aware of his new extracurricular activities was Jonathan. He attended the same debates and had been surprised to find Alex tagging along.

"You're really taking this seriously, aren't you?" Jonathan said, giving his roommate a worried glance.

"Well, I think there is room for me," said Alex defensively.

"Room where? You're not still talking about the army, are you?" Jonathan scoffed.

"Maybe I am. Have you ever thought that it would be good for the military to have people who aren't so convinced they're right about everything, people who genuinely want to help and bring about change?"

Jonathan looked at him sharply. "Who have you been talking to?"

"What's that supposed to mean?"

"It just sounds like someone's trying to manipulate you." Jonathan shrugged. "It's your life, Cameron. If you want to throw it away getting blown to pieces in Kabul, I guess it's your business."

"Yeah, I guess it is."

Alex gritted his teeth thinking about Jonathan and the inevitably similar reaction he was bound to get from his father. *I am an adult*, he told himself, *a university student with my own ideas and opinions. I don't see why my opinions aren't as valid as theirs.*

Alex pulled into his driveway, the car bouncing slightly as one of the front tires hit a small sinkhole. He shut off the car, which sputtered and groaned a bit as he did. He grabbed his bags from the backseat.

"Alex!" His mother was waiting at the door. She'd clearly been hovering at the window, waiting for him to get home. He smiled and folded her into a big bear hug, lifting her slightly off her feet. She was so tiny, he thought, as he swung her around once and then gently placed her back on the floor.

"How was the drive?" she asked.

"Not bad, just cold. I think I need to get the heat checked on the Ford." He rubbed his hands together for warmth.

"You can take it to Joe's garage on Monday; I think it's open until Christmas Eve."

His mom looked down at the bags. "Which one has the laundry in it?"

Alex gave her a sheepish glance. "The blue-and-red one."

She picked it up carefully, as if handling radioactive waste. "How long has it been sitting around?"

Alex blushed. "Two weeks."

She shook her head. "Disgusting. I'll go throw this in. Your dad's just in the shower. There was an incident with jam this morning."

"An incident?"

"You know your father is clumsy. Blueberry jam every-where. Such a mess." She sighed in a good-natured way and turned to the basement.

Alex gathered the rest of his things. He trudged up the stairs to his room, which was just as he had left it. He tossed his bags on the floor next to the desk and looked longingly at the bed, contemplating a nap before supper.

"Alex! You're home."

Alex turned to see his father in the doorway, grinning broadly. He was naked, save for a pink bath towel wrapped precariously around his waist. He reached forward to pull his son into a hug, and it fell promptly to the ground.

"Oops," he said cheerfully, as Alex looked away, mortified. "Sorry. I had a little episode this morning with the jam."

"I heard."

"Damned jar broke and spilled everywhere. All over the paper. Didn't even get to read it."

"I'm sure it would have just made you mad, anyway." The words tumbled out of Alex's mouth like an overturned jar of marbles.

His father raised his eyebrows. "What's that supposed to mean?"

Alex shrugged. He wished he could take back what he'd said. He didn't want to get into it so soon, and not like this, with his father standing before him clutching a towel to cover himself.

"You know," he said finally. "The war and all that."

"Oh." His father's face darkened. "Well, I certainly have my thoughts on that. Just yesterday, I was reading that war-mongering hawk of a columnist, what's-her-name—"

"You know what, Dad?" Alex cut him off gently. "I'm really tired. I'm thinking about a nap."

"Huh?" His father looked momentarily confused at the sudden shift in conversation. He recovered quickly, nodding. "Of course. Of course, you must be tired after the drive. Probably partying all night, too, now that exams are done, eh?" He gave Alex a wink. "I remember my wild college days."

"Right, Dad."

Alex watched his father saunter down the hall, losing hold of the towel once again to reveal his rather sizeable behind. Shuddering, Alex went back into his room and shut the door, grateful that he had his mother's fit frame. There would be plenty of time to talk to his dad about the war later. And it wasn't as if he was *sure* what he was going to do, either, he reminded himself. He was just *thinking* about it, in a serious way. Yawning, he pulled off his sweater and flopped on the bed. His father wasn't entirely wrong—he had been up with friends until past three, but much of that time had been spent silently agonizing over the geometry final. Settling back, he lay his head on his old pillow and gave in to sleep, pushing all thoughts of calculations, war, and his father clear out of his head.

As he settled into the familiarity of being home, Alex thought less and less about the army. He still felt the same rush of irri-tation whenever his father pounded his cereal spoon on the breakfast table over news items that raised his ire, but he put off making any decisions or having any serious discussions.

On Christmas Eve, Alex got an e-mail from Benji: "Alex—grades are UP. Check at your own risk! Geometry's a bitch. Lump of coal in my stocking…prof's an ass. Later, B."

Geometry's a bitch. Alex felt his head spin and stomach drop, as if he were skydiving and his parachute had failed to open. He needed to maintain a least an A average to keep his scholarship and stay in the Honors program. Alex cringed, thinking of how it would feel if he were kicked out. He'd never even got a grade less than an A- in high school, and now here he was, worried about *passing* a damn geometry course.

Hands shaking slightly, Alex logged on to his university account and waited. His heart pounded so loudly, he was sure his mother would be at his door any second asking what all the racket was. He stared at the page in front of him for a moment, paralyzed, before clicking "grade report."

A list of grades appeared before him. Alex had to blink twice; it all looked like a blur to him, as if someone had written the grades in pencil and then wiped a damp cloth across them. He breathed deeply and read out his grades, running his finger along the screen for confirmation: "A…A-…B+…A-…D."

"D." Alex said the last grade aloud. Saying it out loud made it feel worse. "D," he said again, this time practically yelling. Then he quieted down, breathing heavily. "Shit," he whispered, staring at the screen.

Alex quickly added up his five grades and divided them. He felt the room swing from side to side as if he were on a broken elevator or amusement park ride. He double-checked the numbers, but he had been right the first time: he was coming up just short of a B+. *I'm going to get kicked out*, he realized. He felt numb. It took a moment for the reality to sink in, like a burn that takes a second or two to cause pain. He tried to stand up, but he couldn't. He couldn't feel his legs. *Where are my legs?* he thought stupidly, panicked. He looked down, expecting them to have vanished, but there they were. Angrily, he poked his left thigh with a pencil. "Ow," he muttered. So he wasn't paralyzed. Momentarily disappointed—at least if he were in a wheelchair, no one would judge him for getting kicked out of honors math—he stood up and launched himself onto the bed, where he curled up in the fetal position. Checking to make sure his door was closed, he fished under his pillow for his old blanket and held it tightly to his chest. He inhaled its familiar scent and felt a slow-moving wave of calm overtake him, as if the blanket were a fast-acting tranquilizer.

Alex wondered if he could petition to remain in the program. Maybe he could repeat the geometry class. Alex groaned and rolled over onto his other side. He now stared at the wall, at his old *Star Wars* posters and a calendar from 1998 he'd never bothered to take down. It had come free in the mail from a travel agency, but Alex had liked it: each month had a picture from a different destination. The calendar was stuck at December, and happy children eating gingerbread smiled at him from a snow-covered Christmas market somewhere in Germany. Alex stared enviously at them in their handmade hats and mittens. He daydreamed of clearing out his savings and hopping on a plane to Munich and not coming back. He'd have to learn German, sure, but it couldn't be any worse than geometry. Also, he knew a little French, and weren't all European languages pretty much the same?

Alex sat up and reached for the can of Coke on his bedside table. It was from yesterday, and warm and flat, but it was better than nothing. He swallowed the tepid liquid and resisted the urge to gag. Putting the can back down, he knocked his wallet to the floor.

Swearing to himself, Alex bent over to retrieve the wallet and settled back down on the bed. He opened it and took out Rory's card. He read it for the hundredth time, reciting the phone and e-mail almost by heart. He played with the little card, flipping it back and forth between his left and right hands.

That night, Alex waited until his mother had served the soup before making his announcement.

"I've decided to join the army," he said. His tone was matter-of-fact. "I've given it a lot of thought."

His mother made a small noise and put down her wine glass. His father dropped his soupspoon in shock. They all watched as it hit the floor with a loud clatter.

"You. Are. Not. Enlisting. In. The. Army." His father enunciated each word very carefully and slowly. His voice was thunderous, and his face was flushed. Alex felt his resolve crumble but mustered his strength. He thought of his D in geometry, of Jonathan's know-it-all laugh, and of the girls in burkas. Most of all, he thought of his father running away all those years ago. He steeled himself, staring at his father with hard eyes.

"You can't stop me." Alex was calm. "I'm over eighteen. I'm an adult."

"An adult!" His father nearly choked on his words. "You're a child. I don't care what the law says. You spend most of your time playing video games!" His anger was rising. "And what about school? You're just going to drop out of school?"

"The army is going to pay for school. I'm still going to finish, just later." He watched his father's reaction and felt a small thrill of pleasure at his fury.

"This is insanity." His father was shaking his head so quickly, Alex wondered how he managed to stay upright. "How long have you been planning this?"

"I don't know. A while, I guess."

"And you thought you'd do this tonight? On Christmas Eve?"

Alex was silent. He felt a stab of guilt as he stared across the room at the carefully decorated tree. Each year his mother chose a theme: this year, in honor of his first year away at school, it was decorated with little graduation caps and miniature calculators.

"It's just the three of us," muttered Alex, pushing his guilt aside. "It's not like it's a big family holiday dinner."

"That. Is. IRRELEVANT!" His dad was shouting again. He banged his fist on the table and the soup bowls shook, the soup inside swaying slightly from side to side.

"Don." His mother spoke up for the first time. Her voice was quiet and trembling. She put a hand on her husband's arm. "Please."

She paused to breathe and spoke up again. "Please calm down, both of you." Her voice was stern now. She turned to Alex. "Alex, I know 9/11 was upsetting and that you feel like you need to do something. But your father is right. You're young, and you're not thinking clearly. You need to finish school."

Alex started to protest, but she cut him off abruptly. "Maybe you have a romantic view of war from movies and TV, Alex, but I can assure you that's not how it is in real life. I've been through it: it's horrible." She gave her son a hard stare. "You could die, or lose a leg or an arm. Is that what you want?"

Alex was fuming. "I can't believe you think I'm such an idiot!" It was his turn now to slam his fist down hard on the kitchen table, rattling the silverware. "I don't think war is romantic." His face was hot. They sounded just like Jonathan. "And I'm *not* too young to make decisions. And I want to join the army." Obstinate, he folded his arms and glowered at his parents.

His mother began to sob quietly. She got up from the table and rushed out of the room.

"You see?" His father was yelling so loudly now, Alex felt himself shrink back into his chair. "Look what you did to your mother! This conversation is over. No one in this house is joining the army. Understood?"

Alex jumped up. He felt bad about making his mother

cry, but he wasn't going to let his father scream at him like he was eight years old and tell him how to live his life. "You can't stop me," he said calmly, glaring at his father. "I'm going to join. I'm not a coward."

The unsaid words *like you* hung in the air. Alex immediately regretted what he'd said. He backed away from the table and stared at the ground.

His father turned red and looked hard at this son. He stared at Alex, mutely, his eyes filled with sadness.

"I didn't mean…" Alex's voice trailed off as he looked at his father, abashed. Still, his father said nothing; he just kept looking at him with that same sorrowful stare. Alex tried again.

"Dad, I'm sorry you don't like it but…it's important to me. Same as *not* going to Vietnam was important to you. Don't you get it?"

His father stood up from his chair and called out after his mother, then left the room. Alex stared at the half-eaten bowls of soup, now cold and unappetizing. He waited to see if his parents would come back. Ten minutes passed. Alex collected the soup bowls and dropped them in the sink. He went back to his room and opened his e-mail. He had an important message to send.

There was a soft knock at the door. Alex looked up from the laundry he was folding, startled. His mother stood in the doorway, leaning against it. She looked tired; her eyes were shadowed with gray and her shoulders sagged slightly inward.

"Alex?" Her voice was tentative.

"Mom." He set down a shirt and turned to her. "What is it?"

"I just—" Her voice faltered. "Your father—"

"I don't want to talk about him." Alex's voice hardened, and he turned away. His dad hadn't spoken to him since the episode Christmas Eve. He hadn't yelled or fought or even tried to persuade Alex. He had just stopped talking to him, as if Alex didn't exist. Alex had tried to engage him, tried to talk to him, to convince him he knew what he was doing, but his father ignored him. When Alex spoke, he stared right through him as if he were invisible, a ghost.

"He just—he wants what's best for you. He doesn't want to see you get hurt or lose your legs or…" Her voice trailed off, and she looked away.

"He wants what's best for *him*. If he really cared about me, he'd think of what I want and not just what he wants."

"But sweetheart, I don't believe you're thinking this through enough. It's a war in the desert somewhere, and you could be killed. Why do you want to do this? I think that's what we don't understand. Why?"

Alex gritted his teeth. "I want to fight the Taliban. They're evil. And I want the people who plotted the 9/11 attacks to pay for what they did."

"But Alex, they don't even know if the people behind the attacks are *in* Afghanistan."

"So you think the Taliban are okay?" Alex ignored her point and turned to her, arms folded. "You think their form of government is good?"

"I don't. But I also don't know if this is a winnable war. I'm worried it will be like Vietnam. So many lives lost, and the country all but destroyed…. It's a foreign war, Alex." His mother spread out her hands helplessly. "I don't know what the right thing is. But I don't want my son killed."

"What if the Americans had said that in World War II? Do you think the concentration camps were okay, Mom? That was a foreign war. And Vietnam—it was bad, fine. But it got you out of there, didn't it? It brought you here. You wouldn't have *me* if someone had held that attitude."

His mother sighed. She looked weary, as if she didn't have the strength to fight anymore. "I just hope you've thought this through. I don't think it is as black-and-white as you believe it is. And I don't know if this is the right choice for *you*, Alex. The army? You never even liked being on a baseball team."

Alex's face twisted. "I don't think sports and the army have anything to do with each other."

"I understand your principles, but is this really the right choice for you, personally? For Alex Cameron?"

"Everyone is so sure I'm not cut out for this." Alex resumed folding his shirts with ferocity. "I'm going to be just fine."

His mother sighed again. Her shoulders seemed to bend inward as she did so. "I'll leave you, then," she said softly. She turned quickly and left the room.

Alex didn't turn his head. He folded another shirt and shoved it into his duffel bag. Then he took a deep breath and looked around the room to see what else needed packing. He couldn't take much to the basic-training camp, but he didn't want to forget anything important, either. He walked over to his desk and began opening and closing drawers, rifling through them. He remembered the last time he had done this, barely four months ago. How he'd changed since then, he thought. He was practically a different person. He'd been younger then, naive, innocent about stuff like war and politics and history.

Alex was about to slam the final drawer shut when he noticed the soldier doll. It peered at him from the dusty space, half covered by a pack of yellow Post-it notes. It had a somber look on its little face.

Alex pulled it out and studied it. It was a soldier, and he was going to be a soldier. He held it, considering. Was it silly to bring along a doll? Would the other guys laugh?

It's from an American soldier who was in 'Nam, he decided. *No one's going to laugh at that.* Alex grabbed his backpack and stuffed the wooden figure inside.

The sky poured freezing rain the day he left. He waited for his parents to come to the door to say good-bye, but they didn't. He unlocked the door very slowly and went outside, closing it with force behind him. He waited, but still nothing. He waited longer, his wool hat turning to ice. He felt his eyelashes freeze and the vapor drip into his eyes. He blinked and stared hard at the door, waiting. Still nothing. Not even his mother. She spoke to him less and less now—his father had seen to that. She still looked at him with sad eyes, but she didn't say much.

"I'll write you," she'd whispered last night. "And please call. Call my cell phone."

Alex had turned away in disgust. She was so afraid of his stupid father that she didn't even want him, her only son, to call the house. At that moment, he hated her, hated her as much as he hated his father. He was glad they refused to see him off, to say good-bye.

Alex wrapped his scarf tighter around his neck as he lugged his bag down the driveway. Icy rain whipped his face, stinging his cheeks in needles of pain. At the bottom of the incline, he lost his footing and slipped, landing on his back with a sickening crunch. When he'd caught his breath, he righted himself, dusting the snow off his soaking jeans. He shook off his backpack to see if there was any damage, but the crunching sound had just been a half-open bag of pretzels. He started to close the bag and then noticed the soldier doll.

He picked it up and stared hard at it. His mother hadn't even come downstairs to say good-bye. "I don't need you," he said to it. "I don't need anyone." He tossed the doll on the side of the road and walked quickly to the bus stop.

CHAPTER 13

Toronto, Canada
2007

"Mom?" Elizabeth kicks off her shoes and walks into the house, carefully stepping over her discarded footwear. Her mother sticks her head into the hallway from the kitchen, frowning at the haphazardly dumped yellow platform sandals.

"Someone could kill themselves on those things," she says disapprovingly.

Elizabeth kicks the shoes to one side. "Who ever got killed by a killer pair of shoes?" she quips.

"Those aren't just shoes. Look at the size of the heels! You could sustain a concussion if you tripped in them."

"Yeah, if you're a total spaz, maybe," Elizabeth snorts. "Death by fashion."

"It's been known to happen." Her mom leans against the

doorway and folds her arms across her chest.

"Right."

"There was a dancer once; I can't remember her name. She was wearing a really long fashionable scarf, and it got wound up in the wheel of the car she was in, and she was strangled."

"Come on." Elizabeth casts her eyes heavenward in mock exasperation.

"I'm telling you. Look it up on your Wikipedia or whatever."

Elizabeth raises her eyebrows. "Even if it's true, it doesn't prove anything. She could have been wearing a practical, warm scarf and the same thing might have happened."

Her mother gives a resigned sigh. "You'd make a good lawyer, Liz. You have an answer for everything."

Elizabeth grins triumphantly. "Does that mean I win?"

"No. You still have to put your shoes away."

"Boo." Elizabeth sticks out her tongue.

"I'm the boss of this house."

"What about Dad?"

"He's not here right now, remember? So I'm in charge."

Elizabeth is quiet for a moment. Her father left a week ago, but she still isn't used to his absence. It's as if something isn't quite right in the house without his silly jokes or enthusiastic laugh. It feels strange, now that it's just her and her mom in this new house; it suddenly makes the space feel much larger than it did a month ago.

"I miss Dad." The words tumble out before she can stop them.

"Oh, honey." Elizabeth's mother comes over and puts an arm around her daughter's narrow shoulders. "So do I."

Elizabeth lets her mother hug her for a minute before pulling away. "Did he call today?"

"Yes. And he sent an e-mail. He's had a lot of interesting replies to his article on the soldier doll."

"Oh yeah?" Elizabeth looks at her with interest. Her dad and Dr. McLeod had co-written an article on the discovery of the doll for a national newspaper, and it had been published last week.

Her mother motions for Elizabeth to join her at the kitchen table.

"Most were just Margaret Merriweather fans," her mom said. "But there was one really interesting one. It was from an older woman who'd had the doll at a concentration camp called Terezín. It was near Prague," Her mother leans back in her chair. "Her name is Eva Goodman. Here, I printed it for you." She reaches into her back jeans' pocket and retrieves a folded square of paper.

"Thanks." Elizabeth snatches the paper from her mother and unfolds it, smoothing it against the wooden surface of the tabletop.

The e-mail is quite long. Mrs. Goodman begins by explaining to Elizabeth's father how a fellow prisoner, a German Jew named Franz Roth, had presented her with the doll as a small gift.

He told me the doll was a good-luck charm, that his friend had given it to him on the battlefield in the Great War. He said they'd found it on an English soldier, wrote Mrs. Goodman.

Elizabeth looks up at her mother. "An English soldier?" she asks excitedly. "Do you think it could be Ned?"

"Your father certainly does. He was beside himself over this e-mail. Like a little boy." Her mother grins.

"I can imagine," says Elizabeth. She goes back to reading.

After the War, Mrs. Goodman concludes, *before I immigrated to America, I gave the small toy to an orphanage in Prague. A dear friend of mine, who I later learned had perished at Auschwitz, had spent time there. I donated it in her memory.*

Elizabeth finishes reading the e-mail to herself, which includes further details of life at Terezín and Mrs. Goodman's deportation to another camp called Treblinka, just before she was finally liberated by the American army in 1945. She had then married an American soldier and immigrated to New York.

"Wow," says Elizabeth when she's finished. She looks shaken. "Did you read this?"

"I did," says her mother in a somber tone. She looks at her daughter curiously. "You learned about the Holocaust in school, didn't you?"

"We did," says Elizabeth, frowning. She has a faraway look in her eyes. "It's different, though, when you read it like this. In an e-mail. When you read the books and stuff, it just seems so long ago."

Her mom nods. "Makes it seem more real. More personal." They sit quietly for a moment, contemplating.

"Dad must have been so excited to get this," Elizabeth says

again. She smiles, thinking of how thrilled her father would have been to receive the message.

Her mother laughs. "Look at all the exclamation marks in the subject line when he forwarded it to me."

Elizabeth rolls her eyes and scans the top of the e-mail for her father's words. "He doesn't really say much, though," she observes. "It would be nice to get a little more information."

"He'll probably call again tomorrow," says her mom. "He's got a lot going on there, and the Internet connection is slow. I'm sure he'll be in touch whenever he can. And he did promise we're all going to go to England on his first leave."

"That's true," says Elizabeth, brightening. It's what she's looking forward to most—going to London. She looks around the kitchen. "Is there anything for supper?"

"Yes!" Her mother rises proudly from her chair and opens the fridge, gesturing triumphantly.

"What is it?" Elizabeth looks suspiciously at the casserole dish inside.

"Lasagna." Her mom beams.

Elizabeth eyes her skeptically. "Where's it from?"

"I made it!" Her mother looks very pleased with herself.

"Seriously? Like with noodles, from scratch?" Elizabeth walks over and pokes at the dish in disbelief, prying open the lid to look inside.

"And vegetables."

"No!" Elizabeth steps back from the fridge and feigns shock, fanning herself with her hands as if she might faint. "I don't believe it."

"Believe it." Her mom looks smug. "*Now* what can you say about me, since I'm no longer forcing you to eat pizza?"

"Me?" says Elizabeth innocently. "What did I say?"

"Ha." Her mother slides the lasagna out of the fridge and carefully places it in the oven.

"Do you even know how to turn that on?" Elizabeth cocks her head to one side and grins slyly.

"Funny." Her mother elbows her gently in the ribs as she switches on the heat and sets the timer. Impatient for the generous topping of cheese to begin to bubble, the two stare at the glass oven door while the dish inside slowly cooks.

"Would anyone really buy this?" Elizabeth holds up a hardcover book, displaying the cover for Evan. She looks doubtful. "Maybe one for the free book table?" She nods in the direction of the door. Outside, unwanted books, cast off even by Sam, sit, forlorn, on a table marked "Free to a Good Home."

"*Soap: A History*." Evan reads the title. "I'm not so sure. It could be interesting. How it was discovered, how it became popular. You know, people didn't bathe until recently. Like, doctors didn't even wash their hands."

"Gross." Elizabeth wrinkles her nose. "But if they didn't wash their hands, then that wouldn't really be part of the history of soap, would it?"

"I don't know," says Evan pointedly. "You'd have to read it to find out."

Elizabeth sighs. Evan is protective of the books. He treats them like children, reluctant to banish them to the free book table. She peels off a price sticker and carefully places it in the top left-hand corner. "It's a dollar book, then."

Evan winces. "Poor soap book."

Elizabeth laughs. "No wonder Sam wanted to hire someone else to help you with this," she says. "You're impossible. He'd never be able to turn over inventory with you here alone."

Evan looks wounded. "Untrue," he says, pouting. "I got rid of all those atlases."

"Evan, they were so old that most of the European countries in them don't even exist anymore."

"Exactly. They were antiques." He jumps up. "They could be worth something! I'm going out to get them."

"Oh, sit down." Impatiently, Elizabeth pulls him back down to the floor, where they've been sorting books for hours. Sam had hired her to work with Evan these last few weeks of summer to help clear out the old books to make room for new ones in the fall. It's been fun working together as a couple, and they often spend their evenings together, too.

"You have no appreciation for antiquities," grumbles Evan, picking up an old volume of *Encyclopedia Britannica* and examining it critically.

"Me? How dare you. You're talking to the current owner of the soldier doll."

"Which you had never heard of until I mentioned it."

"Stop sulking, it's annoying."

Evan sticks his tongue out, and Elizabeth laughs. She whacks him gently on the head with an old paperback destined for the twenty-five-cent pile.

"So did your dad get any more feedback on that article?" Evan asks. Elizabeth had told him about the e-mail from Eva Goodman.

"Yes, actually." Elizabeth puts down the book she is holding. "I meant to tell you. We heard from another guy who says he used to have the doll. Here in Toronto."

"Really!" Evan looks at her eagerly. "Tell me."

"He's a vet," says Elizabeth. She looks slightly uncomfortable.

"A vet?" Evan frowns. "Like an animal doctor?"

"Um, no." Elizabeth snorts. "Like a veteran. From the war. In Afghanistan." She's still not making eye contact.

"Ah," says Evan, blushing. "Right."

"His name is Alex. He lost a leg over there." She looks worried.

Evan puts an arm around her. "Your dad will be fine," he says.

Elizabeth ignores him. "He said his mom gave him the doll. He said an American soldier gave it to her in Vietnam."

"Wow," says Evan. He sits back. "It's really been around, huh?"

"I know," says Elizabeth. "It's crazy, isn't it? My dad's been updating Margaret Merriweather. He's obsessed."

"So are you going to London soon?"

"Yes!" says Elizabeth, perking up. "We booked our tickets yesterday! I forgot to tell you. We're going to go when my dad has leave, in October."

"So lucky!" Evan looks at her enviously. "I've never been to England."

"I know, I wish you could come. But it's kind of a family thing. Dad's meeting us, from Afghanistan…"

"I understand." Evan squeezes her hand.

"I promise." Elizabeth squeezes back. "I'll text you the entire time."

"Make sure you get me an autograph. I'll give you my copy of *Autumn Evening*. It could be worth something someday."

"You're obsessed. Anyway, you'd *sell* it?"

"Of course not. It's *knowing* it's worth a lot."

Elizabeth shakes her head. "You're crazy."

"You love it." He grins slyly.

She tilts her head coquettishly. "Maybe."

Smiling, he pulls her to him, knocking over a stack of books. Elizabeth groans loudly. "There goes an hour's work. And you almost killed Boris."

Evan looks down at the large rabbit, who stares up at him indignantly, flexing his front paw.

"Sorry, my furry friend," he says apologetically. He ruffles Boris's back and reaches again for Elizabeth. He narrowly misses hitting her head against the desk as he pulls her in for a kiss.

Elizabeth lugs the heavy shopping bag home, grunting with the effort. *I should have just let Mom drive me to the mall to get this stuff.* She winces as the overstuffed bag pinches her shoulder, as if the handle were alive with teeth or claws. The bag brims with pens, pencils, notebooks, and a variety of other school supplies. Elizabeth secretly enjoys back-to-school shopping. There is something about crisp, new, yet-to-be-opened notebooks and fresh, unused pens with their caps still in place that makes her feel excited and optimistic about the upcoming academic year. She had gone to the store with Emily, who spent most of their outing quizzing her on the finer points of her relationship with Evan.

"So when you guys are at work together and no one's around, do you ever, you know—" Emily raised her eyebrows suggestively.

"Em!" Elizabeth cut her off. "No! It's a store. People can walk in at any time!"

"Not even a kiss?" Emily looked at her friend knowingly. Elizabeth blushed, and Emily grinned triumphantly. "I knew it!"

"Sh," said Elizabeth, scandalized, looking around the office supply store. "Someone will hear you!"

"No one's listening to us," said Emily impatiently. She leaned in toward Elizabeth conspiratorially. "You're sure you're just kissing?"

"Yes! Shut up!"

Elizabeth grins now at the memory of her friend. She shifts the bag to her right shoulder, revealing an ugly, red, welt-like mark on the other one. "Ugh," she says, shuddering. She's almost home now. She drops the bag to the ground and drags it behind her up the front stairs.

The house is unusually quiet when she walks in. She's grown accustomed to having her mother around—she's been wrapping up her days early lately, even making it home before Elizabeth. Her mother is the kind of person who likes background noise and often has the television or radio blaring, regardless of whether she's actually watching or listening. Today, though, there is silence.

Probably seeing a late patient, Elizabeth reasons. She slips off her shoes and stares at the bag at her feet, tempted to leave it for now. Then she considers her mother's reaction to the bag and, sighing, hauls it up the final flight of stairs to her room.

"Liz?"

Elizabeth blinks, surprised. Her mom is home after all. She peers into the hall from her bedroom. *Why is she in her room with the lights off?*

"I need to talk to you."

Heart hammering, Elizabeth makes her way to her mother, who is lying on top of the made bed. She reaches over to turn on a bedside lamp, and Elizabeth can see her eyes are red and puffy, her cheeks stained black with running makeup.

"Mom?" Elizabeth's voice is small. "What is it?"

"Oh, honey." Her mother takes a deep breath. "It's Dad."

Elizabeth feels dizzy, as if she has been knocked off her feet. "No," she whispers. Her heart pounds loudly in her chest in an unnatural rhythm, and she can feel the blood rushing in her ears.

"It was a bomb of some kind at the base, a terrorist attack—"

"No!" Elizabeth's voice is shrill. "He's just an engineer!"

"I know, sweetheart, I know. It was a terrorist attack, there was nothing—"

"He said he'd be okay, that he was just an engineer!" Elizabeth is crying now.

"It's a terrible tragedy," her mother says robotically, crying now, too.

"How do they know for sure? Are they sure?" Elizabeth collapses onto the bed.

"They know, Liz. There was a—"

"Don't say it!" Elizabeth's voice rises again in pitch. She can't bear to hear the word *body*, to hear her father described as an inanimate object, as an *it* instead of a *he*.

"Oh, Elizabeth." Her mom's voice breaks. "I'm so sorry."

Elizabeth stares helplessly at the wall. Her parents' wedding portrait hangs there, her parents smiling at her from another time, a happier one. She looks into her father's unseeing, laughing eyes and feels the grief overtake her like an avalanche from within.

"Are you all right?" Her mom looks worried.

"I can't breathe." Elizabeth shudders.

"Just let it out," her mother replies gently.

Elizabeth does, wailing noisily into her mother's pillow. Her mother strokes her hair and makes soothing noises, the way she used to when Elizabeth was a little girl.

"I'm sorry, Mom." Elizabeth sniffles, turning to look at her mother. "I should be doing this for you."

"Don't be silly," her mom says, waving her hand.

Elizabeth sits up. She huddles close to her mother, drawing her knees to her chest and hugging them tightly.

"What are we going to do?" Elizabeth's voice is quiet again. She stares out the window now. In the backyard below, she catches sight of her father's little shed. She quickly looks away, feeling as if her heart might actually break.

"We have to be strong." Her mother grasps her hand tightly. "I need you to be strong."

"What if I can't?" Elizabeth's voice is dull. "I don't think I can, Mom."

"Don't be silly," Her mother's tone is sharper now. "I need you to be strong, Liz." She takes a deep breath. "I—I have something else to tell you."

Elizabeth stares at her mother, her eyes frantic. "What?" she cries. "What is it? You're not sick, are you?" She searches her mother's face for signs of illness. Her heart is thudding hard again, and she feels as if she might be sick.

"No! Not like that, anyway." Her mother pulls Elizabeth to her and holds her hard against her chest.

"What do you mean? What does that mean—not like that?" Elizabeth pulls back slightly and looks at her mother suspiciously. She's still frightened.

"I'm pregnant." Her mother says it quietly. Her hands go to her stomach.

Elizabeth stares at her, dumbfounded. "What?"

"I'm pregnant." Her mom gives her a weak smile.

"Does—did Dad know?" Elizabeth winces at the past tense. *Pregnant!* Her mind reels with shock.

"Yes—we were hoping to tell you together. I didn't find out until after he left. Right after, actually."

"When—when is the baby due?"

"April."

"How did this happen?" Elizabeth shakes her head, struggling to come to terms with the news.

Her mother manages a small smile. "Are you sure you want to know the answer to that question?"

"Come on. You know what I mean. After all this time?"

Her mom shrugs, exhales. "I don't know. It's a miracle, really."

"Is it—should we—" Elizabeth struggles to find the right words. She remembers the darker days of her childhood, the days when her mother shut herself up in her room and Elizabeth could hear the crying. "Is it too soon to…talk about it?" she says finally. Her voice is tentative.

"The doctor says everything looks good," her mother replies. "I had an early scan, and it looked good."

"Wow," says Elizabeth. "A baby."

"I know." Her mother is crying again. "I'm going to need your help, Liz."

Elizabeth folds herself into her mother's arms and cries, her heart heavy with joy and sorrow, sorrow and joy. She cries for her father, who is gone, and for the little unborn brother or sister who will never hear his laughter or know his love.

CHAPTER 14

Toronto, Canada
2007

"Liz, can you get that?"

Elizabeth stares hard at the phone, mentally willing it to be silent. She slumps in her seat, pretending she hasn't heard her mother yelling from upstairs.

"Liz!"

With a sigh, Elizabeth rises slowly from her seat and reaches for the phone, still hoping that it will cease its incessant ringing. *You'd think whoever's on the other end would get the point*, she mutters to herself in irritation. She waits for one more ring—the tenth—before resigning herself to the caller's inexplicable persistence.

"Hello?" Her tone is rude and harsh. She doesn't want to talk to this person—or anyone, for that matter. She just wants to be left alone.

"Oh—hi!" The voice sounds surprised. "I didn't think anyone was going to answer."

"Who is this?" Elizabeth is short.

"Oh, sorry. Um, my name is Mike Stepanek. I'm looking for John Bryant. I'm calling about his article in the paper. The one about the soldier doll? I saw it online."

"Oh," says Elizabeth quietly.

"The editor gave me his contact information. I tried e-mailing that address, but it's been weeks, and no one replied, and I thought, well, maybe I'd try calling..." His voice trails off as he waits for a response.

No one replied. The words pierce Elizabeth, and it's as if she's just learning the bad news all over again. It's like this each time.

"Hello?" The man sounds awkward now. "Are you still there?"

"Yes," says Elizabeth quietly. "It's just, he's not here. John Bryant. He...went to Afghanistan. And we're not really inter-ested in the doll anymore." She feels a twinge of guilt as she says this, but pushes it aside. It's the truth. She isn't interested in the soldier doll any longer. What was the point? She doesn't want to go to London, either. She's been pressuring her mother to cancel the trip. Her mother strongly disagrees with her on this, of course, as does Evan. She doesn't agree with them on much now.

"But Liz," Evan had said, shaking his head. "Your dad was so *into* the soldier doll. He'd have *wanted* you to go to London."

"What do you know about my dad and what he wanted?" she'd shot back. "You didn't even know him."

Hurt, Evan had dropped the subject. He didn't provoke her much these days—when she agreed to see him. Most days, she wasn't in the mood. She had quit the job at the bookstore the day before the funeral and now spent most of her time in her pajamas in front of the television.

Her mother acted the same way as Evan. "Dad would have wanted us to go to London and see Ms. Merriweather," her mother had said firmly. "I think we should still go."

"I don't care about the doll," Elizabeth had snapped back. "It's just a stupid toy. And I can't believe you want to do anything like that now that Dad's gone."

"So we should spend the rest of our lives lying around here? In our pajamas? Watching crappy reruns of reality TV?"

"Leave me alone."

But now, Elizabeth finds herself second-guessing her decision to abandon the matter of the soldier doll: the man on the phone seems disappointed at her words.

"Really?" The man, Mike, sounds dejected. "I was really hoping to get some information on that doll. I think it's the one I had; it was from my aunt, from Czechoslovakia, well, the former Czechoslovakia I guess, and I gave it to this kid in 'Nam, and I always—"

"Czechoslovakia? Vietnam?" Elizabeth's curiosity gets the better of her. "Did you say your aunt? Was she near Prague?" She thinks of Eva Goodman's e-mail to her father.

"Yes! She was in Prague. Does that mean you're still

interested?" Mike Stepanek sounds hopeful.

"I guess I am," admits Elizabeth quietly. She realizes she's said the words out loud and continues hastily. "I mean, yes, please, go ahead. I'd like to hear your story." She adopts a more businesslike tone.

"Okay, great." Mike's voice is eager now. "Where should I begin?"

"Um, at the beginning, I guess." Elizabeth rolls her eyes. "How did you get it?"

"It's kind of a long story. I think you should hear the whole thing though. Do you have some time?"

Elizabeth looks down at her pink-plaid flannel pajamas, then up at the TV. She reaches for the remote and shuts it off.

"Actually," she says, "I do." She tucks the phone under her chin and settles back on the sofa.

"I was one of the first to be drafted," Mike explains. "Today, people talk about Vietnam; they talk about how it was an unnecessary war. My son—he can't understand why I went. But it wasn't so simple. I wasn't sure what the right thing to do was. I don't think the right thing was that clear. I guess it never is, not in a war, really."

Elizabeth thinks of her father and feels her stomach tighten.

"I think you're right," she says softly. It's the first thing she's said since Mike began talking, and he seems startled to hear her voice. It's as if he's forgotten there is anyone else there, someone on the other line to whom he is bearing his soul. Pausing to exhale loudly, he continues with his tale, going on to inform Elizabeth about the horrors of Vietnam: the fighting, the misery, the friends whose blood had been fatally mixed with the slippery mud of the jungle.

Mike reaches the end of his story. "I gave it to a girl in a village…a little village where we were sent off to check for weapons." His voice sounds far away now as he remembers. "She was just a little girl, and she was hungry. She was begging for food."

Elizabeth waits for him to go on, but he is silent for a moment.

"I gave her the doll," he says, speaking up again. "I thought—I thought it would remind her that she was just a little girl. I don't know. It sounds stupid." He sounds embarrassed.

"It doesn't," says Elizabeth sincerely. She pauses. "The girl—I might know who she is. I mean, she might live here. In Toronto."

"She—you know her?" Mike sounds shocked.

"Maybe. A guy got in touch with us, an Afghan vet. He said his mother got the doll from a soldier in Vietnam. I guess that's her, then. She's a consultant of some kind now, I think." Elizabeth hoped she wasn't babbling.

"That's—that's wonderful." Mike's voice catches, and Elizabeth worries for a second that he will cry. She can't cope with anyone else crying right now, not when she always feels on the verge of tears herself.

"Do you want to get in touch with her? Because I could ask—"

"No. No." Mike responds quickly, and Elizabeth can almost hear him shaking his head. "No. She wouldn't—it's not a good idea. No, just knowing she's well and a mother…that's enough for me. That's wonderful," he says again, and Elizabeth can tell he's definitely crying now. She looks over at the soldier doll on the fireplace mantle and is suddenly overwhelmed by what it has witnessed.

Elizabeth feels awkward. Mike is clearly crying on the other end of the phone, and she isn't in any state to offer him words of comfort or advice.

"Thank you for listening," says Mike sincerely. "I was so disappointed when I didn't hear anything after my e-mail."

Elizabeth takes a deep breath. "I'm sorry about that," she says. "My dad…it's my dad's e-mail. Was," she corrects herself. "He—he was killed a few weeks ago. In Afghanistan."

"Oh," says Mike. It comes out more of a groan, and it is full of knowing and understanding. "I'm so very sorry."

"Thank you," says Elizabeth quietly.

"It never goes away, but it does get better," Mike says. His voice radiates with sympathy. "I—I remember. It's hard to be the one who lives. The guilt at still being alive, and the pain because they're not."

Elizabeth fills her mother in over supper that night. It's another lasagna; only this time, it's Elizabeth who prepared it. After the phone call with Mike, she spent some time thinking.

It's hard to be the one who lives. It was true. She found it hard to understand how, when her father was gone, she was expected to continue on, to recreate something like the life they'd had before, only with him missing.

But Mike had done it. Eva Goodman had done the same. They had all managed, Elizabeth realized, to be the ones who lived. And she would have to do it, too. For her sake and for her mother's and, most of all, for the baby.

Elizabeth had left the house for the first time that week, unsure of her destination but happy to be outside. She drank in the warm air, which, as September approached, was no longer humid but quite pleasant. She noted that some of the trees had begun to turn already, little dots of red and yellow in a sea of green. It would start to get chilly at night now. She watched a squirrel dart by and wondered if it was already foraging for the long winter.

She found herself at the bookstore, tapping on the glass. The store was closed for lunch, but she could see the shadow of Evan's legs underneath the desk. She held her breath as he came over to unlock the door.

"Well," he said, raising his eyebrows. "You left the house."

"I did," she said. There was a pause. "I've missed you."

"Oh, Liz," he said. He pulled her to him. "I know it's so hard."

"I'm sorry," she sniffed, burying her head in his shoulder. "It's just been so bad."

"I know," he said, and held her. "I know."

They stayed that way for a while. Then Evan cheered her up with some new tricks he was trying to teach Boris.

"Watch this," he said, waving a piece of lettuce in the air. "Jump, Boris!"

Boris gave him a look and hopped in the other direction.

"It worked before," said Evan, frowning.

"Can you teach a rabbit tricks?" asked Elizabeth, trying not to laugh.

"Maybe not," Evan admitted. He tossed the lettuce at Boris and grinned sheepishly at her.

On her way back from visiting Evan, Elizabeth passed the grocery store and, on impulse, went inside. She'd never cooked anything in her life but macaroni and cheese or chocolate chip cookies, but she figured it couldn't be that complicated. She'd find a recipe somewhere on the Internet. Elizabeth tossed items into the cart: noodles, a jar of sauce, some cheese, a couple of red peppers, some mushrooms. The mushrooms even came all sliced and ready to go, wrapped in plastic on a little Styrofoam tray. As she passed the prepared food section, Elizabeth resisted the temptation to buy a ready-to-eat lasagna and pass it off as her own. Once home, Elizabeth had painstakingly followed online directions and cobbled together what looked, once it was done, like an actual, real lasagna! Elizabeth stood back and admired her handiwork. *Cooking wasn't so bad.* Then she looked around the kitchen. The counter was covered with spilled sauce; crumbs of cheese littered the floor; and the left-over noodles were now stuck, congealed, to the bottom of the pot. It then took Elizabeth longer to clean the kitchen than it did to make supper.

"This is great, Liz," says her mom at dinner, reaching for another serving. "Does that mean you'll be taking over the cooking now?" She smiles.

"Ha," says Elizabeth. "I'd have to drop out of school. It took me, like, the entire day to make it and then clean up. Cooking is so messy."

"The trick is to clean as you go," her mother says, scooping her last bites into her mouth.

"I think the trick might be to buy the ready-made one at the store."

Elizabeth finishes telling her mother about Mike. "He seemed like he was going to cry when he talked about the doll," says Elizabeth, twirling melted cheese around her fork. "I wonder why."

Her mother shrugs. "Who knows? Things are complicated in war."

"I'll say." Elizabeth reaches for another serving.

"You seem better." Her mother's voice is cautious. "Did something else happen?"

Elizabeth finishes chewing and nods. "It was something he said."

"Mike?"

"Yeah. He said 'it's hard to be the one who lives,' or something like that."

Her mother nods. "It's true."

"Yeah. So it made me think, maybe I need to be stronger—I need to *live*."

"It's great to hear you talk like that." Her mother looks

relieved. She puts her fork down and reaches for Elizabeth's hand. "Does that mean you want to go? To London?"

Elizabeth winces and looks away. "You really think we should?"

"I do." Her mother is firm. "It's what your father would have wanted."

"It feels so weird though, without Dad." Elizabeth's voice quavers as she stacks their plates.

"I know. But I think we should go, the two of us. It's important."

There is silence for a moment. Elizabeth scratches her fork along her plate, thinking. "Okay," she says finally. "You're right."

"Good." Her mother smiles approvingly. "It's the right choice, hon. If we wait much longer, may never have another chance. Margaret Merriweather is an old woman; she isn't going to live forever."

"I guess you're right," Elizabeth says quietly. She's still staring down at her plate.

"I have some good news, too."

Elizabeth looks up at her mom, who is smiling now. "What is it?"

"I got the test results back. You know, about the baby. Everything is fine; the baby is healthy and normal."

Elizabeth perks up. "That's great! Thank goodness."

"And…"

"And what?" Elizabeth looks at her, curious.

"It's a girl."

A girl! Elizabeth tries to imagine what it will be like, after all these years, to have a sister. She laughs. Her mother looks at her, surprised, and laughs too.

EPILOGUE

London
2007

Elizabeth looks at the scrap of paper in her hand and compares it to the number painted in black script above the large glass entryway.

"Twenty-three," she says to her mother. "I guess this is it."

Her mother nods, and Elizabeth presses a button. A loud buzzer sounds, and the door swings open slowly.

"Hello." A young woman dressed in pink scrubs greets them with a pleasant smile. "Are you Mrs. Bryant and Elizabeth? Here to see Ms. Merriweather?"

"Yes, thank you," says Elizabeth.

"I'm Janet," she says. "Meg's nurse. Come along this way."

Elizabeth and her mother follow Janet down a series of hallways. The nursing home looks like a cross between a hospital and a stately old home. There are nurses' stations and medical equipment tucked into corners, but also elegant molding and grand-looking furniture.

Janet leads them to a room labeled 2A and knocks on the door. "Meg?" she calls out. "Your visitors are here." Then she opens the door.

The woman in the room is indeed very old. Her face is etched with deep lines, like those on a map, and her white hair is tied in a neat knot near the top of her head. When she smiles, though, she suddenly looks much younger, and Elizabeth can't help but smile back at the transformation.

"You must be Elizabeth and Mrs. Bryant," the woman says. "Please, come in."

"Thank you, Ms. Merriweather," says Elizabeth's mother, nudging her daughter forward.

Elizabeth stammers her own thanks and steps into the room, her mother close at her heels. Janet takes their coats and leaves the room, and Ms. Merriweather motions for them to sit with her around a little wooden table. Elizabeth glances around, taking in the scene before her. A vase of fresh flowers rests on the windowsill, and an ancient-looking secretary's desk sits in the corner. She wonders if it's Ms. Merriweather's, and commits it to memory.

"Memorize every detail," Evan had instructed her before she'd left for the airport. "I want a full report. Don't leave anything out."

"I won't," she'd promised.

He'd pulled her to him, kissing her gently at first and then more urgently. It was the kind of kiss you felt all the way down to your toes. Elizabeth feels flush with happiness recalling it. She turns back to Mrs. Merriweather, who is eyeing her with a smile.

"That's my old escritoire," she says, as if reading Elizabeth's mind. "I brought it with me to the nursing home. They were very accommodating. Please," she says, "make yourselves comfortable. And call me Meg. Everyone does."

They sit down, and Meg pours them tea. Elizabeth watches the old woman's hand tremble ever so slightly as she handles the small china teapot. It's white with gold piping and painted with delicate pink and green flowers. Meg offers her a cup, and Elizabeth handles the delicate vessel with great care; it looks very expensive. Elizabeth has a brief mental image of the teacup shattering, its fragments scattered and mingling with tea on the carpet. She shudders and holds the teacup tighter.

Meg clears her throat and looks solemnly at mother and daughter. "Please accept my sincere condolences on your loss," she says softly.

Elizabeth winces and says nothing. She has been trying not to think of how much her father would have liked to be here, to have sat at this table and drank tea with the famous author.

"Thank you," says Elizabeth's mother immediately. "John would have loved to be here." She looks at her daughter, but Elizabeth is staring hard at her teacup, still silent.

Meg is watching Elizabeth. She reaches out suddenly and puts a wrinkled hand on the girl's arm, gripping it gently. "I understand," she says simply.

Elizabeth looks up at her, startled. Their eyes meet for a moment. Neither says anything, but the mood changes; the atmosphere becomes more relaxed, less awkward. Elizabeth nods slightly and puts her own smooth hand on top of Meg's withered one, resting it there for a moment.

Elizabeth takes a deep breath. "I have the doll," she says. She places her teacup cautiously in its saucer and reaches for her bag. She retrieves the small figure from within. She's wrapped it again in the baby blanket, and she unravels it carefully now as her mother and Meg watch.

"Here it is," she says. The doll stares, unblinking, at Elizabeth. Elizabeth feels a small pang of regret as she hands it back to its rightful owner. She has a fleeting thought, not for the first time, that if only her father had taken the doll with him, it would have protected him, kept him safe. She shakes her head at her own foolishness and looks away.

Meg exhales audibly as she takes the doll from Elizabeth, leaning in close to examine it. Elizabeth and her mother turn to look as the older woman inspects the doll, touching its fingers, its toes, its hair.

"This is certainly my little Will," Meg says. Her eyes are tearing, and her voice catches slightly. "That's what I used to call him, before I painted him and gave him to my Ned."

"We're sorry for your loss, as well," says Elizabeth's mother kindly. "I'm sure it's still difficult, even after all this time."

Meg turns to look at her. "The pain, it does lessen with time," she says softly, a faraway look in her eyes.

She pats the little doll and smiles at it. "My father made it for me," she tells them. "My mother had died. He was a good friend to me in those days. And what an adventure he's had! I never could have guessed it, not back then." She turns to the two younger women. "Thank you for bringing him back to me. I am ever so grateful."

"You're welcome." Elizabeth speaks up now. "It was our pleasure."

"I'm glad," Meg replies, smiling. She's looking at the doll again, tracing the shape of its left boot with her index finger.

Meg straightens and turns to Elizabeth again. She holds out the doll in her hands, in an offering gesture. Elizabeth stares at her, surprised.

"Thank you for finding him for me," says Meg again. "I'm so happy to have seen him one last time." She places the doll back in Elizabeth's arms.

"But—it's yours," stutters Elizabeth, confused. "We brought it back here, to you."

"Oh, no," says Meg. She shakes her head. "It was mine, once, and I most definitely did want to see it again. But the doll is yours now. It belongs to you."

"No!" says Elizabeth. She jumps up, her face red. She's on the verge of tears. "I saved it for you, to bring it here to you!" Her voice is shaking now. "I would have given it to my dad, when he shipped out, it might have…" Her voice trails off, and she turns away, avoiding the woman's stare.

"Elizabeth!" says her mother, scandalized, but Meg nods at her.

"It's all right," says the ancient woman. "I understand." She looks at Elizabeth, who still refuses to meet her gaze. "Elizabeth. I understand. I had the same hopes for the doll when I gave it to my Ned. But it didn't save Ned, and it couldn't have saved your father." Elizabeth looks up at her slowly, her cheeks red and damp. Meg continues. "A doll cannot save someone. I know you know this. You're a smart girl."

Elizabeth nods slightly. "I'm sorry," she says, accepting the offer of a tissue. "I can't help it."

Meg nods. "I understand," she says again.

There is quiet for a moment. Elizabeth speaks up. "But Ms. Merriweather—Meg—the doll is yours. It belongs to you. Don't you want it?"

Meg smiles at her. "I'm a very old woman, past a hundred," she says simply. "My time on this earth is running out. A doll doesn't need an old woman. It needs a child to care for it."

"I'm not a child!" protests Elizabeth automatically, looking offended. She ignores her mother's glare and crosses her arms.

Meg laughs. "I know you're not." She looks over at Elizabeth's mother's belly, which already shows signs of pregnancy. "You might find you have use for it, though, in a few months' time."

Comprehension dawns on Elizabeth's face, which lights up at the mention of the baby. "It's a girl," she says softly. "A sister."

Meg smiles. "The soldier doll is, at its heart, still a doll," she says. "And a doll needs someone to love it. A little girl should do just fine, don't you think?"

Elizabeth smiles and takes the doll. "I'll keep it safe for her," she promises. Looking into the doll's blue eyes, she grins again and tucks it back in her bag.

ACKNOWLEDGMENTS

This book wouldn't have been possible without the assistance and support of many people, so I will try to thank them all here: To Ibi Kaslik, without whose mentorship this book would never have been possible; to my editor, Kathryn White, who tirelessly plowed through version and version of the manuscript and always seemed cheerful about it; to Margie Wolfe, Kathryn Cole, Emma Rodgers and the staff of Second Story Press for having faith in the book and making it a reality; to authors Karl Marlantes, James Webb, Tim O'Brien and Philip Caputo for saving me a trip to Vietnam; to Judy Cohen and Carla Pearson, my third and tenth grade English teachers, for encouraging me to write; to Dara Laxer and Cheryl Ellison, my best friends and beta readers; to Paul and Jess Gold for their technical support and endless enthusiasm; to my husband, Adam Goodman, who never doubted *Soldier Doll* would be published, and who took our son to the museum fifteen weeks in a row so I could attend writing workshops; to Teddy and Violet, for inspiring me to write and making me want to be a better person; and finally, to my parents, Howard and Karen Gold, for a lifetime of love and encouragement that made it possible for me to believe I could do this.

ABOUT THE AUTHOR

JENNIFER GOLD is a lawyer and mother of two young children living in Toronto. A history buff, she also has degrees in psychology, law, and public health. *Soldier Doll* is her first book. Visit her online at www.jennifergold.ca.